Kalki's
PONNIYIN SELVAN

Dr M. Rajaram is an exceptional IAS Officer with balanced views on administration. His efficiency in administration has brought him many prestigious awards, notably the Best Collector Award, Malcolm Award, Anna Award, etc., from the government. He has authored more than 40 books: *Quality Educational Administration: Who Will Bell the Cat?*, *Thirukkural: Pearls of Inspiration*, *The Elemental Warriors*, *Food for Thought*, *Passport for Success*, *Blossoms in English*, *The Yellow Line*, *Glory of Thirukkural*, *Higher Education for Better Tomorrow*, *Better English*, *Glory of Tamil*, *The Success Mantra in Bhagavad Gita*, *Tic-Toc-Tic*, *Bosses: The Good, the Bad and the Ugly*, *Corporate Wisdom in Thirukkural*, *Oriental Wisdom*, etc. His English translation of *Thirukkural* earned him a well-deserved tribute from Dr Abdul Kalam, the late President of India. His book is so popular that it has been added to the White House Library.

Praise for the book

'*Ponniyin Selvan*, a popular Tamil novel unfolds an epic story based on historical facts and characters with lot of twists and turns keeping the readers spellbound reflecting the glory of Indian literature.'

—**Sri M. Venkaiah Naidu**
Hon'ble Vice President of India

'*Ponniyin Selvan* is an outstanding historical Tamil novel rendered in simple and elegant style by Dr M. Rajaram.'

—**Ki Rajanarayanan**
Sahitya Akademi Award Winning Tamil Writer

'*Ponniyin Selvan* is a story of plots within plots highlighting the greatness of the Chola Empire rendered in elegant style without losing its original flavour.'

—**Dr Avvai Natarajan**
Former Vice Chancellor, Tamil University, Tanjore

Kalki's
PONNIYIN SELVAN
Volume 1

Translated by M. Rajaram

RUPA

Published by
Rupa Publications India Pvt. Ltd. 2022
7/16, Ansari Road, Daryaganj
New Delhi 110002

Sales centres:
Allahabad Bengaluru Chennai
Hyderabad Jaipur Kathmandu
Kolkata Mumbai

Translation and Abridgment Copyright © M. Rajaram 2022
Cover Illustration Copyright © Maniam Selven

All rights reserved.
No part of this publication may be reproduced, transmitted,
or stored in a retrieval system, in any form or by any means,
electronic, mechanical, photocopying, recording or otherwise,
without the prior permission of the publisher.

This is a work of fiction. Names, characters, places and incidents are either the
product of the author's imagination or are used fictitiously and any resemblance to
any actual person, living or dead, events or locales is entirely coincidental.

ISBN: 978-93-91256-10-4

Tenth impression 2022

15 14 13 12 11 10

The moral right of the author has been asserted.

Printed in India

This book is sold subject to the condition that it shall not,
by way of trade or otherwise, be lent, resold, hired out, or otherwise
circulated, without the publisher's prior consent, in any form of
binding or cover other than that in which it is published.

Contents

Foreword by M. Venkaiah Naidu	*ix*
Author's Note	*xi*
Historical Backdrop of Ponniyin Selvan	*xiii*
Publishers' Note	*xxiii*
1. Season of Aadi	1
2. The Bravest of the Brave	4
3. Vinnagara Temple	7
4. Kadamboor Fort	10
5. The Folk Dance	14
6. Midnight Meeting	18
7. Women's Rule	21
8. Mysterious Palanquin	24
9. True Friend	28
10. Astrologer	31
11. Sudden Entry	34
12. Nandini–A Mystery!	39
13. Vandiyathevan and Astrologer	42
14. Crocodile in the River	45
15. Affectionate Brother and Sister	49
16. Self-Respecting Horse	53
17. Idumban Kari–The Dark Man	55
18. Enemy's War Memorial	58
19. Our Foremost Enemy	61
20. The Curtains Parted	64
21. Emperor's Bodyguards	66
22. Chendan Amudan	70
23. All-Powerful Paluvettarayars	72

24. Tanjore Fort	74
25. Court Poets and Bards	78
26. Our Honourable Guest	81
27. Palace Art Gallery	83
28. Thieves! Thieves!	85
29. A Vampire on the Tree	88
30. The Fragrant Garden	90
31. A Sorcerer	92
32. Do You Remember?	96
33. Battle of Roaring Lions	99
34. Nandini's Drama	102
35. Paluvettarayar's Infatuation for Nandini	105
36. Dark Underground Passage	109
37. Is This Friendship?	112
38. Palayarai—Chola's Old Capital	115
39. Queen Mother	118
40. The Young Spy	121
41. People Grumbled	123
42. Romantic Moment	126
43. Surprise of Surprises	129
44. Paranthaka Hospital	132
45. A Dream City	134
46. Agitated Crown Prince	139
47. Poison of Passion	142
48. My Lover	145
49. Unexpected Incident	149
50. No Peace on Earth	152
51. Kodikkarai Lighthouse	155
52. Is She Mad?	159
53. Poonkulali's Midnight Lovers	162
54. Poonkulali Is Peculiar	164

55. Ocean Princess	169
56. Ghost Island	172
57. Honourable Prime Minister	176
58. Beloved Son of Ponni	181
59. Two Full Moons	184
60. Distressed Midnight Call	187
61. Emperor's Hallucination	191
62. Which Is the Worst Betrayal?	197
63. The Spy Is Caught!	200
64. Tigress versus Tigress	203
65. Infamous Tanjore Dungeons	206
66. Royal Mint	210
67. Nandini's Letter	214
68. Wax in Fire	217
69. Blood Thirsty Sword	222
70. Rogue Elephant	225
71. Her Word Is Gospel	228
72. The Elephant Driver	232
73. Fistfight	236
74. The Prince's Dinner Party	239
75. City of Anuradapura	243
76. Throne of Lanka	247
77. Is It Nandini?	252
78. Goddess Cauvery	254
79. Eloquent Paintings	257
80. Amazing Sword Fight	260
81. Conspirators	264
82. One and Only Duty	267
83. The Rogue Elephant	271
84. Prison Ship	274

Foreword

भारत के उपराष्ट्रपति
VICE-PRESIDENT OF INDIA

MESSAGE

I am happy to know that Dr. M Rajaram has translated into English Kalki Krishnamurthy's famous Tamil novel, 'Ponniyin Selvan'.

'Ponniyin Selvan', a very popular and widely read book in Tamil literature, unfolds an epic story based on some historical facts and characters with lot of twists and turns keeping the readers spellbound. It is set in the life and times of the great Emperor Rajaraja Chola, reflecting the glory of Indian culture.

I am sure, the English version of this soul-stirring novel will rekindle interest in the younger generation and others to know more about our rich cultural heritage and legacy. Non-Tamil readers, especially, will, definitely enjoy reading this epic story.

I congratulate Dr. M Rajaram for translating this epic as well as Rupa, New Delhi for publishing this book.

(M. Venkaiah Naidu)

New Delhi
29th April, 2021

Author's Note

The world is at the feet of the benevolent ruler who reigns with love for people's welfare.

—Kural-544

Rupa Publications has rendered yeoman service to Tamil and Tamil literature by taking my book, *Thirukkural–Pearls of Wisdom*, the greatest ancient Tamil classic, to every nook and corner of the world including the White House library. When this renowned 100-year-old publishers asked me to translate Ponniyin Selvan into English, I couldn't refuse.

Initially, I found it to be a Himalayan task. But after I completed a few chapters in the first volume, it became very interesting, thanks to the amazing twists and turns in the story, even though I had read it in my college days.

Like a mother rejoicing the birth of a child after delivery, I too rejoiced after the completion of the work. Having been the erstwhile district collector of Tanjore, I feel even more proud of my work as the story of Ponniyin Selvan revolves around the city of Tanjore, the capital of the great Cholas.

This is a book of five volumes published in a Tamil weekly called *Kalki*, continuously, for more than two-and-a-half years in the 1950s. It was a challenge to condense the Tamil version consisting of 500 chapters and 2,400 pages into three volumes. I had to burn the midnight oil to complete the work within a period of eight months, making good use of the COVID lockdown.

No Tamil book or novel has been as grandly celebrated and fondly remembered as Kalki's *Ponniyin Selvan* in Tamil literature. The fascination for the Chola royalty also accounted for its stupendous success.

The novel has been republished innumerable times as books, audio books, comics, stage plays, etc. *Ponniyin Selvan* continues to fascinate people and remains an evergreen novel for all Tamilians across the globe. There are no book fairs without the *Ponniyin Selvan* spread. The names of the characters in the story are household names. The diehard fans of *Ponniyin Selvan* have a Facebook group of their own and go on conducted tours to the places mentioned in the novel.

This is a story of Prince Arulmolivarman alias Ponniyin Selvan, who, later on, ascended the Chola throne as Raja Raja Chola! the Great. It is a story of romance, wit and wisdom, suspense, thrill, sacrifice, turns and twists, plots within plots, etc.

Kalki is a trendsetter in writing historical fiction. He made it as interesting and engaging as any contemporary genre. It is amazing the way he has woven imaginary characters into the mainstream of historical events.

Popularly known as Kalki, Krishnamurthy is the narrator of *Ponniyin Selvan*. It has been the most widely read historical fiction from the date of its commencement and even now, after 60 years, its glory is still intact. This work of fiction has become a part and parcel of the life of the Tamilians who are its avid readers.

As a student of English literature, I have read innumerable plays and novels but nothing ever came near to *Ponniyin Selvan* with its rich content presented in a lucid and flamboyant style.

I would not have been able to complete this Herculean task in a limited time but for the tireless support of Sri V. Rajagopal, Smt K.R. Swarnalakshmi and Sri Sagar Pentela.

Historical Backdrop of Ponniyin Selvan

The Chola dynasty was a great Tamil empire of south India, one of the longest ruling dynasties in the world's history. The earliest references of this dynasty are seen in the inscriptions from the third century BC and they continued to govern until the thirteenth century.

Vijayalaya Chola was one of the greatest Chola kings who ruled between AD 848–871. Under his reign, the Cholas were a small kingdom. After him, his son, Aditya Chola came to the throne. He defeated the Pandiyas and the Pallavas.

After Aditya, Paranthaka I ascended the Chola throne. He ruled for forty-six years. During his times the Chola nation expanded from the shores of Cape Comorin in the south to the banks of the Krishna-Tungabadra rivers in the north. For some time, the tiger flag flew over Lanka also. The Rashtrakutas who were very powerful in the north tried to contain the growing powers of the Cholas.

Paranthaka I had three sons. The eldest among these sons was Rajaditya. Expecting an invasion from the north, Rajaditya was stationed with a large army in Thirumunaipadi and he utilized those soldiers to construct the huge Veera Narayana Lake, in the name of his father, at Veeranarayanapuram, which was beneficial to the farmers of that region.

The Rashtrakutas invaded and a fierce battle was fought at a place known as Takkolam, near present day Arakonam in Tamil Nadu. In that battle, Rajaditya fought valiantly but he lost his life on account of his magnanimity and the treacherous game played by his enemies.

If Rajaditya had not died on the battlefield, he would have ruled the Chola nation after his father Paranthaka-I. His descendants would have ascended the throne after him. But since he died without any offsprings, his brother Kandaraditya was crowned as the king and it was decided that his younger brother Arinjaya and his descendants would succeed.

This decision was made because Kandaraditya's wife had died without having given birth to any children, several years before he came to inherit the throne and he did not marry again. However, his younger brother Arinjaya had a handsome, capable and intelligent son, Sundara.

After all such arrangements were made, Kandaraditya married the jewel among the maids, the beautiful, modest and pious Sembiyan Madevi. As a result of this marriage, a child was born. They named the child Madurandaka and cherished him. But both the king as well as the queen did not wish to change any of the arrangements they had made earlier about the succession to the kingdom. They wished to raise their son spiritually. Arinjaya, who ruled after Kandaraditya, died within a year.

Thus, bypassing the descendants of the elder brothers Rajaditya and Kandaraditya, the line of Arinjaya Chola became heirs to the Chola throne and Sundara Chola became the king. In the early years of his reign, he performed various deeds of valour, and defeating the Rashtrakutas and the Pandiyas, he expanded the kingdom.

Aditya Karikalan and Arulmolivarman, sons of Emperor Sundara Chola were able warriors. Both the sons cooperated and helped their father with complete devotion. These sons gained valorous experience in battlefields and wars at a very young age. In every campaign they participated in, the goddess of victory stood by their side.

The story of Ponniyin Selvan (*The Son of River Ponni* [The Son of River Cauvery]) is a historical novel written by Kalki set against the backdrop of these 11th century historical events. Most of the characters and events are real.

It tells the story of the early days of Arulmolivarman who later became the greatest Emperor of the Chola dynasty as Raja Raja Chola I, and ruled during the period AD 985–1014. Kalki took more than three years to complete the story.

Ponniyin Selvan is the greatest historical novel ever written in Tamil. It was first published as a series in the Tamil magazine Kalki, during the 1950s (for two-and-half-years) and was later integrated into a novel.

CHARACTERS

Vandiyathevan: The brave, witty, adventurous warrior and prince of Vaanar clan. He is a close friend of the crown prince, Aditya Karikalan.

Sundara Chola: The emperor of Chola Empire. Handsome and valourous. Afflicted with paralysis in old age.

Vanamadevi: Empress of the Chola Empire. Wife of Sundara Chola. Daughter of Thirukovalur Malayaman.

Thirukovalur Malayaman: Father-in-law of Sundara Chola. He was advisor for Aditya Karikalan in Kanchi.

Aditya Karikalan: Eldest son of Sundara Chola, the crown prince and the commander of northern troops stationed at Kanchi.

Kundavai: The Chola princess. Only daughter of Sundara Chola. Admired much by her father and the people for her intelligence, wit and beauty.

Arulmolivarman/Raja Raja Chola I/Ponniyin Selvan: The youngest son of Sundara Chola. He was said to be saved by Mother Cauvery/Ponni from drowning in the river when he was five. This gave him the title 'Ponniyin Selvan' or 'Son of Cauvery'. He was loved by all for his nobility, ability and valour.

Vanathi: Kodumbalur princess and daughter of the younger chieftain of Kodumbalur who died in the battle in Sri Lanka. She is the most beloved friend of Princess Kundavai and deeply in love with Prince Arulmoli.

Chendan Amudan: The real heir to the Chola throne, son born of Kandaraditya and Sembiyan Madevi. Due to circumstances, grows up in a humble home doing flower service to a temple.

Sambuvarayar: Chieftain of Kadamboor—a part of Chola Kingdom.

Kandamaran: Son of Sambuvarayar and close friend of Vandiyathevan who became a bitter foe later on. They served together in the army.

Manimekalai: Younger sister of Kandamaran and daughter of Kadamboor Sambuvarayar, deeply in love with Vandiyathevan.

Aniruddha Brahmarayar: Sundara Chola's childhood friend and classmate. When Sundara Chola ascended the throne, he requested him to be his prime minister and assist him in administration. He knew the personal secrets of all the royal members.

Alvarkkadiyan Nambi: A Vaishnavite spy who works for Prime Minister Aniruddha Brahmarayar. He is the foster-brother of Nandini and also a close associate of Vandiyathevan.

Sembiyan Madevi: Wife of Emperor Kandaraditya and Madurandakan's mother. Pious and well respected by everyone.

Madurandakan: Growing up as the son of Sembiyan Madevi as a humble spiritual person. Taught not to desire for the throne. Actually is a Pandiya prince groomed at Chola palace.

Senior Paluvettarayar: The finance minister of the Chola Kingdom who was respected for his valour and the 64 scars he got in battles. He is married to the young and beautiful Nandini in his old age, gets seduced by her beauty and gets used by her as a puppet for her plot to destroy the Chola Empire.

Junior Paluvettarayar: The commander of Tanjore Fort, younger brother of Senior Paluvettarayar. He is the father-in-law of Mathurandakan.

Nandini: Young queen of Paluvoor and wife of Senior Paluvettarayar. She grew up in a priest's family along with the royal children in Palayarai. She had a deep hatred towards the royalty for their ill-treatment of her and also had a desire for the throne.

Boothi Vikrama Kesari/Elder Kodumbalur Chieftain: Uncle of Vanathi. The commander of the southern troops during Sundara Chola's reign. He has a desire to marry Vanathi to Prince Arulmoli and thus make her the queen.

Poonkulali: Daughter of the lighthouse keeper at Kodikkarai. She was an adventurous and fearless boat girl.

Murugaiyan: Son of lighthouse keeper and elder brother of Poonkulali.

Rakkammaal: Murugaiyan's wife. Sister-in-law of Poonkulali. A Pandiya conspirator.

Mandakini: The deaf and mute woman whom Sundara Chola fell in love with and secretly married in his teens but had to leave her due to unavoidable circumstances. She is the sister of the Kodikkarai lighthouse keeper and aunt of Poonkulali and Chendan Amudan.

Vaani: The deaf and mute sister of Mandakini, foster mother of Chendan Amudan.

Parthibendra Pallava: Friend of Aditya Karikalan, who comes from the lineage of Pallavas. He fought along with Aditya in his battles.

Pinaakapani: Palayarai doctor's son sent by Kundavai with Vandiyathevan to collect medicinal herbs from Kodikkarai.

Ravidasan: Bodyguard of the slain Pandiya king, Veerapandiya, conspiring to avenge his death by killing the members of the Chola royalty, disguised as a sorcerer.

Idumban Kari: Pandiya conspirator working in Sambuvarayar's palace.

Theveralan and Soman Sambavan: Accomplices to Ravidasan.

Karuthiruman: A boat man close to Pandiya king, Veerapandian and prisoner in the dungeons of Tanjore. Claims to know the location of Pandiyan crown and scepter hidden in Sri Lanka.

Kumbakonam Astrologer: Famous due to his correct predictions and very close to the royal family.

STORYLINE

Vandiyathevan was a warrior prince whose ancestors were great kings and once ruled the Vallam territory of Tamil Nadu. He was a close friend of the crown prince, Aditya Karikalan. He embarks on a secret mission to Tanjore as per the directive of the crown prince carrying messages to Emperor Sundara Chola in Tanjore and Princess Kundavai in Palayarai. On the way he reaches Veeranarayanapuram in the Chola Empire and was awestruck with the beauty and fertility of the land.

He had a glimpse of Senior Paluvettarayar, the most powerful man in the Chola Empire on the banks of the Veeranam Lake. He also meets Alvarkkadiyan Nambi a Vaishnavite devout and spy of Prime Minister Aniruddha Brahmarayar.

He proceeds to Kadamboor to spend the night in his friend Kandamaran's palace. Kandamaran was the only son of Sambuvarayar, chieftain of Kadamboor—another powerful man in the Chola Empire.

An important meeting was going to take place in the Kadamboor Palace and all the powerful chieftains of the Empire have assembled there.

Senior Paluvettarayar had married a young girl of his daughter's age and takes her along with him in a closed palanquin to all the places of his visit.

While serving in the army, Kandamaran had told Vandiyathevan much about his sister Manimekalai and his desire to give her hand in marriage to him. Kandamaran had also said much about Vandiyathevan to Manimekalai who falls in love with him at first sight. But Vandiyathevan considers her only as his sister.

During his overnight stay in Kadamboor, Vandiyathevan discovers that all the powerful men in the kingdom were conspiring against the emperor and his sons under the leadership of Senior Paluvettarayar. The emperor is bedridden with paralysis. They don't want Aditya Karikalan to inherit the throne. Instead, they propose the emperor's first cousin Madurandakan to be crowned. For some reason, Madurandakan's father, late king Kandaraditya, and mother, Sembiyan Madevi, did not want him to inherit the throne. They wanted him to lead a spiritual life. He was leading such a life until then. But on getting married to the daughter of Junior Paluvettarayar, Commander of Tanjore Fort, he was instigated by Nandini to claim his right to the throne. Now, under the leadership of Senior Paluvettarayar, he is secretly gathering the support of the chieftains and hence this meeting at Kadamboor.

Other than Vandhiyathevan, Alvarkkadiyan also witnesses the midnight conspiracy by the Chola chieftains and yet another conspiracy—a plan to avenge death of King Veerapandian by assassinating the emperor and his two sons and bring the Chola Empire under Pandiya rule. The young queen of Paluvoor, Nandini, who was once betrayed by Karikalan, was helping them secretly.

Princess Kundavai and Princess Vanathi, on their visit to astrologer Kumbakonam's house, meet Vandiyathevan. It is love at first sight for Kundavai and Vandiyathevan even without knowing each other's identity.

Vandiyathevan enters the Tanjore Fort with the help of the junior queen of Paluvoor, Nandini. He befriends Chendan Amudan, a humble young man doing flower service to a nearby temple.

While delivering the letter to the emperor, Vandiyathevan realizes that the emperor is being held hostage in his own palace and no one can reach the emperor without the knowledge of the Paluvettarayars. He escapes from the custody of the commander of the fort, Junior Paluvettarayar, who suspects Vandiyathevan to be a spy.

Junior Queen Nandini's maid mistakes him to be a sorcerer and takes him inside the queen's palace and he meets the junior queen.

She casts a seductive net but Vandiyathevan escapes from her through the underground treasury only to find his dear friend Kandamaran being stabbed in the back by Paluvettarayars' guard. Unfortunately, Kandamaran believes Vandiyathevan tried to kill him. Vandiyathevan leaves his wounded friend under the care of Chendan Amudan's mother and reaches Palayarai and delivers the letter to Princess Kundavai.

The princess sends him to Lanka to deliver a letter to her younger brother, Prince Arulmoli, and bring him back to Tanjore.

He reaches Lanka with the help of a boat-girl, Poonkulali, who is also Chendan Amudan's cousin.

He meets Prince Arulmoli, wins his trust and becomes his friend. Prince Arulmoli is loved by the people of Lanka and much respected by the Buddhist monks there. Vandiyathevan realizes that the prince's life is in in danger. But a mute old woman saves him from all dangers in Lanka. Suddenly ships sent by Senior Paluvettarayar come to arrest the prince on charges of trying to usurp the Lankan throne. He decides to go back to Tanjore and surrender to his father, the emperor, and prove his innocence.

Vandiyathevan and the prince get caught in a storm in mid sea. Poonkulali saves them and brings them to Kodikkarai. But the prince gets a fatal delirious fever.

Meanwhile, in Tanjore, Chendan Amudan gets arrested for helping a spy (Vandiyathevan) to escape. Princess Kundavai helps to get him released and sends him to Kodikkarai to meet Vandiyathevan and Prince Arulmoli.

The conspirators follow the prince to Kodikkarai and attempt to kill him there. Princess Kundavai had sent instructions through Chendan Amudan to take the prince to a Buddhist monastery in Nagapattinam.

There is chaos in the kingdom when people get to know that their beloved prince was lost at sea. They blame the Paluvettarayars.

Prince Arulmoli recovers from the delirious fever with the help of the Buddhist monks only to get caught in a deadly tsunami.

Nandini lures Aditya Karikalan to Kadamboor to sort out the succession issue. But her real intention is to kill him to avenge the death of Veerapandiya. She succeeds in her mission and the blame falls on Vandiyathevan. But Manimekalai claims that she killed the crown prince.

Prince Arulmoli escapes from the tsunami, and reaches Tanjore and enters the fort disguised as Princess Vanathi's mahout. Prince Arulmoli and Princess Vanathi fall in love.

The conspirators try to kill the emperor. But the mute woman, Mandakini, who was the emperor's first love saves him and dies. The emperor decides to crown Madurandakan but the Queen Mother opposes. The Emperor gets to know that Madurandakan was not the son of Kandaraditya and the Queen Mother. He also gets to know that Chendan Amudan was actually their son, but he is not interested in ascension to the throne. He wishes to marry his cousin Poonkulali and lead a pious life serving the temple in Kodikkarai. It is decided that Prince Arulmoli should be crowned.

Finally, Senior Paluvettarayar reveals the mystery behind the murder of Karikalan and accepts his failure to save the crown prince. He kills himself and Vandiyathevan's innocence is proved.

But at the last minute, to everyone's surprise, Chendan Amudan is crowned as the emperor by Arulmoli himself.

Arulmoli sets off on an overseas expedition leaving Vandiyathevan to assist the new emperor.

Princess Manimekalai goes insane and dies on account of her love towards Vandiyathevan and the ordeal she faced when her lover was arrested for the murder of Karikalan. Princess Vanathi decides to wait for Prince Arulmoli's successful return from his overseas expedition.

Publisher's Note

Ponniyin Selvan has universal appeal and acceptability. To publish a book of such immense interest is a great privilege for us. The reason for bringing out this book is its simplicity, lucidity, elegance and universal appeal.

We sincerely acknowledge Dr M. Rajaram, IAS (Retd) for his commendable efforts in bringing out this book in a stunningly impressive style.

Ponniyin Selvan by Kalki is an absolute varied flux of bravery, friendship, romance, eternal love, revenge, religious fervour, art and sculpture, smart and clumsy rulers and so on.

It makes every reader desiring to be a part of that era of bravery, romance and culture to behold all occurrences that happened in those days. Every reader would like to get this book tucked away in his or her book shelf as it is entertaining, engrossing and styled adeptly, glamorizing a variety of suspenses and mysteries. It reflects history vividly with flavoured romanticism and portraying the required virtues of the Chola emperors.

Dr M. Rajaram is an exceptional IAS officer of 1992 batch with seasoned and practical approach in administration. He belongs to the scholar-civil servant tradition with strong roots to our rich and undiscovered cultural and spiritual heritage.

His efficiency in civil administration brought him many prestigious awards, including the Best Collector Award, Poet Laureate, etc.

He has published more than 40 books, to mention a few: *Quality in Educational Administration, Who Will Bell the Cat?, Elemental Warriors, Food for Thought, Passport for Success, Blossoms in English, Yellow Line, Better Tomorrow, Towards Better English, Glory of Tamil, Success Mantra* in *Gita, Tic Talk Tic, Corporate Wisdom,* etc. Dr A.P.J. Abdul Kalam, former president of India, has paid a very well-deserved tribute to his literary works.

Publishers

I

Season of Aadi

We request our readers to board the ship of imagination and travel with us briefly into the glorious past of Tamil Nadu, dating back to a few thousand years.

In the kingdom of Chola Nadu, near the town of Chidambaram, lies a great lake known as the Veera Narayana Lake or Veeranam Lake. Standing on the banks of this mighty lake one might feel pride at the foresight of the Cholas, the legacy they have left behind.

A young warrior, mounted on a horse, was riding down the banks of Veera Narayana Lake. He belonged to the famous Vaanar clan known for their bravery. Vallavarayan Vandiyathevan was his name. Tired after a long journey, his horse was walking slowly. He was relishing the sight of the vast expanse of the lake.

It was the eighteenth day of the Tamil month Aadi, known as *Aadiperukku* and all the rivers in the Chola Kingdom were spatting with flood waters touching both the banks. The lakes were full to their brim. Veera Narayana Lake appeared as a mighty ocean.

The water rushing out of the seventy shutters of Veera Narayana Lake was flowing a long way making both sides fertile. Farmers were busy ploughing the land, sowing seeds and transplanting saplings. As they were working, the men and women were singing joyously.

Listening to this sweet music, Vandiyathevan rode on his horse leisurely, witnessing the picturesque view of nature and the festive activities around the lake.

'Oh! What a magnificent lake! The lakes in other kindoms would look like pools and puddles in front of this one!'

Adding to the joy of festive activities, men, women, children and the elderly were bubbling with enthusiasm in their colourful costumes. Vandiyathevan was basking in the joy of the people.

He was overjoyed at the sight of young women, giggling shyly, looking at him.

Suddenly, the sight of seven or eight large boats gliding swiftly, like white swans floating on the lake with wide spread wings, caught his attention.

All eyes fell on those boats. One of the boats reached the shore swiftly with several well-built soldiers carrying sharp and shiny spears. Some of them jumped on to the lake shore and started shoving the people with shouts of 'Go! Move away!'

Vandiyathevan was perplexed at this and approached an elderly man.

'Sir, who are these men?'

'Young man! Do you see the flag in the boats, embossed with the palm tree symbol? Don't you know that the palm-tree flag belongs to the Paluvettarayars?' asked the elderly man.

'Is it the great warrior, the Chieftain of Paluvoor?' asked Vandiyathevan with eyes wide open, looking in the direction of the approaching boats.

The brothers—Senior Paluvettarayar and Junior Paluvettarayar—were renowned from Lanka in the south to the kingdom of Kalinga in the north. Paluvoor, situated on the northern banks of the Cauvery, near the city of Uraiyoor was their capital. The Paluvoor family was famous for their valour and loyalty to the Cholas. Because of this, they enjoyed royal status and were allowed to have their own flag and emblem.

The senior Paluvettarayar had fought in twenty-four battles. There was no warrior in the Chola Kingdom to match him. He was over sixty years old now and did not go to the battlefield anymore. Nevertheless, he held several eminent positions in the government of the Cholas. He was the finance minister and head of food supply in the Chola Empire.

He had the right to levy taxes from any subordinate kingdom and nobleman. Therefore, next to the emperor, Sundara Chola, he was the most powerful man in the Chola kingdom.

Vandiyathevan was eager to see this powerful senior Paluvettarayar.

At the same time, he recalled the words uttered in privacy by the crown prince and commander of the northern forces, Aditya Karikalan.

'Vandiyatheva, I know you are a brave and intelligent man. I give you this great responsibility. Of the two letters I have given you, deliver one to my father, the Emperor, and the other to my sister, Princess Kundavai.

There are all kinds of rumours going on, even about the higher officials of the Chola Kingdom. Nobody should know you are carrying my letters. Don't pick a fight with anyone even if provoked. Never reveal that you are a great warrior. Be very cautious with the Paluvettarayars and my uncle Madurandakan. They should never know who you are and what your mission is.'

Therefore, Vandiyathevan suppressed his desire to see the senior Paluvettarayar. He nudged his horse to move on quickly. But his tired horse merely plodded ahead. Having decided to spend the night at the Kadamboor Palace of the chieftain, Sambuvarayar, he resolved to procure a better horse before resuming his journey the next morning.

2

The Bravest of the Brave

Vandiyatheven was riding on his horse, his heart was dancing with joy like the boats dancing on the waves of the lake. His intuition revealed that his mission was going to be extremely adventurous.

He was delighted to see the beautiful Chola Kingdom with so many rivers, reservoirs, clear streams and the beautiful ponds with the lotus and lilies winking their eyes in invitataion. Trees laden with flowers and with colourful birds were a treat to his eyes.

The city of Tanjore and Palayarai! What would its magnificent palaces, towering columns, big armouries, bounteous granaries and busy markets be like? The monumental temples! Vandiyathevan had heard about the songs sung by music exponents in these temples, enthralling the listeners to a state of rapturous devotion. He was going to hear all that very soon.

And that was not all. He was going to meet the mighty emperor, Paranthaka Sundara Chola, who was very brave and stunningly handsome. He had never thought all this would happen, not even in his wildest dreams. And was that all? No. He was also going to meet the emperor's beloved and graceful daughter Kundavai.

He wanted to reach the town of Kadamboor by sunset but before that he reached the Vaishnava temple at Veeranarayanapuram.

There was a huge crowd at the temple with vendors selling varieties of fruits and flowers. There were mounds of coconuts, tender coconuts, betel leaves, jaggeries, puffed rice, etc. for sale.

Fun games were being played. There were palm readers, astrologers and sorcerers making predictions. Vandiyatheven was walking along enjoying the beautiful sights of the village fair.

He noticed a large crowd and heard loud voices engaged in heated arguments. He was curious to go near and hear the argument. He got down from his horse and began making his way towards the crowd.

He found only two persons arguing between themselves. The large crowd gathered around them had taken sides and were loudly cheering the person they supported.

Of the two persons arguing, one was a Vaishnavite (worshipper of Lord Vishnu), Alvarkkadiyan Nambi. He had sandal markings all over his body and a tuft of hair on his head. He held a short wooden staff in his hand and he was short, stout and strong.

The other man was a Saivite (worshipper of Lord Siva) with markings of ash all over his body.

They were involved in a heated argument as to who (Siva or Vishnu) was greater. The argument was leading to a fist fight.

Watching all this, Vandiyathevan wondered if he should grab the staff from the fellow with the tuft on his head and hit him.

He came forward and said, 'Gentlemen! Why are you quarrelling? Don't you have any other work? If you are itching for a fight, go to Lanka and join the big war going on there.'

'Who is this fellow trying to make peace?' remarked Alvarkkadiyan, quickly turning towards him. People in the crowd liked Vandiyathevan's heroic charismatic face.

'Siva is a great god. So is Vishnu. Both are equal. Worship whomever you want. Why quarrel?' said Vallavarayan.

'How can you say that? Where is the proof that Siva and Vishnu are equal?' chided Alvarkkadiyan.

'Proof? I will give you proof. Last night I asked both Siva and Vishnu directly. Do you know what they said? "Vishnu and Siva are one and the same. Those who don't know this should have their mouths filled with sand!" Saying so, they gave me this fistful of dirt to throw in the mouths of the idiots who quarrel about it.'

Vandiyathevan opened his fist to show a handful of dirt. He then threw it on them. Upon this all hell broke loose. The men in the excited crowd started picking up dirt and rubble and began throwing it at each other.

Luckily, just at that moment, the arrival of Senior Paluvettarayar was announced and the commotion came to a halt.

'The best of the best, bravest of the brave, he who destroyed the very roots of the Pandiya army with sixty-four battle-wounds on his heroic body, the Chola minister of finance and food has arrived. Make way! Make way!' announced a thundering voice.

The heralds who made these announcements came first. Then came the drummers, followed by men carrying the palm-tree flags and smart soldiers with arms. Behind all these men came a dark, well-built man seated on a finely decorated elephant.

People stood on both sides of the roadway and watched. Vandiyathevan guessed that the man seated on the elephant was the senior Paluvettarayar.

Behind the elephant came a palanquin with silken drapes. Before he could wonder who could be inside, Vallavarayan saw a fair hand full of bracelets and bangles come out and slightly part the curtains. The dazzling face of a woman could be seen inside the palanquin, like the moon shining forth from behind a shifting cloud cover.

Though he was an admirer of beautiful women, Vandiyathevan was not impressed by that captivating face for some unknown reason. At the same time the eyes of the woman in the palanquin were focussing on someone behind Vandiyathevan; she let out a scream and the screens closed.

Vandiyathevan looked around him. He saw Alvarkkadiyan leaning against a tamarind tree with a horrible expression on his face.

3

Vinnagara Temple

Sometimes trivial incidents lead to events of great significance. One such incident now occurred to Vallavarayan Vandiyathevan. He was standing by the roadside watching the procession of the senior Paluvettarayar and his entourage. His horse stood a little way from him. Some men at the rear end of the entourage sighted Vandiyathevan's horse and bullied it by twisting its tail. The horse began running helter skelter amidst the festive crowd, knocking down several people.

'Young man, did you see the work of those Paluvoor brutes? What happened to the boldness that you showed earlier? Could you not show your valour against them?' Alvarkkadiyan asked pointedly.

Though Vandiyathevan was very upset, he restrained his emotions and went towards his horse. His horse stood in a tamarind grove nearby, with a stricken look in its eyes. He quietened the horse by patting its back and then took it back towards the road.

'Young man, which way are you going? Perhaps, if you are planning to stay at the palace of Kadamboor, I have a task to be done there ...' asked Alvarkkadiyan.

Vandiyathevan was furious to see Alvarkkadiyan following him.

'What? Do you know magic or witchcraft? How did you know that I was going to Kadamboor Palace?' asked Vandiyathevan.

'What is so surprising about it? Tonight, several dignitaries from various places are going there. Senior Paluvettarayar and his entourage are also going there.'

'Is that true?' asked a surprised Vandiyathevan.

'Yes, it is true.'

Vandiyathevan pondered whether he ought to proceed to Kadamboor. The opportunity to stay in the same lodgings as Senior Paluvettarayar was not that easy to come by. He may even get a chance to make the acquaintance of that esteemed warrior.

Alvarkkadiyan interrupted these thoughts in a pleading voice, 'Young man, please, take me to Kadamboor Palace tonight?'

'Why? Is there a fanatic Saivite coming there? Are you going to continue your fight there?'

'No, no. Do you think that getting into arguments was the only thing I do? Tonight, there will be a lavish banquet at Kadamboor. After the feasting, there will be several entertainments: music, dance and drama. I wish to see the folk dances. You could say that I am your servant.'

Vandiyathevan felt as though his earlier doubts had been confirmed.

'Find someone else for such fraud. I do not need a servant like you. Anyway no one will believe it; from what you say, I doubt if they would even let me enter the palace tonight.'

'That means you are not going to Kadamboor upon invitation?' enquired Alvarkkadiyan.

'Well, of course I have an invitation from my friend, the Crown Prince of Kadamboor, Kandamaran, son of King Sambuvarayar. But not for this occasion. He invited me several times to come and stay in his palace.'

'Is that all? Then your entry into the palace is doubtful tonight!'

Both walked together in silence for a while followed by a long conversation.

'Why are you still following me?' asked Vandiyathevan.

By now they had reached the Vinnagara temple on the other side of the lake.

Inside the temple, Alvarkkadiyan started singing some devotional songs. Vandiyathevan was very moved by them. His biased opinion about Alvarkkadiyan immediately changed.

When they came outside the temple after their worship,

Vandiyathevan said, 'Nambi Alvarkkadiyan! I did not realize that you were such a devout and learned person. If I have annoyed you, please forgive me.'

'I forgive you, young man. Please, do me a favour? I will give you a small note. If you stay at Kadamboor Palace, you must find an appropriate time to give it to someone,' Replied Alvarkkadiyan.

'To whom?'

'To the lady who was in the closed palanquin behind the senior Palavettarayar's elephant.'

'Nambi! I am not the fellow for such activities!'

And Vandiyathevan mounted his horse to proceed towards Kadamboor.

4

Kadamboor Fort

Vandiyathevan reached Kadamboor Fort in no time. Sengannan Sambuvarayar was a very influential nobleman in the Chola Kingdom. His palatial mansion resembled a fort with tall gates and towering walls.

Lot of elephants, horses and bulls were tied in the courtyard. Men were attending to them—feeding and grooming them. Several others were holding torches giving light to these activities; some were pouring oil to the torches.

All these activities stunned Vandiyathevan. That night an important event was happening inside the palace. This was not the right time for him to visit his friend. But he was curious to know more about the happenings inside.

The gates of the palace were well guarded by soldiers with sharp spears. As Vandiyathevan rode towards the gates, the alert guards stopped him.

He was enraged. He raised his voice and asked, 'Is this the hospitality of your land? Stopping guests at the gate and making enquiries?'

'Young man, you speak smartly. Who are you and where are you from?' asked a guard.

'I hail from the Vaanar clan. My name is Vallavarayan Vandiyathevan.'

'Whoever you may be, you cannot go inside. All the guests expected today have already arrived. We cannot allow anyone further.'

Vandiyathevan quickly made up his mind. He told the guards,

'Let go the reins of my horse, I will go back.'

When the guards did so, he nudged his horse to charge forward and entered the palace premises swirling his sword menacingly at the guards.

His horse mowed down the guards. The guards fled in all directions to save themselves from the attack.

The palace doors were shut. There were screams of 'Thief, thief, catch him'. He jumped down from the horse swirling his sword and screamed, 'Kandamara! Kandamara! Your guards are killing me!'

On hearing the name of their young prince, the guards stepped back in shock.

Just then a thunderous voice came from the upper floor of the palace, 'What is that noise there?'

'Master! A young man tried to break into our palace. We caught him but he is shouting the name of our prince,' replied the guard.

The thundering voice of Sambuvarayar ordered, 'Kandamara, go down and see what is happening.'

The guards made way for the approaching young man. Vandiyathevan stood there wielding his sword heroically. The young man looked at Vandiyathevan with pleasant surprise.

'Vallava! My beloved friend! Is it really you?' said the young man and ran to embrace him.

Pointing at the guards, Vandiyathevan said, 'Kandamara! This is the reception I get for accepting your invitation to visit your palace.'

Kandamaran dismissed the guards by saying, 'You fools! You have the brains of a wooden grain-pounding stick.'

He was jumping with joy as he held Vandiyathevan's hand and took him inside the palace.

As they walked in, Vandiyathevan asked Kandamaran, 'What is the occasion today? Why is your palace full of activities and so well-guarded?'

'I will tell you about it later. When we were together in the army, you always used to say you wanted to have a glimpse of the

Paluvettarayars, to see this person, that person and all that? All of them are here today. You can meet them!' said Kandamaran.

Kandamaran took him to the upper chambers where the guests were seated and introduced him to his father Sambuvarayar, 'Father, I always used to tell you about my good friend, Vandiyathevan, belonging to the Vaanar clan. Well, this is him.'

Vandiyatheven paid his respects with folded hands but Sambuvarayar was not very happy.

'Oh! So, he is the one who created so much of commotion at the gates.'

'No father, my friend is not the reason for the commotion; the fools employed by us as our guards are.'

'Anyway, he need not have chosen today to enter into our palace, that too so late in the night.'

Kandamaran did not want to get into an argument with his father. He took his friend to where the guests were seated. The senior Paluvettarayar was seated on a tall chair in the middle.

'Uncle, this is my dear friend, Vandiyatheven, of the noble Vaanar clan. Together we served in the army. He always wanted to meet the bravest of the brave, our senior Paluvettarayar and wondered if it was true that you got sixty-four war wounds on your body. And I used to say, "One day you can count it for yourself."'

Paluvettarayar frowned at this and said, 'Is that so young man? Won't you believe it unless you count them yourself? Can none other than the Vaanar clan be brave?'

Both the friends were taken aback. What was meant to be a compliment had been misconstrued.

Vandiyathevan was annoyed but controlled himself and uttered, 'Sir, the fame of the bravery of your clan is well known to all. Who am I to judge?'

'Good answer! Smart fellow!' said Senior Paluvettarayar.

The friends quickly moved away from the guests. Sambuvarayar called his son and whispered in his ears, 'Your friend must be tired after a long journey, give him some food and a room in a quiet place to sleep, as early as possible.'

Kandamaran nodded his head sadly and moved on.

Kandamaran took his friend to the ladies' chambers and introduced him to his mother. Vandiyathevan paid his respects with folded hands. He assumed the girl hiding shyly behind her mother must be Kandamaran's sister. Kandamaran had often mentioned his sister and Vallavarayan had imagined much about her beauty.

In the crowded ladies' chamber, Vandiyathevan's eyes were searching for the lady whom he had seen in the palanquin behind Senior Paluvettarayar's elephant.

5

The Folk Dance

When the friends came out of the ladies' chamber, a shrill voice called, 'Kandamara! Kandamara!'

Kandamaran turned to Vandiyathevan, 'Mother is calling. Please wait here. I will be back.'

Once inside the chamber, Kandamaran was struggling to answer several questions asked amidst laughter and merriment by the womenfolk.

Vandiyathevan asked his friend, 'There was much laughter when you were inside the ladies' chamber. Were they all happy to see me?'

'They were very happy to see you. My mother likes you very much. But the reason for their laughter is not you.'

'Then what else?'

'At this age, Senior Paluvettarayar has married a young woman. He has brought her here in a closed palanquin. He always keeps her locked inside his room instead of sending her to the ladies' chambers. One of the maids who saw the young queen of Senior Paluvettarayar through the balcony described her beauty to all the women. There is a debate going on in the ladies' chamber whether the new bride is from the kingdom of heaven.'

'When did Senior Paluvettarayar marry this mysterious woman?'

'Three years back. He never leaves her alone, even for a while. He takes her along in a closed palanquin wherever he goes. The whole kingdom is making fun about this.'

'That may not be the reason, Kandamara! I will tell you the actual reason. Women are generally jealous. The women of your family are not as fair as the young bride of Senior Paluvettarayar. That's the reason for all the rumours and comments.'

'How do you know about her complexion? Have you seen her? If Senior Paluvettarayar gets to know about this, you may not stay alive.'

'Kandamara! There is no need to fear as I have done no wrong. I was amidst the crowd near the Veeranam Lake witnessing the entourage of Paluvettarayar with elephants, horses, palanquin…You had sent them to receive him.'

'Yes, we sent them all… So what?'

'I was only comparing the reception you gave Paluvettarayar to the reception I received at the gates of your palace!'

'He was received with full honours meant for a high-ranking official of the kingdom and you were given the welcome of a true warrior. When you become the son-in-law of our family, we will receive you with due honour. Well, how do you know that Senior Paluvettarayar's mistress is very fair?'

'Paluvettarayar was seated majestically on an elephant you had sent to receive him. Following the elephant was a closed palanquin. Just as I was wondering who could be inside, a fair hand slightly parted the curtains and I could barely see the fair face of the woman inside. The hand and face were golden in colour. This is all that I managed to see. From what you say, I guess she must be the young queen of Senior Paluvettarayar.'

'You are a lucky man, Vandiyatheva! No man in this kingdom has seen that young queen. You at least had a glimpse of her fair hands and face.'

Just then, the sounds of musical instruments were heard. All kinds of drums, trumpets and flutes were being played.

'What is this noise?' asked Vandiyathevan.

'Oh! They are starting the performance of folk dance. Would you like to see the dance or go to bed early after dinner?'

Vandiyathevan cheerfully replied, 'I would like to see the folk dance!'

They walked ahead a little. The guests were already gathered.

The courtyard was surrounded with high walls. The stage was set in the middle of the courtyard, well-decorated with different paintings and well-lit with torches. Musicians were briskly playing their instruments.

When the audience were seated and settled down, nine female dancers came on the stage. They greeted the audience first and began to sing and dance bewitching all the guests. The performance was concluded with a prayer for a life of no hunger and no disease but bounteous rain and prosperity.

Next was a powerful form of dance performed by a man and a woman. The man was called Thevaralan and the woman, Thevaratti. They were dressed in bright red costumes, wore red flowers in their hair and had a red kumkum marking on their foreheads. Their mouths and lips were red like their eyes.

The dance started slowly and gracefully. As it progressed, the dance became fast and violent. The woman picked up the spear kept at the side of the stage and danced, while the man tried to grab it from her. This went on for some time. Finally, the man jumped with all his might and let out a deafening roar, shaking the auditorium. A spark flew from the eyes of Thevaralan and his body shook in ecstasy as if possessed.

After some time, a priest spoke to Thevaralan, 'Oh God! Please answer your devotees!'

'Ask me!' roared Thevaralan.

'Will the rains fill our rivers, ponds and reservoirs this year? Will there be fertility and prosperity? Will all our wishes come true?'

'It will, but Goddess Durga demands a human sacrifice of royal blood from a dynasty of kings who have been on the throne for a thousand years without a break.'

The dignitaries sitting in the front row exchanged meaningful glances.

The priest stopped playing the drum. The possessed Thevaralan fell on the stage like an uprooted tree. Devaratti ran onto the stage and took away Thevaralan.

The audience dispersed in silence. Wolves were howling in the distant woods.

Vandiyathevan, who was watching all this with some agitation, looked towards the direction in which the howling wolves were heard. He saw a head atop the outer walls of the palace! It was Alvarkkadiyan's head. He felt horrified for a moment. It appeared as if the severed head of Alvarkkadiyan was placed upon those walls.

He blinked his eyes to look again: the head disappeared! Several emotions were agitating his mind.

6

Midnight Meeting

After the folk dance, the guests were led to a banquet. Vandiyathevan had no appetite. He was tired and mentally disturbed. Kandamaran seated next to him was very excited. All the dignitaries were powerful chieftains of the Chola Empire.

Vandiyathevan should have been elated to see all the important chieftains of the Chola Empire gathered in one place. But he was not.

Why have they all gathered here?

He kept wondering. An unknown feeling was disturbing him.

Filled with such disturbing thoughts, Vandiyathevan went to the lonely open terrace to spend the night.

'You need rest. I will attend to the other guests and come to you later,' said Kandamaran.

Vandiyathevan fell asleep immediately. As he was emotionally disturbed, he could not sleep deeply. His fearful thoughts manifested into a terrible nightmare.

A lone wolf howling at a distance dissolved into thousands and started chasing him. On the other side, there were hundreds of dogs chasing him. Suddenly, the severed head of Alvarkkadiyan was singing.

He awoke from the nightmare.

At a spot, directly in front of his terrace, he could see the head of that very same Alvarkkadiyan Nambi. It was not a nightmare. It was real, the fellow was staring rather intensely at something below, inside the palace.

'What is he looking at...? There is some kind of mystery in this.' Vallavarayan jumped up and walked towards the direction in which he saw Alvarkkadiyan's head.

After walking on for a while, he suddenly heard the sound of voices somewhere nearby. Hiding himself behind a pillar, he peered down below.

In a narrow courtyard, enclosed by tall walls, he saw about ten or twelve men seated comfortably. All the men seated there were the dignitaries he had met at the banquet earlier.

They must have gathered this midnight to discuss an important matter. Alvarkkadiyan must be trying to spy on them by hanging on the outer walls. Indeed, Alvarkkadiyan must be a shrewd fellow. Somehow, the fellow had selected such a perfect spot that nobody could notice him.

He recalled the words of Sambuvarayar saying, 'He need not have come here today'. It was clear that they wanted no stranger to know about their discussions. He thought to himself, 'In such a situation if they suddenly see me, they may suspect me. I will definitely put Kandamaran in a tight corner. Even Kandamaran is part of this meeting; he is seated at the back. I can get to know from him in the morning.'

As these thoughts ran through his mind, Vandiyathevan saw a covered palanquin resting in one corner of the courtyard below him. Is this not the same palanquin he had seen earlier? Why was it here? He decided it was none of his business. He turned to go back to bed.

Suddenly he heard his name being uttered down below. He, immediately began to eavesdrop on their talk with some interest.

'Where is that fellow who came in saying that he was a friend of your son? He should not hear anything uttered here. Remember that he serves the Crown Prince. None should know about our plans. If there is even the slightest suspicion, that this fellow knows something, he must not be let outside this palace. In fact, it would be better to put a complete end to his activities...'

Vandiyathevan was shocked to hear these words. But he did not move away from the spot. He made up his mind to listen to all their talk. What was their plan that must be kept secret from the Crown Prince, who was next in line for the throne?

At that moment, Kandamaran intervened for his friend: 'Vandiyathevan is fast asleep in the corner terrace. He cannot hear the discussions. He will not poke his nose in things that do not concern him. Even if he hears something, he will not hinder your plans in any way. I will be responsible for that.'

'I am glad that you trust him so much. Even if one whisper gets out, it may lead to dire consequences,' said Senior Paluvettarayar.

7

Women's Rule

Vandiyathevan had had a premonition earlier that something mysterious was taking place in that palace.

Even Kandamaran, my most dear friend, did not tell the truth. He sent me to bed so that he could attend the secret midnight meeting. I won't let him off so easily tomorrow.

By now, Senior Paluvettarayar had begun to speak. Vandiyathevan listened carefully from his hiding place.

'I am here to announce a very grave news to you all. That is why Sambuvarayar has convened this meeting. Right now, Emperor Sundara Chola is seriously ill. According to the palace doctors, he is not likely to survive. Therefore, we have to decide upon the next course of action.'

'What is there to decide now? Hasn't Aditya Karikalan been coronated as the crown prince two years ago?' said a hoarse voice.

'True. None of us were consulted before the coronation, though all of us belong to well-established clans that have strived for more than four generations to acquire the eminence of this Chola Empire. But the Emperor did not consult us for the decision on a successor to the throne. He consulted Queen Mother Sembiyan Madevi and Princess Kundavai on this issue. My heart burns and my blood boils. The soothsayer who danced in frenzy asked for a human sacrifice of a prince from a thousand-year-old dynasty. My clan is more than a thousand years old. Offer me as sacrifice to Goddess Durga.'

Senior Paluvettarayar spoke the above words with much anger. An eerie silence prevailed for a short while. The whistling of the western breeze and the whispering of the trees were the only sounds to be heard.

'You are our leader without an equal. We are all ready to carry out your orders,' spoke Sambuvarayar.

'If you all may recall, two hundred years ago, our kingdom was small and insignificant. Vijayala Chola broke the power of the Muthuaraya kings and captured Tanjore. During the battle of Thirupurambiyam, he helped the Pallava army and destroyed the legions of Madurai Pandiya. From that moment, the Chola Kingdom has been expanding day-by-day. All kings have accepted the supremacy of the Cholas today. The Chola tiger flag flies in many countries. Even Lanka in the south as well as the Rashtrakuta in the north should have come under our rule. I need not give you the reasons why it has not. You know the cause for failure.'

Maluvarayar intervened, 'Yes. All of us know the reason. The Emperor's sons. Crown Prince Aditya Karikalan and the commander of the southern armies, Prince Arulmoli Varman.'

'I agree with the reasons given by you. The elder prince, Aditya Karikalan, is the commander for the northern armies. What is he doing? He is not planning invasions to win territories. He sits in Kanchi building a golden palace for his own dwelling!'

'Has the construction of this golden palace been completed?'

'Yes. The elder prince, Aditya Karikalan, sent a letter to the Emperor inviting him to come and stay for a while in that newly constructed golden palace.'

'Is the Emperor going to Kanchi?' asked another alarmed voice.

'You need not have any concern about that. I have stopped all letters from reaching the Emperor through my brother Junior Paluvettarayar, the commander of Tanjore Fort. Nothing happens there without my knowledge.'

'Hail the Chanakian political astuteness of the Paluvoor king!' all shouted in chorus.

'Please, listen, as I relate to you, the activities of the Emperor's younger son, Prince Arulmoli, who has gone to Lanka. When we invade enemy territories, the food supplies and payments for our armies have to be procured from those enemy lands as per tradition. The wealth to pay our army must be captured in those enemy regions. Excess treasures should be sent back to the homeland. But Prince Arulmoli wants food supplies to be sent from here by ships to feed our soldiers in Lanka! For the last one year, I have sent several shiploads of supplies, draining our resources.'

'Most unusual! We cannot tolerate such stupidities!' Several voices rose.

'Listen to the reasoning of Prince Arulmoli for this peculiar behavior. If we try to procure supplies for our armies from the enemy territories, it would cause a lot of inconvenience to the civilians. The dispute is with the royalty of Lanka and not with Lankan people.'

Someone from the meeting protested, 'I have never heard anything of this sort in the past.'

'Due to the follies of both the princes, the treasury and granary at Tanjore is getting emptied! I am forced to levy more taxes and also collect tributes from all of you. Perhaps that is why the Cholas have appointed me as their finance minister. If I had not considered the welfare of this country as most important, I would have given up my positions long ago!'

'Why not speak about these things to the Emperor?'

'Yes, I have personally spoken to him about it several times. "Ask the Queen Mother Sembiyan Madevi and Princess Kundavai," he says. Their words are gospel to him. The Emperor has lost reasoning power. He never asks our opinion. I, along with other ministers, have to go and stand in front of that small girl who knows nothing about politics. How long can I tolerate such humiliation? If you all unanimously agree, I shall give up my official positions which trouble me to levy taxes.'

'No! Never do that! You should not forsake us. The nation will be lost in confusion within a short time if you do that,' said Sambuvarayar.

'Well then, what is the solution to the women's rule?' asked Senior Paluvettarayar.

8

Mysterious Palanquin

For a while, the men in that meeting continued to have heated arguments. Vandiyathevan could not hear anything clearly.

In a louder voice, Sambuvarayar said, 'What is the point of each one talking like this? It is already past midnight now.'

'I have a certain doubt. I would like to ask one question, if you don't mind,' said a hoarse voice.

'Is that you, Vanangamudi Munairayar? Please ask any question without any hesitation. I won't mind it,' said Senior Paluvettarayar.

'We all know that Paluvettarayar married a young girl about three years ago…'

In an angry voice, Sambuvarayar interrupted, 'We object to such words. It is totally indecent to ask such improper questions to our beloved leader.'

'Please remain patient. Let us allow him to speak freely. It is true that I married a young girl in my fifty-seventh year. But I never declared myself as a reincarnation of King Rama who vowed to have only one wife! I loved that girl and she returned my love. Willingly, we married each other. What is wrong with that?' asked Senior Paluvettarayar.

'Nothing wrong!' replied several voices.

'I never said there was anything wrong about this marriage. But… but…'

'But what? Ask without hesitation.'

'People say that in all matters, Senior Paluvettarayar consults and acts according to the wishes of the Young Queen, even in matters of the state. It is said that he takes his young queen wherever he goes.'

Paluvettarayar continued, 'Munairaya, is it a crime to take my legally wedded wife wherever I go? It is not true to say that I consult the Young Queen in matters of the state.'

'If so, I request Senior Paluvettarayar to clear just one more doubt. Why has this palanquin, which should have stayed in the women's courtyard, come here to our confidential meeting? Is there someone inside the closed palanquin or not? If there is no one inside, how is it that I heard somebody clearing their throat?'

A curious silence prevailed after Munairayar asked these questions. Since these doubts had occurred to most of them, nobody spoke up against the words of Munairayar.

Senior Paluvettarayar said, 'Good question. I am obligated to clear your misgivings. I am happy to have the trust you have all posted in me. Let us come to a conclusion.'

'Yes, we do. We have complete trust in you,' said Sambuvarayar.

'Let no one think that my loyalty to Senior Paluvettarayar is less than that of anyone else. Since he invited us to speak freely, I asked,' said Munairayar.

'I know about Munairayar. I also recognize the trust you have all placed in me. Therefore, let us now come to a conclusion about the matter for which we convened this meeting. Let Emperor Sundara Chola live long and rule this Chola Empire. However, unfortunately, if something happens to him, we have to decide who has to succeed the Chola throne,' said Paluvettarayar.

'We request you to voice your opinion. None of us will say anything against your views.'

'That is not correct. Each one of you must express your opinion.

'Permit me to remind you about some old history. Twenty-four years ago, Emperor Kandaraditya who ruled the Chola Kingdom died unexpectedly. His son, Madurandakan, was only one year old. Kandaraditya, on his deathbed, had named his younger brother, Arinjaya, as the successor. This was revealed to us by Kandaraditya's wife, Queen Sembiyan Madevi. Unfortunately, Arinjaya, too, died within a year. Kandaraditya's son Parantaka Sundara Chola became the emperor. Until two years ago, he ruled the nation with justice.

Now, the health of Sundara Chola is not good. We have to decide the successor. Madurandakan, the cherished son of Emperor Kandaraditya, is now grown up with all the qualities of a person worthy of the throne.

Sundara Chola's son, Aditya Karikalan, who is younger to Madurandakan by one year, is stationed in Kanchi as commander-in-chief. Who, between these two, has the right to succeed the throne?'

'Madurandakan, the son of Emperor Kandaraditya has the right to succeed. That is legal, justice, traditional,' said Sambuvaraya

'We all agree,' so rose several voices.

'Before that, we need a clarification. What are the feelings of Prince Madurandakan? Is he ready to accept the throne and rule this Empire? We have heard that the cherished son of Kandaraditya has renounced the world and is fully devoted to Lord Siva with no interest in political affairs. We have also heard that his mother, Queen Sembiyan Madevi, is totally opposed to him ascending the throne. We wish to know the truth about this from you.'

'In due course, his mind has slowly undergone some transformation. He is ready to accept the throne if you all support him.'

'What proof do we have for this?'

'I will produce proof to satisfy you all.'

Senior Paluvettarayar rose from his seat and went near the closed palanquin.

'Prince! Please come out and show your face,' senior Paluvettarayar spoke in a subdued tone.

Vandiyathevan, sitting behind the pillar on the upper terrace was listening to all these discussions with curiosity. As he peeped down, he saw a dazzling face, comparable to the full moon.

Oh, is this Prince Madurandaka, son of Kandaraditya? I mistook him to be a woman because of the closed palanquin. But did Alvarkkadiyan Nambi also make the same mistake?

Vandiyathevan looked around to see if Nambi was still thrusting his head above the wall. That spot of the palace wall was now shrouded by shadows cast by the trees. He could see nothing.

By now, he could hear some shouts from below. 'Long live Madurandaka!'

9

True Friend

Vandiyathevan went back to bed that night in Kadamboor with bitter feelings after witnessing the midnight conspiracy. The dangers from external enemies to the Chola Empire had been overcome only a few years ago but the internal political conspiracy was rising up now.

Most of the important officials, ministers, chieftains and famous warriors of the Chola Kingdom were involved in this political conspiracy. Senior Paluvettarayar must have secretly taken Prince Madurandakan, the rival of Crown Prince Aditya Karikalan, to several other places also in a closed palanquin. The fact of his marrying a young girl in his old age had helped him in this conspiracy!

What is the legality? Who is really eligible to succeed? Prince Karikalan or Prince Madurandakan? The more he thought about it, the more he felt that both sides had equal rights. Vandiyathevan could not sleep for a long time. After much struggle, he fell asleep only at dawn.

Vandiyathevan did not get up even after the sun had risen. He was woken up by Kandamaran.

'It is already so late; it must be several hours past sunrise. I have to leave immediately. Kandamara, tell your servants to prepare my horse.'

'How can you leave so soon? What is the hurry? You must be my guest for at least ten days before you go,' said Kandamaran.

'No, my dear friend! My uncle in Tanjore is very sick. I must see him before he is gone.' Vandiyathevan lied with conviction to escape from Kadamboor.

After breakfast, both friends mounted their horses and left Kadamboor Palace. The ride was pleasant. The friends didn't mind even the dust from the swift winds. They were lost in old memories. After some time, Vandiyathevan said, 'Kandamara! Even though I spent just one night in your palace, it was very useful to me. You used to say much about your sister while we were in the army camp. I could not even see her properly yesterday.'

Kandamaran wanted to say something. But no words came out.

'Never mind. Kandamara, what is your sister's name?'

'Manimekalai.'

'Oh! A delightful name!'

Kandamaran interrupted and said in a guilty tone, 'My friend! Please take my sister off your mind and forget her.'

'Why Kandamara? Has everything has turned upside down? Even last night you hinted that I may become the son-in-law of your family!'

'Yes, I did say so. But the situation has changed since then. My parents have arranged to wed my sister elsewhere and she has also agreed.'

Vandiyathevan had no trouble in guessing who the bridegroom might be. They must have engaged her to Madurandakan who had stepped out of the closed palanquin. They were perhaps arranging such a marriage alliance in order to strengthen Prince Madurandakan.

'Oh! You have fixed an alliance with one of your rich guests who came last night. Kandamara, I am neither surprised nor disappointed. In a way it was expected.'

'Expected? How is that?'

'Who would give their daughter to an ordinary man like me? What is the use of my glorious ancestry?'

'My dear friend! Enough of this! Don't think low of me or my family. What you say is not the reason. There is a strategic reason for this. You will agree when you get to know of it.'

'Kandamara, you're talking quite mysteriously today.'

'Forgive me for that. It is a big secret which I cannot reveal now. Whatever happens, trust me that nothing will come between us. When the time comes, I will disclose all the details. I will never let you down.'

Within a few minutes the friends reached the river bank. The river was swollen with floods. Trees on the other bank looked like small plants. The river water was red with silt from the distant lands, flowing with thunderous whirlpools trying to break through the high banks on both sides, rushing towards the eastern sea. Vandiyathevan was amazed at this majestic sight.

Both friends got off their horses. 'Can I take the horse in the boat?' asked Vandiyathevan.

'No need. Look! Two of my soldiers are following us. One of them will take your horse back to Kadamboor. The other fellow will accompany you in this boat and get another horse for you on the other side,' said Kandamaran.

'Aha! How thoughtful. You are my true friend.'

The two friends took leave of each other with a hearty embrace. Vandiyathevan walked down the river bank and got into the boat. One of Kandamaran's soldiers also entered the boat. The boat was ready to leave.

Suddenly, from a distance they could hear shouts of 'Stop! Stop!'. The boatmen stopped the boat. Vandiyathevan recognized the approaching man as Alvarkkadiyan Nambi.

10

Astrologer

River Ponni (Cauvery), born at the Kudagu Hills, was eager to embrace her beloved. She went swiftly crossing hills and dales, rocky mountains and canyons. As she came closer and closer, with joyous anticipation of meeting her beloved, the Ocean King, she extended her arms widely to reach out to him. These arms were the many tributaries crisscrossing the Chola Kingdom. Chola women celebrated her in many wondrous ways. They clothed her with beautiful paddy fields and colorful flowers.

One of the arms stretched out by Ponni to reach out for her beloved the Ocean King is known by the name Arasalar River. One could not easily see this small river from a little distance on account of the thick groves of trees growing on both its banks.

A boat, laden with beautiful girls singing, floated gently down the river and stopped amidst the woods. Two women stepped out. One was a royal lady, the other was her companion who played the veena. Though both were beautiful, there was a difference between the two of them. One had the dignity of a lotus in full bloom; the other had the softness of the evening water lily. One was the radiant full moon; the other was the young crescent of late evening. One was the dancing peacock; the other was a nightingale.

Of the two ladies, the one with dignity in her posture was Princess Kundavai, the beloved daughter of Emperor Sundara Chola. She was the elder sister of Prince Arulmolivarman, who later becomes the historically famous Raja Raja Chola. She was the lady revered by the people as the young royal princess. As a distinguished daughter of the Tamils, she laid the foundation for the greatness of the Chola Empire. She was the capable lady who moulded the ambitions of Raja Raja's son Rajendra and made him the greatest among the South Indian kings.

Her friend was Vanathi, a princess from the clan of Kodumbalur, a small kingdom in the Chola Empire. She was fortunate in being a part of Kundavai's household. In the future, she would attain greatness unparalleled in history. She was young, modest and gentle. After alighting from the boat, Kundavai turned to her other companions and said, 'You can all wait here. We will be back in an hour.'

All her companions were princesses from the families of the aristocrats and chieftains in the Chola Kingdom. They had come to the Palayarai Palace as maids of honour to Kundavai. After Kundavai left, along with Vanathi, the others were envious of Vanathi.

A horse-drawn chariot awaited on the shore. When both were seated, the chariot moved on swiftly.

'Sister! Where are we going?' asked Vanathi.

'We are going to the house of the Kumbakonam astrologer to ask about you! For some months now, you have been lost in some dream world and losing weight.'

'Sister! Nothing is wrong with my health. Let's go back.'

'No, my dear! I am not going to ask him about you alone. I am going to ask him if I will ever get married or am I going to spend all my life a spinster!'

'Sister! Why ask the astrologer about it? Just nod your head; princes from all the fifty-six kingdoms would queue up, vying with each other for your hand. You have to decide and not the astrologer.'

'Vanathi, even if I accept all that you say as truth, there is one obstacle. If I marry any one of these princes from another land, I will have to go with him to his kingdom. My dear, I don't like to go away from this beautiful Chola Kingdom where the Ponni flows! I have vowed that I will never go out of this kingdom.'

'That is not an obstacle! Any prince who marries you will stay at your feet as your slave. If you order him to stay here, he will remain here.'

'Oh God! How can we retain an alien prince in our land? If I have to be married, I will choose an orphan Chola warrior without any kingdom. He will remain here, in this Chola Kingdom.'

'I too have no heart to leave this prosperous Chola Kingdom!'

'Once you are married, won't you have to leave?'

'I am not going to marry anyone, sister. I love this Chola Empire.'

'You deceiver! I know everything! The Chola Empire, my loving brother whom you love, is bearing sword and spear and has gone to Lanka to wage a war! Don't I know your secrets?'

The house of the astrologer was situated in the outskirts of Kumbakonam, in an isolated spot, near a Kali temple. The chariot entered the city, through a circular route and reached that house quickly. The astrologer and one of his disciples received the royal guests.

'Astrologer! I hope none else will come here now.'

'People seek the astrologer only when they are troubled. Nowadays, under the rule of your great father, the Emperor Sundara Chola, people have no troubles at all!'

Kundavai and Vanathi entered the astrologer's house. The astrologer turned to his assistant and said, 'Wait outside and allow no one in.'

After both ladies were seated, the astrologer asked. 'Your majesty, please tell me now the purpose of your visit?'

'I have come to ask about this girl. She came to the Palayarai Palace about a year ago. For the first eight months, she was very cheerful and happy. Amongst all my companions she was the most joyous, always filled with laughter. For the last four months, something has happened to her. Often, she is depressed.'

'Is she not the beloved daughter of the chieftan of Kodumbalur? Is her name Vanathi?' asked the astrologer.

'Yes, you know everything.'

'I even have the horoscope of this young lady. I have it in my collection. Please wait a little.'

The astrologer opened an old casket and searched awhile. He then picked up a palm leaf and went through it.

II

Sudden Entry

Kumbakonam was known as Kudanthai during those days. Besides being a pilgrimage centre, it was also famous for the astrologer. A little away, to the south of Kumbakonam, was located the interim capital of the Cholas, i.e, Palayarai, with its temple towers reaching the skies.

After reading the horoscope, the astrologer stared at Vanathi's face, then again looked at the horoscope. He kept on doing this without uttering a single word!

With a little impatience Kundavai asked, 'What, sir? Are you going to say something or not?'

'Your majesty, this is a very fortunate horoscope. Her horoscope is better than even your horoscope! I have never seen such a lucky horoscope till now. Four months ago, something that seemed like a bad omen occurred. Something slipped and fell. But in truth, that is not a bad omen. It is from that incident that this princess has obtained all her good fortune.'

Kundavai gave a mischievous smile to Vanathi and asked.

'Where will her husband come from? Can you tell us all these things from the horoscope?'

'Your majesty! A husband for this maid does not have to come from very far! He is quite nearby. That brave warrior is not here now. He has gone across the seas.'

Upon hearing these words, Kundavai looked at Vanathi. Vanathi tried to contain the joy bubbling in her heart; however, her face revealed it.

'Who is he, then? Which clan?'

'Oh yes. A fortunate prince with the conch and discus on his palms.'

Once again Kundavai looked at Vanathi. But Vanathi was looking down, hiding her face. 'Any signs or lines on her palms as well?' asked Kundavai. 'Tell us something about the man who is to be her husband.'

'Yes. The fortunate youth who will take her hand is the bravest among brave and a king of kings. He will rule the kingdom for many years with the praise and support of a thousand kings. But there will be several dangers for the young man who will marry this princess. He will have several enemies...'

'Oh!'

'But all the dangers will fly away at the end. Enemies will be totally destroyed. There is something much more important than even this! You should look at the stomach of this girl sometime, there will be a mark shaped like a banyan leaf on her stomach. If it is not there, I will give up my practice.'

'Sir, what is special about the sign of a banyan leaf?'

'The son who is to be born to this lady will have no deterrents. His touch will be golden; wherever he sets foot, the Chola tiger flag will fly high over them. The fame of his clan will last as long as this world exists!'

As the astrologer spoke these words, Kundavai was looking at him with rapt attention.

'Sister! Something is happening to me,' said Vanathi in distress and suddenly, fainted.

'Sir! Please fetch some water quickly,' saying this, Kundavai lifted Vanathi onto her lap. Kundavai sprinkled water on her friend's face.

'Nothing will go wrong! Don't be worried,' said the astrologer.

'I am not worried. She will open her eyes soon. Upon waking she will ask if this is earth or paradise,' said Kundavai.

Then, in a much softer voice she asked, 'Sir! I came to ask you something else also. Have you any answer?'

The astrologer's manner changed; he said some words to her very precisely and quickly.

Then, Kundavai asked, 'I hear that people in the countryside and cities are talking about all sorts of things. The long-tailed comet has been appearing in the skies for some time. Is there some danger to the empire?'

'Your Majesty, in general, this period is full of confusion and danger. All of us have to be a little careful.'

'Sir! About my father, the Emperor... I am quite worried ever since he moved to Tanjore from Palayarai.'

'I have told you earlier, Your Majesty. This is a period of grave danger for the Emperor. All your family members will face great danger. With the grace of Goddess Durga all troubles will be overcome.'

'Sister, where are we?' asked the faint voice of Vanathi.

Vanathi, who was lying on Kundavai's lap, blinked her eyes several times like a buzzing bee and looked around.

'Darling, we are still on this earth. The flower-laden flying chariot has not yet come to take us to the heavens. Get up! Let us get into our horse-drawn chariot and go back to the palace.'

Vanathi sat up and asked, 'Did I faint?'

'No. You did not faint. You took a nice nap on my lap. I even sang a lullaby. Did you not hear it?'

'Please bear with me sister. Suddenly, I felt dizzy.'

'Yes. You will feel dizzy. If this astrologer predicts all those grand fortunes for me, even my head would become dizzy.'

'Get up. Let us go. Can you walk to the doorstep? Or, should I carry you on my hip?'

'No. I can walk very well.'

'Please have a little patience, Your Majesty! I will give you some offerings of the goddess,' said the astrologer.

'Sir, you described all sorts of things for me. But you said nothing for sister? About the bravest of warriors who is to marry sister...' asked Vanathi.

'Doubtless. A very capable prince. He who has all the thirty-two signs of good looks will take her hand!'

'When will that handsome prince, deserving our majestic Kundavai come and where from?' asked Vanathi.

'How will he come? Upon a horse or elephant? On a chariot or on foot? Or, will he rip open the roof and jump down from the skies?' asked Kundavai with a mocking voice.

At this moment, voices could be heard outside the door.

'Is this the astrologer's house?'

'Yes. Who are you?'

'I must see the astrologer.'

'Come later.'

'I cannot come later; I am in a great hurry.'

'Sir! Please! Don't enter!'

The confused shouts came closer and closer. The wooden front door opened with a bang and a young man made a sudden entry.

Yes, it was the youthful hero, Vandiyathevan. All the three pairs of eyes inside the house looked at that warrior.

Vandiyathevan looked at the people inside—no, he looked at only one person inside. Not even that. He did not see Kundavai completely. He just saw her golden face. Not even that! He saw the petals of her coral red lips, opening slightly with surprise; he saw her wide-open eyes brimming with surprise; he saw her dark eyebrows; he saw the sandal-coloured forehead; he saw the rosy dimpled cheeks; he saw the throat shaped like a smooth conch-shell. He saw all these at the same time and individually! They became imprinted in his heart.

All this took place in just a second. He quickly turned towards the astrologer's assistant and said, 'Why didn't you say that there were ladies inside the house? Had you said it, I would not have come in like this.' With these words he crossed the doorstep and quickly left the house but not without stealing another quick glance at Kundavai.

'Oh my god! What a storm that was!' said Kundavai.

'Listen. The storm has not stopped!' said Vanathi.

The argument between the astrologer's assistant and Vandiyathevan was continuing.

'Sir! Who was that?' asked Kundavai

'I don't know. He looks like a foreigner.'

Kundavai suddenly thought of something and laughed brightly. 'Why are you laughing, sister?' asked Vanathi.

'Why am I laughing? We were just talking about my bridegroom—whether he would come on horseback, riding an elephant or jump down from the sky; I thought of that and laughed!'

Vanathi also began to laugh irresistibly. Their laughter rose like waves on the ocean shore. Because of their laughter even the argument outside stopped.

Immersed in silent thoughts, the astrologer gave kumkum to both ladies. After receiving it both women rose and walked outside. The astrologer went along. Vandiyathevan who was standing aside near the doorstep, saw them and said loudly, 'I beg your pardon. This genius did not tell me that ladies were inside. That is why I entered in such a hurry. Pardon me for that.'

With a pleasant face and mischief-filled, teasing eyes, Kundavai looked up at him. She did not say a single word in reply. She took hold of Vanathi's hand and walked towards her chariot under the banyan tree.

12

Nandini—A Mystery!

When the boat reached the opposite bank, the soldier who accompanied Vandiyathevan went away to get a horse. Alvarkkadiyan and Vandiyathevan sat down under a large banyan tree on the river bank. They tried to elicit information from each other. For a while, the conversation continued in a roundabout manner.

'Youg man, you went to Kadamboor without taking me along.'

'I gained entry into the palace with great difficulty.'

'What happened there? Who else had come there?'

'Many dignitaries had come including Senior Paluvettarayar with his young bride. There are no words to describe the beauty of that young queen!'

'Did you see her?!'

'Yes. I saw her. My friend Kandamaran took me to the women's chambers. I saw her there. Among all the dark-colored beauties, that queen's face was like a radiant full moon. All the heavenly beauties—Ramba, Urvasi, etc.—are no match for her.'

'Young man! What happened then? Did you see the folk dance?'

'Yes. It was very fantastic. I thought of you at that time. The "divine-man" and "divine-woman" came upon the stage as if possessed and danced with fury.'

'Did the spirit manifest? Any predictions?'

'Yes, he said something about political affairs. I did not listen to that at all. All the dignitaries at Kadamboor had a midnight meeting to discuss the successor to the throne. Who will be the next king? What is your opinion?'

'I know nothing about politics. I am a devout Vaishnavite. I sing devotional songs to spread Vaishnavism.' After uttering these words, Alvarkkadiyan started singing hymns in praise of Lord Narayana.

Vandiyathevan interrupted him, 'Please, stop this. I think your devotion to god is false. I suspect it to be a big masquerade!'

'Oh! God what are you saying?'

'You put on such guise to hide your lust!'

'Young man, I am not a hypocrite. Your suspicion is incorrect.'

'Then why did you ask me to deliver a note to the girl who came in the palanquin? That too, how can you lose your heart to a woman who is already married? You have come to Kadamboor mainly to see her. Don't deny it.'

'I won't deny it. But your reasoning is incorrect. You have misunderstood me. It is a long story.'

'My horse hasn't arrived yet. Tell me that story. I can listen.'

'By story I do not mean an imaginary tale. It is a true and astonishing story. You will be shocked if you hear it. Do you want me to tell you?'

'Yes.'

'Alright. Though I am in a hurry to go elsewhere, nonetheless, I will tell you that story before I go. I may need your help sometime later. You should not refuse it then.'

'If it is justified, I will help you.'

'I will surely tell you the story of the young bride of that demon, Senior Paluvettarayar. Her name is Nandini.'

Alvarkkadiyan started narrating the story of Nandini.

Alvarkkadiyan Nambi was born in a village on the banks of the river Vaigai in the Pandiya Kingdom. All his family members were ardent Vaishnavites. One day, when his father was walking in the garden along the river bank, he found an abandoned baby girl and brought her home. The child was very attractive and all in the family loved her deeply. Since the child was found in a garden (*nandavanam*), they named her Nandini. Alvarkkadiyan considered her as his own younger sister and loved her very much.

As Nandini grew in years, her devotion to Lord Narayana also grew. She captivated the hearts of all the people with her devotional songs. After his father's death, Alvarkkadiyan took up the responsibility of raising her. Once Alvarkkadiyan had gone on a pilgrimage to Tirupati. His return was delayed.

The final great battle between the Chola and Pandiya kings was fought near the city of Madurai. The Pandiya armies were totally destroyed. King Veerapandiya was defeated. His personal guards found him with wounds all over his body and they brought him to Nandini's house which was nearby. Nandini was filled with pity and she nursed King Veerapandiya in the sickbed. The crown prince, Aditya Karikalan, found him and killed him. Nandini went missing. It was learnt that Senior Paluvettarayar was captivated by the beauty of Nandini and took her away with him.

All this happened three years ago. After that Alvarkkadiyan never got to see Nandini at all. From that day, Alvarkkadiyan had been trying to meet her.

Upon hearing this tale, Vandiyathevan's heart was rather moved. For a moment, he thought of telling Alvarkkadiyan that the person inside the covered palanquin in Kadamboor was not Nandini, that it was Prince Madurandakan. Something in his heart prevented him as he disbelieved Nambi and his story. By then, the soldier brought a horse for Vandiyathevan.

Before parting, Vandiyathevan asked Alvarkkadiyan once again.

'Can you say who will succeed to the Chola throne, if something happens to the Emperor?'

'What do I know about political matters? Perhaps the Kumbakonam astrologer may be able to tell you something,' said Alvarkkadiyan

'Oh? Is the Kumbakonam astrologer that capable?'

'Very capable. He will make correct predictions. He knows the worldly activities and gives his predictions accordingly.'

Vandiyathevan was curious to learn about his own future and made up his mind to go see the astrologer.

13

Vandiyathevan and Astrologer

The astrologer took Vandiyathevan into his house.

'My son! Who are you?'

Vandiyathevan laughed.

'Why are you laughing, my son?'

'Nothing. You are such a famous astrologer. You ask me such a question! Find out using your astrology.'

'If I were to tell everything on my own, who will pay for my services?'

Vandiyathevan smiled and then asked, 'Sir! Who were those women who came before me?'

'My son! Several people will visit an astrologer's house. One should not talk about one visitor to another. I won't tell you anything about the women who left just now. Neither will I disclose a single word about you to anybody else.'

'Ah! Everything that Alvarkkadiyan Nambi said about you seems to be true!'

'Oh! That Vaishnavite devout has a different name in different towns and he dons different roles for different persons.'

'Do you mean to say he is a bad fellow?'

'We cannot say that! He is good to the good and bad to the bad.'

'Ok, predict my future. I am in a hurry.'

'I need some basis to predict; I need a horoscope to study; if there is no horoscope, I must at least know the day and star under which you were born. If you do not know even that, I need a name and address.'

'My name is Vallavarayan Vandiyathevan.'

'Aha! Of the Vaanar clan?'

'Yes, I am that very same person.'

'Young man, why did you not say this before?'

The astrologer started singing a song in praise of Vandiyatheven's Vaanar clan.

'How was the song?' The astrologer asked him.

'The song was very pleasing! But now I have to climb a tall tree to find my kingdom,' said Vandiyathevan sarcastically.

'Today your situation is like that. Who knows what will happen tomorrow?'

'What do the planets and stars foretell about me, sir?'

'Ask something specific; I will answer specifically.'

'Tell me, the mission on which I am going to Tanjore, will it succeed?'

'If you are going to Tanjore on your own, the endeavour will succeed; if you are going on someone else's behalf, I have to see that person's horoscope before I answer.'

Vandiyathevan uttered in astonishment, 'I have never met as smart an astrologer like you.'

'Do not flatter me, young man.'

'Ok. I will ask what I want, clearly. I want to meet the Emperor in Tanjore. Is that possible?'

'There are two astrologers greater than me in Tanjore. You have to ask them.'

'Who are they?'

'One is Senior Paluvettarayar, the other is his brother, Junior Paluvettarayar.'

'I want to go on a ship and travel to distant lands...'

'Your wish will definitely be fulfilled. You will cross the seas very soon.'

'Sir, about the commander of the southern armies, Prince Arulmolivarman, who is now waging a war in Lanka, what do the planets and stars foretell about him?'

'Young man, Prince Arulmoli is like the pole star. He has a charming face like that of a baby. He is the darling of the goddess of good luck. Just as sailors take direction from the pole star, you take direction from Prince Arulmoli.'

'Sir! Your description of Prince Arulmoli sounds like a lover describing his sweetheart!'

'Young man, ask any fellow of the Chola Kingdom, they will tell you the same thing.'

'Sir! Many thanks. I take leave of you! Please accept this small gift of gold coins along with my heartfelt thanks.'

'The benevolence of the Vaanar clan never dies!' said the astrologer, accepting the gold coins.

14

Crocodile in the River

Vandiyathevan left for Tanjore riding on his horse. The scenery around the river Arasalar appeared to him more beautiful than what he had heard about the Chola Kingdom.

Emerald green paddy fields, ginger and turmeric gardens, sugarcane and banana plantations, coconut groves; streams, rivulets and brooks; tanks, pools and canals—all these dotted the landscape like a mosaic pattern.

Blooming water lilies in creeks and other flowers were abundant in riotous display on still-water ponds and pools. He had never seen such flowers before! White storks and herons flew in large groups like soft clouds. Red-legged cranes stood on one leg performing penance. Crystal clear water rushed and frothed along conduits. Farmers were ploughing their paddy fields, manuring it with bio fertilizers. Women were transplanting seedlings from nurseries, singing melodious folk songs.

Sugar mills were seen next to the cane plantations, extracting sweet sugarcane juice. The aroma of the fresh juice combined with the smell of jaggery filled the air and tingled the nose.

Tiny cottages with thatched roofs and tiled roofs were seen amidst the coconut groves. In the front yards of the tiny cottages, the new paddy had been spread out to dry. Hens and roosters were pecking at the grains and ran hither and thither with cries of 'Koko ro ko!' The little girls, set to guard the grain, were not bothered about that.

Smoke rose from chimneys on rooftops. The fragrance of paddy being cured, millet-grain being parched and meat being roasted in hot spices tempted Vandiyathevan's taste buds.

Blacksmiths on the roadside were busy preparing tools for farming and battlefield. Farmers and soldiers were vying with each other to buy the tools of their trade.

The sounds of bells and drums and pipes inside the temples were heard mixed with the pleasant music of devotional songs.

Men, tired from their labours, were resting beneath shady mango trees watching goats fight.

Priests, carrying their guardian deities, amidst songs and dances were added attractions.

Vandiyathevan was enjoying the graceful dance of peacocks and the melodious songs of cuckoos on his way. Yet his mind was preoccupied with thoughts of the girl he had seen at the astrologer's house.

Alas! Why didn't that girl open her pearly lips and utter a few words when I pleaded apology for suddenly entering the astrologer's house? What would she have lost by saying a few words? Who could she be? Am I a fellow to be ignored? That Kumbakonam astrologer never revealed who that girl was! He is very clever. He made a good prediction about my rising lucky stars.

Finally, he reached the banks of the river Arasalar and suddenly heard the screams of women asking for help.

'Oh help! Help! Crocodile! Crocodile!'

He whipped his horse and sped towards them. He saw the faces of several women filled with fright. To his surprise, he saw the very same girls he had seen in the astrologer's house!

He saw a crocodile with its jaws wide open, half in the water and half on the bank very close to those women. He swiftly threw the spear on the crocodile's back.

He heard the women laughing. The sound was very repulsive to Vandiyathevan. 'Why do these foolish girls laugh at this dangerous moment?' he thought.

The one he had seen in the astrologer's house spoke in a sweet voice, 'Girls, stop it! Why are you all laughing?'

He moved closer to the crocodile and then hesitated as he raised his sword. He turned to look at the faces of those women once again with a suspicion, which filled his heart with shame. By now, that girl, who had been dwelling in his thoughts for some time now, stood before him, in front of the crocodile as if guarding it!

'Sir! I am very thankful to you. Please don't trouble yourself unnecessarily.'

Earlier in the day, there was much back-biting and bickering when the other maids were left behind by Princess Kundavai who took only Vanathi with her to the astrologer's house.

'Hi! All see how fortune favours that Kodumbalur girl! Why does our princess love her so much?'

'No, nothing like that! For the past four months this girl has been behaving strangely; she often faints. Our princess is worried because she is fatherless. She is taking Vanathi to the astrologer to find out what troubles her.'

'I agree with you. All those fainting fits of Vanathi are only big deceptions.'

'She is a pretender and a skillful actress.'

'Fortune favours the deceivers only.'

'There is no need to go to an astrologer. It is lovelorn fainting!'

Upon hearing this, all of them giggled.

'When our Prince Arulmoli comes back from Lanka, she will again play her tricks on him. We should not give room for that.'

'Come on. Let us do what our princess asked us to do.'

They pulled a stuffed crocodile from underneath the boat and placed it among the tree roots.

One maid asked, 'Why did our princess want us to leave the crocodile here?'

'To get rid of Vanathi's fear and make her brave,' said another sarcastically

'If we consider all these things, it seems as if the Princess really intends to wed this foolish Vanathi to our prince!' commented another maid.

'Let us also play our trick and impress our prince. What this Vanathi does, we can also do!'

15

Affectionate Brother and Sister

About a thousand years ago, the best of the kings, Sundara Chola (AD 957–973) ruled as an emperor, without an equal, in South India. Chola territories were spreading in all directions with more power during his time.

Sundara Chola had all the qualities of a great king. Being skilled at war, he led an army to the southern region in the very beginning of his reign. A great battle took place between the Chola and Pandiya armies at a place called Chevoor. Mahinda, the king of Lanka, sent a large army to help his friend the Pandiya king, Veerapandiya, who was ruling from Madurai City.

It had been the practice of the Lankan kings to send their men in support of the Pandiya kings in the clashes between the Cholas and Pandiyas. Sundara Chola wanted to put an end to this practice.

Unfortunately, the Chola army did not land in Lanka all at one time as they did not have adequate shipping facilities at the time. The battalions, which had landed first, started advancing without any forethought. Mahinda's Lankan army ambushed the Chola forces in a surprise move and the Chola commander, the chieftain of Kodumbalur (father of Princess Vanathi) lost his life.

A large force was mobilized and a question, as to who should lead the Chola army, arose. Prince Arulmolivarman, the younger son of Emperor Sundara Chola, came forward to lead the army as the crown prince, Aditya Karikalan, was busy guarding the northern frontier.

'Father! I have spent enough time in the luxury of the Palayarai Palace. Please appoint me as the commander of the southern armies.

I shall go to Lanka and lead the Lankan war.'

Prince Arulmoli was barely nineteen years old. All the children born to the handsome Emperor Sundara Chola were attractive and beautiful. But the youngest child, Arulmoli, surpassed all others in beauty. He had a divine and charming face. His elder sister Kundavai loved him more than any other person.

Though she was barely two years older than him, Kundavai felt that the responsibility of rearing this divine child was hers! In return, Arulmoli showered all his love upon his sister. The brother would not cross the line drawn by his elder sister. The Princess had to merely utter one word; even if all the gods were to say something against Kundavai, Arulmoli wouldn't heed their words. The elder sister's words were gospel to the younger brother.

The sister would often look into her darling brother's face not just when he was awake, but even while he was sleeping.

'There is some divine grace in him; it is my duty to bring it to the forefront and make him shine!' thought the young princess.

When her brother slept, she would often hold his hands and study the lines on his palms. To her, those lines would appear to have the signs of the conch and disc.

'Aha! He is born to rule this world! He will bring the whole world under one rule,' she would think.

But there was no possibility of him ascending the Chola throne. There were two others before him eligible to ascend the throne. Then, how could he do so? Who knows divine intentions? The world was big, with several kingdoms and territories, along with a lot of opportunities.

Kundavai was constantly thinking of her brother's future. In the end, she came to the conclusion that her younger brother was the apt commander to lead the Lankan war.

She said, 'My loving brother Arulmoli! I can't be without you even for a moment. However, the time has now come for me to send you to lead the Lankan war.'

Arulmoli joyously agreed. He had been waiting for the day to escape from the life of luxury.

He began preparing to leave for Lanka.

Kundavai arranged for a grand ceremony at Palayarai to bid farewell to her loving brother. The victory drums in the palace courtyard boomed; conches were blown and cheering shouts rose sky-high.

All the maids of honour in Kundavai's court stood on the palace steps carrying golden arti plates, each laden with a lamp. These maids were princesses from noble families. They had all come to Palayarai to be companions to Kundavai. Vanathi, the daughter of Kodumbalur chieftain, was one among them.

When the girls saw the Prince coming down all hearts were pounding. When the Prince came closer, they began waving their arti plates with the lighted lamp before him. At that moment, Vanathi started shivering. The golden arti plate slipped from her hands. The thought, 'Oh dear! What is this ill omen!' rose in the hearts of all. But when they saw the wick burning bright even when the lamp had fallen, they felt it was a good omen after all.

Prince Arulmoli smiled gently at Vanathi who had dropped the plate. As soon as he moved ahead, she fainted with the guilt of having committed a blunder. Upon the orders of Kundavai, the serving maids carried her inside the palace.

Kundavai hurried inside, without even waiting to see her beloved brother mount his horse for departure.

Holding the reins of his horse, the Prince sent a soldier inside to find out the condition of the girl who had fainted.

Kundavai sent the soldier back asking him to bring her brother inside for a moment. Prince Arulmoli came in. The sight of his sister trying to revive the young girl lying on her lap touched his heart.

'Sister! Who is this girl?' he asked.

'She is Vanathi, daughter of the chieftain of Kodumbalur.'

'Oh! Now I understand why she fainted. Was it not her father who led the earlier war to Lanka? Didn't he die in the battlefront over there? Perhaps she remembered that.'

'Maybe. But don't worry about her. I will look after her. I called you back to wish you well. Come back soon with victory.'

By now, Vanathi was regaining her consciousness and heard the pleasant voice of Prince Arulmoli! Upon glancing at the Prince, her eyes opened gently and her face became brighter. Her coral red lips smiled and her cheeks dimpled. Her shyness also returned and she felt sorry for having acted inappropriately.

But the Prince consoled her, 'Don't worry Vanathi! You have every reason to be agitated.'

As the Prince, who never spoke to any woman, was talking to her, Vanathi wondered whether it was all really happening.

'Sister, my men are waiting. Permit me to leave. When you send me news from here, let me know of this girl's condition.'

Saying this to his sister, he departed. The other maids and companions were watching all these happenings from the windows and balconies. The flames of jealousy were blowing from their eyes.

From that day onwards, Kundavai started pouring more love on Vanathi by keeping her by her side always. She engaged tutors to teach her and took her wherever she went to share her secrets and her dreams about her younger brother. All this made the other girls in the palace all the more jealous.

16

Self-Respecting Horse

Kundavai decided that Vanathi would be the bride for her loving brother. But Vanathi was too timid. Kundavai decided to make her fit to be her brother's bride. So, she had arranged a stuffed crocodile to give her a shock treatment. But Vanathi easily passed that test.

After meeting the Kumbakonam astrologer, Kundavai and Vanathi left in their swan-shaped boat downstream for a short distance, with a plan for some fun amidst the thick groves of trees. After reaching their destination, they climbed down. Suddenly, one girl screamed—'Crocodile! Help! Help!' Soon all other girls started crying for help. But Vanathi remained unperturbed.

'Sister, the crocodile is powerful only in the water and not on the land. Tell these girls not to be scared!'

'You thief! Somehow you have come to know that it is a stuffed crocodile!' said one of the other maidens.

'I won't be scared of the crocodile on land. I am only scared of lizards.'

Having heard the cries for help from the women, Vandiyathevan arrived there to save them from the crocodile! He threw his spear and attacked the crocodile in one go. When Vandiyathevan saw the lady whom he had seen at the astrologer's house, his joy knew no bounds.

But, the crocodile behind her with jaws open created a suspicion in him. Why is she standing before the crocodile? Why is she asking me not to bother? And why is that crocodile not moving.

The lady continued, 'Sir! In Kudanthai, you apologized for having barged into the astrologer's house. We left without even replying you.

You might have misunderstood us. I was in confusion as my friend had suddenly fainted just then. That is why I could not respond. I feel sorry for that.' His disappointment melted when she uttered these consoling words.

Oh! What a sweet voice this is! Why is my heart pounding like this? Why is my throat parched?

As Vandiyathevan's heart raced with excitement, Kundavai said, 'You threw the spear at the crocodile. It is rare to find a warrior like you who can handle the spear with such speed and accuracy.'

All the other maids laughed and their laughter annoyed Vandiyathevan. He examined the crocodile again to find it to be a stuffed one. He felt as if his pride had fallen. His horse neighed as if mocking him along with those girls. He jumped upon his horse and whipped it without even looking back at the girl who captivated his heart. The self-respecting horse quickly galloped away. For a while, Kundavai stood looking in his direction till the dust raised by the horse had settled down.

Then she addressed her companions, 'Girls! You have no manners! You should not have laughed like that. Never show discourtesy to a stranger. What would he think of the Chola women?'

17

Idumban Kari—The Dark Man

After Vandiyathevan left for Kumbakonam, Alvarkkadiyan Nambi stood on the banks of the Kollidam murmuring, 'This youth is very sharp. I am unable to assess him. Luckily, I have sent him to the Kumbakonam astrologer. Let him find out who he is.'

'Hello Sir! Are you talking to that pipal tree or to yourself?'

Hearing this sudden voice, he turned around to see the soldier from Kadamboor who had come to get a horse for Vandiyathevan.

'Oh! I wasn't talking to myself. I had a brief chat with a vampire sitting on this tree, what is your name, my dear man?'

'My name is Idumban Kari,' he said hesitatingly.

Then, Idumban Kari did something very peculiar! He placed the spread out palms of both his hands one upon the other and wriggled his thumbs. As he did this, he looked at Alvarkkadiyan's face.

'Friend, what is this sign? I don't understand...?'

Idumban Kari's dark face darkened further.

'I made no sign at all,' he said.

'You did. You did something like the classical dancers do, holding a certain posture with their fingers, symbolizing the fish!'

'Very good! Your eyes are something special! On an ordinary tree, you can see a vampire, and on my empty hands, you see a fish.'

'No. No! Don't sidetrack me. Where are you going?'

'I have to go back to Kadamboor. My master will pluck my eyes out if I don't show up.'

'If that is so, go quickly. The boat is about to leave.'

He bid farewell to Alavarkkadiyan and started walking towards the ferry landing. He looked back when he was half way down but Alvarkkadiyan was missing.

By then Alvarkkadiyan had quickly climbed the pipal tree on the shore and reached the topmost branch and completely hid himself.

Idumban Kari reached the ferry landing.

The boatman asked, 'Are you coming back to the other shore?'

'No. I will come in the next boat. You can go,' said Idumban Kari.

Alvarkkadiyan saw Idumban Kari coming back to the pipal tree. 'Aha! My guess was right! This fellow did not go on the boat. I must see where he goes and what he does. I clearly saw his hands making the sign of the fish. What does it mean? Fish! A symbol on the Pandiya flag? Let me wait with patience.'

Idumban Kari looked up at the pipal tree from where he stood. His eyes were searching in all directions to ensure that Alvarkkadiyan was not there. His eyes were looking around searching for someone. But he did not look up into the branches of the tree. Even if he had looked up, he would not have noticed Alvarkkadiyan easily.

About an hour passed in this manner. Alvarkkadiyan's legs turned numb. He could no longer remain amidst the tree branches. Idumban Kari did not leave the place. How to escape? However carefully he descended on the other side of the tree he would be noticed.

What can I do? Can I make a horrible noise like a vampire and jump down on him to scare him off? I too can run and escape.

While Alvarkkadiyan was considering these options, another man came to join Idumban Kari. On seeing the new man, Idumban Kari made the sign of the fish and the newcomer also made the same sign.

'What is your name?' asked the newcomer.

'Idumban Kari. What is yours?'

'Soman Sambavan.'

'Where should we go?'

'To the enemy's war memorial, near Thirupurambiyam.'

'Don't talk loudly. Someone may hear us.'

'There is no one here. I checked.'

'Ok. Let us leave. I don't know the way very well. You go first. I will follow you. Stop and ensure that I am behind you.'

'Fine. It is a very bad road full of stones and thorns. We have to walk through the thicket forest. Watch and walk carefully.'

'That's alright. You leave now. Hide yourself if you notice anyone.'

'Yes.'

Idumban Kari started walking westward along the banks of the Kollidam. Soman Sambavan followed him. Alvarkkadiyan waited on the tree till both disappeared from his sight.

All sorts of unexpected things are happening. I may witness some mysterious activities. God has given me the strength to find out. Now, gathering information depends on my resourcefulness. I could not get all the information at Kadamboor. I should be very careful this time.

Thirupurambiyam Memorial refers to the memorial temple built for the Kanga king, Prithvipathi of Kanga Kingdom. It was more than a hundred years old and appeared dilapidated now!

Why are these men going there? Why did they refer to the memorial as enemy's memorial? Whose enemy was Kanga Prithvipathi? Let me find out.

He walked through the dense forest. He met nobody on the way and he reached the memorial temple by sunset.

18

Enemy's War Memorial

A war memorial was erected in memory of Kanga king, Prithvipathi, who died a heroic death in a great battle near Thirupurambiyam.

Like the battles of Waterloo and Panipat, which changed the very course of world history, the battle of Thirupurambiyam had great significance in South Indian history. That battle changed the destiny of the Chola Kingdom, laying the foundation for the great Chola Empire.

Before this battle, the Chola Kingdom was a very small region between the kingdoms of the Pandiyas and the Pallavas. War broke out between the Pandiyas and the Pallavas. The Cholas, under the leadership of King Aditya Chola, supported the Pallavas and their ally Kanga king, Prithvipathi. The battlefield was spread across several miles. After a fierce fight lasting over three days, the field looked like a sea of blood. Dead horses and elephants were piled like mountains. Lifeless bodies and broken chariots were heaped in dunes. Only a very tiny battalion of the Pallavas remained intact. But Pandiya forces attacked again and again.

The Pallavas and Cholas could no longer oppose the enemy and decided to retreat to the north of the Kollidam.

At that point, a miracle happened on the battlefield. Aditya Chola's father, Vijayala Chola, though weak with old age, somehow came to the battlefront. His thunderous roar inspired the remaining Pallava and Chola forces, instilling in them a new hope.

Vijayalaya Chola, seated on the shoulders of two brave soldiers, entered the fight. He rushed into the midst of the enemy area, with a thunderous sound, swirling two large swords held in each hand, killing all enemies. His forces, which had retreated earlier, came back to fight fiercely cheering each other. Enemies were thunderstruck at the brutal bravery of Vijayala Chola.

The goddess of victory changed her mind; her favour fell on the Pallava and Chola armies.

As King Prithvipathi of Kanga Kingdom lost his life after the heroic victory, a stone memorial temple was built in his memory. Over the years, the memorial crumbled and became a totally deserted ruin in the midst of the forest.

When Alvarkkadiyan reached the ruined memorial, it was in total darkness. The structures on the upper walls of the memorial tried to frighten him. He climbed on to the roof of the structure and hid himself carefully amidst the branches of a tree that covered the roof, keeping a watch in all directions. His eyes were able to peer into the darkness and his ears were able to hear even the tiniest of noises.

The darkness around him was suffocating. Alvarkkadiyan was looking up at the stars and started speaking gently,

'Oh! My dear star friends! Today you are laughing at the foolishness of these humans on this earth. Even a hundred years after a man's death, these people consider him as "enemy" and his memorial as Enemy Memorial.

They are going to meet near the enemy's memorial and conspire to do more harm to the living in the name of the dead! What was that? Someone is coming here with a torch along with another person. My waiting is not at all wasted.'

The two men reached the memorial temple. One man sat down and the other one, holding the lighted twigs, was watching in all the directions. After sometime, two more joined them. They were talking amongst themselves. But, Alvarkkadiyan could not hear a single word.

Soon two more men joined them. One man opened the bag in his hand and poured gold coins on the ground and laughed like he was possessed.

'My friends! We are going to destroy the Chola Kingdom using Chola gold! Isn't it funny?' He laughed loudly again.

'Ravidasa, don't shout! Talk softly,' said another.

'Fine! What does it matter if we talk loudly in this place? If anybody hears us, it will be only owls and bats; wolves and wild dogs!' Ravidasa laughed even more loudly.

'Maybe. But it is better to talk softly.'

A while later they were speaking very softly. Alvarkkadiyan could not hear them. He decided to go down. While climbing down the tree, his stout body made a slight rustling sound which was heard by the conspirators.

One of the men in the clearing jumped up quickly, saying, 'Who is that?' Alvarkkadiyan's heart stopped beating for a few seconds. He had no other option except to run. Running would cause more noise. They would surely catch him. At that moment, a vampire bat on the tree created a loud noise by spreading its huge wings.

19

Our Foremost Enemy

Alvarkkadiyan silently thanked the vampire bat for its timely help. The conspirators did not probe further.

'Hey fellow! This bat has frightened us. Kill it!' said one man.

'No. Let us spare our weapons for our enemies! Bats and owls are not our enemies,' said Ravidasa

Alvarkkadiyan quietly inched forward, step by step, and reached an old tree. He bent his body and hid himself in one of the hollow spaces in the hundred-year-old tree.

'We need not worry about funds as long as the royal treasury in Tanjore exists. All we need is the determination to successfully accomplish our task. We have to divide ourselves into two groups. One group must travel to Lanka immediately. The other must go to the northern regions and wait for an opportunity to achieve our goal.

'Where is Soman Sambavan?' asked Ravidasa.

'Here, I am coming.' The voice came from a spot very close to the hollow where Alvarkkadiyan was hiding. Alvarkkadiyan squeezed his body further inside the tree trunk.

Two more newcomers came and joined the group. Alvarkkadiyan peeped out from his hiding place. He recognized the late comers as the men he had seen on the banks of the Kollidam.

Ravidasa welcomed them saying, 'I was afraid for your safety, which route did you take?'

'We walked along the banks of the Kollidam.'

'Let us destroy our enemies without a trace. Here are the tools to achieve our mission!' said Ravidasa pointing at the heap of gold coins which were emblazoned with the tiger symbol of the Chola treasury.

'Any other news?' asked Ravidasa.

'Yes, I have joined the staff at the palace of Sambuvarayar. Yesternight a huge banquet was organized at Kadamboor. Several guests including Senior Paluvettarayar were there. They were discussing the issue of succession as Emperor Sundara Chola is sick and he will not live long. All the dignitaries favoured Madurandakan to succeed the throne and not Prince Aditya Karkalan.'

'They are going to crown that brave fellow roaming around disguised as a woman! Let them crown him! Everything is happening according to our plans. Idumban Kari, you have brought very important news. But, how did you come to know all this? How did you get the opportunity?' asked their leader, Ravidasa.

'I work in the inner chambers of the palace, guarding the courtyard. While on duty, I made good use of my eyes and ears to observe the happenings.'

'Did you learn of anything else there?'

'Yes, a stranger was spying on that midnight meeting hiding on the outer ramparts of the palace.'

'Who was he?'

'A fanatic Vaishnavite fellow with a topknot on his head.'

'What did you do with him? Did you report him to your masters?'

'No. I did not do that. I thought that he might be one of us sent by you.'

'You made a big blunder! He is not our man. He is short and stout with a quarrelsome nature. His name is Alvarkkadiyan Nambi.'

'Yes. That very same fellow. I realized my mistake later today. I thought he was waiting for me on the banks of the Kollidam. I made our secret hand-signal to him but he did not understand. I realized then that he was not our man.'

'You have committed a blunder! You should not make our hand-signal to strangers. Our assignment is in Kanchi and Lanka. Our greatest enemies are in these two places. But our foremost enemy is

Alvarkkadiyan Nambi. He is capable of destroying all of us and our mission. He is trying to kidnap our matchless Queen, who is our leader. If any one of you see him in the future anywhere, finish him off! He is a spy impeding our mission. We should kill that Vaishnavite fellow like an evil creature!' said Ravidasa, in an agitated voice.

Alvarkkadiyan overheard all this from where he crouched, hidden. His body was drenched in sweat and he was shivering in fright. He doubted if he could escape from them. To top it all, he felt a sneeze coming just at that time. He tried as much as he could to control it. He stuffed his scarf against his face and sneezed.

At that very moment the gentle breeze had died. The whispering trees were quiet. The muffled sneeze was heard very clearly by the conspirators. Ravidasa looked up and said, 'There was some sort of noise near that tree. Take the light and see what it is.'

The man holding the lighted twig came closer and closer towards the tree. Had he taken just one more step, Alvarkkadiyan would have been caught. His heart was beating fast. His eyes were looking up and down searching for some way of escape.

Alvarkkadiyan sighted a giant bat on the tree branch above him. He plucked the vampire bat and threw it on the face of the torch bearer. The torch fell from the man's grasp and the light dimmed. The man, beaten by the strong wings of the huge bat, started screaming. The sound of several men rushing towards him was heard. Alvarkkadiyan ran into the forest and soon disappeared.

20

The Curtains Parted

Vandiyathevan was travelling through the bountiful and fertile lands of the Cholas. It was the season of floods and all the rivers and streams overflowed with fresh water rushing in the canals, conduits and waterways. There was water, water everywhere.

Indeed, it was a sight to behold. But the thought of the dangers surrounding the Chola monarch flashed in his mind.

Why should I interfere in this discord between royal cousins? How does it concern me, who sits on the Chola throne? In a way, these Cholas are my ancestral enemies. They destroyed the very existence of the kingdom of my forefathers. How can I forget all that injustice just because Prince Aditya Karikalan is my friend?

It is natural for kings to fight with each other. Victory and defeat are common. What is the use of the defeated group grudging the victorious?

At this juncture, he thought of the woman he had met at the Kumbakonam astrologer's house. He could not stop thinking about her for even one moment.

While his outer mind was brooding over the complications of the Chola Empire, his inner mind was rejoicing upon having met that woman. He started comparing every beautiful sight to that woman. He recalled her graceful arms in the visual grace of tender bamboos swaying in the breeze and compared her dark eyes with water lilies. Even the lovely lotus was no match for her golden face. Likewise, the sweet melody of bees humming over flowers reminded him of her honeyed voice. The very memory of her face made his heart beat faster!

In his heart of hearts, he had a feeling that this lady might be the daughter of Emperor Sundara Chola since her face resembled

Crown Prince Aditya Karikalan's.

Engrossed in these thoughts, Vandiyathevan reached the town of Thiruvaiyaru. He stood on the southern banks of the mighty Cauvery, looking across the river at the town on the northern bank. The fertility and beauty of the land enchanted his heart. *Look at those luscious groves of trees on the Cauvery bank. How big are the fruits hanging from the trunk and branches of the jack tree! There is nothing quite like this in my homeland, the Thondai kingdom! Look at those monkeys rejoicing in these fertile fields. I hear the sounds of music and dance! This town must have been created by the gods just for music and dance!* So enchanted was he that he decided to stay that night in Thiruvaiyaru.

Just then, he noticed a palanquin coming from the west. Guards marched in front and behind the covered palanquin, the screens of which were embossed with the sign of the palmtree.

The palanquin turned towards Tanjore. Vandiyathevan abandoned the idea of staying at Thiruvaiyaru. He thought that Prince Madurandakan might be inside the palanquin and followed it and its entourage on his horse, hoping to make acquaintance with the Prince.

When the palanquin was approaching the fort, he decided to play a trick to expose to the world that the person inside was Prince Madurandakan and not the young queen of Paluvoor. While he was considering various options to execute his intentions, one of the guards questioned him. 'Who are you? Why are you following us?'

'I am not following you! I am going to Tanjore. Does this road lead to Tanjore?'

'Yes. This road leads to Tanjore but it is meant only for important persons and not for the commoners,' said the guard.

In the course of this conversation, Vandiyathevan came closer to the palanquin and pushed his horse towards the palanquin. The guards turned to him with a frightening look.

Vandiyathevan immediately started shouting, 'Oh beloved Prince! Your bearers are pushing against my horse!'

The screens of the palanquin shook and parted.

21

Emperor's Bodyguards

The screens of the palanquin parted and the golden hand seen earlier by Vandiyathevan was visible again. Vandiyathevan dismounted from his horse and ran up to the palanquin saying, 'Prince! Prince! Your bearers...' and looked up to see the most beautiful face of a woman. He blinked his eyes. It was the young queen of Paluvoor and not Prince Madurandakan. He started blabbering. 'Pardon me, Princess! Your bearers and their horses dashed against my horse...'

By now the guards had surrounded Vandiyathevan. But he could not take his eyes off the dazzling face of the queen behind the curtains! Such a stunning beauty she was!

Suddenly he came to his senses and a brilliant idea flashed into his mind. 'Pardon me, beloved Queen! Aren't you the junior queen of Paluvoor? I came this far only to see you!'

A smile blossomed on the gentle face of the young queen of Paluvoor. The radiance of her smile bewildered him; the guards were waiting for the command of their queen. At a sign made by the Queen with her finger, they moved away a little and stood apart.

That jewel among women, looked at Vandiyathevan with piercing eyes from inside the palanquin.

'Yes! I am the junior queen of Paluvoor,' said the Queen in an intoxicating voice. His head started spinning on hearing her speak.

'You said something about my palanquin bearers dashing against your horse?'

The smile on her coral red lips indicated that she had enjoyed the joke and Vandiyathevan gained a little confidence.

'Yes. Great Queen! My horse was frightened because of…'

'You look more frightened than your horse! Go to a priest and get exorcised to overcome your fear!'

Vandiyathevan smiled. Suddenly, the Paluvoor queen's smiling eyes blazed in anger!

'Stop jesting. Tell the truth. Why did you push your horse against my palanquin? Give me a straight answer!'

He gave her a convincing answer with a concocted story:

'Our beloved Queen Nandini! He … Alvarkkadiyan … asked me to meet you! That is why I played this trick. Please pardon me!'

The dark brows of the Paluvoor queen shot up in pleasant surprise.

'Fine! It is not safe to stop in the middle of a road and talk. Come to my palace tomorrow. You can explain everything there.'

The junior queen of Paluvoor presented him an ivory signet ring with the sign of the palm tree to enter the palace and then let the curtains fall close.

Vandiyathevan's heart was filled with joy.

He could not believe what had happened and wondered if it were a dream. His brain revolved around the enchanting beauty of the young queen of Paluvoor.

Myths and fables speak of heavenly beauties called Ramba, Urvasi and Menaka, who had disturbed the penance of great saints. No wonder Senior Paluvettarayar was enslaved by her ravishing beauty. What a contrast between the senior Paluvettarayar with his greying hair and this gentle dazzling beauty! To what lengths would the old man go to gain one smile from her?

Brooding over such thoughts he mounted his horse and slowly rode towards the gates of Tanjore.

He passed through the busy market where people were engaged in various trades. All the streets were busy with the hustle and bustle of a large town: people moving hither and thither, merchants bargaining over the prices of goods, bullock carts, horse drawn chariots and palanquins.

Vandiyathevan's heart rejoiced at the sights and sounds of the new capital of the Cholas. With determination, he neared the main gates of Tanjore Fort.

The massive doors of the main gates were closed and the guards and gatekeepers were regulating the queue of people eagerly waiting to see the parade. Vandiyathevan pulled up on his horse near the gateway. A Saivite youth with beads around his neck, ashen marks on his forehead and a basket of flowers in his hand stood beside him. He started a conversation with him.

'Young man, why are all standing on one side of the road? Is there a procession?' asked Vandiyathevan.

'I think you are a stranger to this area, better if you dismount from your horse and stand aside.'

Vandiyathevan jumped off his horse to chat with him.

'Young man, why did you ask me to dismount?'

'The emperor's bodyguards, known as the Velakkara Padai, are returning from the fort after presenting arms to the Emperor. It is dangerous if the men of the Velakkara Padai see you on a horse. Those wicked fellows will abduct you and your horse.'

'And do you think I will allow them to carry away me and my horse?'

'The Velakkara Padai is law in this city with none to question them. Even the Paluvettarayar brothers won't interfere in their affairs. It was a vital organ in the ancient Tamil kingdoms, particularly in Chola Empire. "Velakkaras" are the personal bodyguards of the ruling king. The men of this battalion take oath to personally guard the life and person of the king at any cost, risking their own lives. If something untoward happens to the king, they will cut off their heads with their own swords and offer themselves as a sacrifice to Goddess Durga. Therefore, it is quite natural for these men to enjoy more privileges than others.'

Just then, a noise of marching drums mingled with loud cheers and shouts raised by hundreds of men was heard from inside the Fort.

About a thousand guards came marching, holding all sorts of paraphernalia and hailing, 'Long live Emperor Paranthaka Sundara Chola'.

The loud cheers echoed in all directions and the cheering crowd remained mesmerised.

22

Chendan Amudan

Vandiyathevan slowly approached the fort's gates. But no one was allowed inside after the Velakkara Padai left. Only members of the royal household, ministers, generals and family members of the of Paluvettarayars had that privilege.

He decided to enter the fort the next day and meet the Emperor to deliver the letters. Vandiyathevan walked slowly along the streets surrounding the ramparts of Tanjore Fort enjoying the various sights around him.

Tanjore was, at that time, a new, fast-growing city with hundreds of street lamps and busy streets. Travellers from far and near came to the city to conduct various trades.

People crowded the shops like flies around sugar syrup. Fruits like bananas, mangoes and jackfruit were heaped in little mounds. Flower kiosks with varieties of flowers—gardenia and jasmine, fragrant frangipani, oleander, chrysanthemum and marigold, champaka and iruvatchi, hibiscus and trumpet lilies—were flocked by women, like humming bees buzzing over flowers.

Vandiyathevan and his horse were tired and he was looking for a place to rest that night. Just then, he saw the same young Saivite man with the flower basket and entered into a conversation with him to gather more information about the temples in the town and the activities of the palace including the workplaces of the king, the commander, prime minister and many others down below. He also ascertained the absence of Senior Paluvettarayar and the presence of his young queen in the palace.

He found the Saivite young man to be very intelligent and Vandiyathevan decided to befriend him. It would be very useful. Vandiyathevan said, 'Brother, I am very tired after a long travel and I need a place to rest this night. Where can I stay?'

'There are many places to stay in this city. There are several inns as well as government rest houses. If you would like to stay in…'

Before the youth could finish, Vandiyathevan interrupted him, 'Brother, what is your name?'

'Chendan Amudan.'

'Oh! A very sweet name (*Amudu* means nectar.) You mean to say I could stay in your house?'

'Yes, how did you know I was about to say that?'

'I have special skills! That's how! Where is your house?'

'Our house is in the suburbs in the middle of a flower garden,' said Amudan.

'Yes, surely, I will come with you to stay tonight.'

They reached a small house amidst the fragrant flower garden. Amudan's mother welcomed the new guest with a gentle smile. She served him a sumptuous dinner. Vandiyathevan learnt that Amudan's mother was deaf and mute and many in his family were also mute.

The conversation continued as they ate.

'Brother! Does Prince Madurandakan also live inside the fort?'

'Yes, he is the son-in-law of Junior Paluvettarayar.'

'Good. Is the prince inside the fort tonight?'

'Must be but people cannot see him. He used to spend his time in meditation and worship of Lord Siva but his mind has completely changed after marriage! Why should we bother about that?'

Vandiyathevan wanted to gain more information from Amudan but the tiredness of the long journey forced him into a deep sleep with the thoughts of the dazzling beauty of the young queen of Paluvoor and the majestic beauty of the woman he saw at the Kumbakonam astrologer's house. Both were beautiful yet totally different from each other.

23

All-Powerful Paluvettarayars

Vandiyathevan woke up after the sun had risen, to the enjoyment of the beauty of the morning breeze, rustling leaves, fragrant flowers and the melodious song being sung by Amudan.

Vandiyathevan pitied Amudan's unfortunate mother who could not hear her son's melodious voice. He got dressed well to meet the emperor and the young queen of Paluvoor. After breakfast, Vandiyathevan and Amudan proceeded to Tanjore Fort, leaving behind his horse to get some rest. During the walk, Vandiyathevan gathered several pieces of information.

He asked Amudan, 'Have you got any other relations besides your mother?'

Amudan replied, 'Yes, of course, my maternal uncle and his family at Kodikarai. He is also the caretaker of the lighthouse on that coast. He has a son and a daughter. That daughter...'

'That daughter? What about her?'

'Nothing. There is something peculiar about my relatives. Some of them are born dumb while others are blessed with a most melodious voice. My uncle's daughter, Poonkulali is a good singer.'

'Can she sing better than you?'

'When Poonkulali sings, the Ocean King quietens and animals become spellbound.'

'What a pretty name!'

'Yes, she is pretty and beautiful. Even the spotted deer and the gorgeous peacocks fall at her feet for her ravishing beauty. Even the heavenly maids perform penance to become as lovely as her.'

Vandiyathevan said, 'She is a suitable bride for you. As your maternal uncle's daughter, you have all the rights for her hand.'

'I am not a match for her at all; the kings of the world and heavenly beings will compete for her hand.'

'Will you refuse if she is willing to marry you?'

'Silly! If the God I worship appears before me and asks', Will you come with me to the heavens or will you remain on this earth with Poonkulali?', I will say that I will stay back with my Poonkulali. But what is the use of my saying this?'

'Why not? Even Senior Paluvettarayar married a young maid at his advanced age! Was that marriage performed with that lady's consent?'

'Dear friend! Those are affairs of the nobility. Why should we discuss them? We are entering Tanjore. Don't utter anything about the Paluvettarayars. It is dangerous. The Emperor is bedridden and will not cross the lines drawn by them. He won't even listen to the words of his sons! There is none to question them. Three years ago, the Pandiya king, Veerapandiya, died on the battlefield. Some of the men, loyal to King Veerapandiya, have sworn vengeance to kill the Chola emperor. The fort in Tanjore is stronger and well-guarded. Under this pretext, the Emperor was moved to Tanjore from Palayarai. The Emperor has paralysis, he cannot use both his legs, he hardly leaves the palace and his mind also is deteriorating.'

'Oh! What a pity!'

'Don't feel pity, my friend! The Paluvettarayars will treat it as treason and put you in prison!'

Paluvettarayar! Paluvettarayar! Everywhere their names crop up. However capable they are, why has so much power been given to them within all departments—the treasury, the granary, policing and intelligence? Because of all these powers, they are plotting against the Emperor. If possible, I will alert the Emperor.

By this time, they had reached the main entrance of Tanjore Fort. Amudan left for the temple and Vandiyathevan approached the gates.

24

Tanjore Fort

The signet ring presented by the junior queen, Nandini, had miraculous powers, like in the fairy tales! In that morning hour, people of all walks of life—milk vendors, fruit vendors, vegetable sellers, butchers, farmers, clerks, cashiers and all petty officials—were entering the fort. The gatekeepers were permitting them in, one by one, through the wicket gate.

As soon as Vandiyathevan showed the palm tree signet ring, they opened the large gate, with deference, to let him in. Several significant events and most important moments were to follow with that entry.

The magnificence of Tanjore Fort was beyond comparison: everything looked new and majestic. Palatial buildings with clusters of rubies, diamonds and pearls, sky-high trees—luxurious tall coconut trees, arecanut palms, asoka trees, laurels, huge banyan trees, fig trees, sacred ficus trees, jack trees, mango trees and neem trees—were all pleasing to the eyes and the mind.

His heart filled with abundant pride to see the new city built by an architect's fancy.

Horses and mount-like elephants walked majestically like tiny, black, moving hillocks, tinkling all around. Huge booming drums and large tolling bells periodically announced the passing hours. The gentle breeze mixed with the melody of musical instruments and the melodious voices of young men and women raised in songs. Everything was festive—like a big carnival!

This was the capital of an empire that was growing day by day! Vandiyathevan did not wish to let anyone know that he was a newcomer or else he would be looked down upon as an uncivilized villager. He mingled with a group of bards and poets and somehow managed to gain access into the chamber of the commander of the fort, Junior Paluvettarayar.

Vandiyathevan entered the audience chamber ahead of the poets and saw the commander, Junior Paluvettarayar, seated on a high throne surrounded by several important persons standing in varied postures with folded hands and sealed lips. One person was standing with several bundles of letters of that day, another was standing with finance ledgers, leaders of the guards awaited instructions for the day, servants were lingering in readiness to execute the commander's orders. A couple of young maids were standing behind the throne, waving peacock feather fans. One fellow stood ready with a box of betel leaves etc.

Even Vandiyathevan, a man of self-esteem and pride, approached Junior Paluvettarayar with some humility. The younger brother was even more imposing than the elder. Upon seeing Vandiyathevan, he asked him,

'Who are you?'

The usually morose Junior Paluvattarayar brightened upon seeing this brave young man as he was recruiting bold young men for the company of his guards.

'Sir! I come from Kanchi. The Prince has sent me with a letter,' Vandiyathevan answered in a humble voice. Upon hearing the word Kanchi, the Commander's face darkened.

'What?' he asked.

'I have come from Kanchi city with a letter from the Prince.'

'Where is it? Give it here!' he ordered with contempt.

Vandiyathevan took out the letter from his pouch and reverently said, 'Sir, the letter is for the Emperor!'

But the junior Paluvettarayar snatched the roll of palm leaf from him and gave it to a subordinate to read.

After listening to the letter, he mumbled, 'Nothing new!' He was immersed in his own thoughts.

'Sir! The letter I brought...' started Vandiyathevan.

'I will give it to the Emperor.'

'No! Sir! The Prince asked me to deliver it personally to the Emperor.'

'Oh! You don't trust me? Did Prince Aditya tell you that?' asked Junior Paluvettarayar with anger.

'The Prince said nothing like that. Your elder brother ordered it.'

'What? Where did you meet my elder brother?'

'I stayed in the house of Kadamboor Sambuvaraya for a night, on the way, and I met him there. He sent me with this signet ring...'

'Ah! Why didn't you mention this earlier? You can go in and deliver this letter to the Emperor and come back soon,' ordered Junior Paluvattarayar.

A servant took Vandiyathevan to Emperor Paranthaka Sundara Chola, who was lying on a reclining bed. Though he had delegated all affairs of the state to his officials and ministers, sometimes he had to receive some indispensable persons like ministers, army generals, captains, leaders of the Velakkara Padai and bards.

Vandiyathevan was saddened to see the sickly appearance of the Emperor who had, once upon a time, performed heroic deeds in various battles and acquired fame as a brave warrior. He was looked upon as the god of love. He bowed low and submitted the letter to the Emperor.

'My Majesty! I come from Kanchi City; I bring this letter from Prince Aditya,' spoke Vandiyathevan in a trembling voice.

The Emperor's face brightened immediately and looking at his wife, Vanama Devi, he said, 'Devi, your son has sent a letter!' He began reading.

'Ah! Aditya Karikalan has built a golden palace at Kanchi! He wants us to come and live there for a while!' saying this, the Emperor's face became dull.

'Devi, look at the activity of your son! My grandfather, that famous Emperor Paranthaka, collected all the gold in the palace to build temples, as temples were more important than palaces. But look at what this Karikalan has done? How can I atone this outrage against gods?' said the Emperor.

Devi's cheerful face fell, she could not reply.

'My majesty! Nothing wrong in what our prince has done! Are not his mother and father the first gods for a son?' Vandiyathevan asked.

Sundara Chola smiled, 'My dear boy, you talk very cleverly. Even if his parents are gods to their son, they are not god for others! Golden temples should be built only for gods!'

'My King! His father is god to the son; the king is god to all his subjects. The scriptures say that a monarch possesses all the qualities of god.'

Sundara Chola, looking at his wife once again, said, 'Queen! Look at this boy's resourcefulness! We need not be concerned about Aditya if he has the council of such friends,' he said

He then looked at Vandiyathevan and said, 'We cannot come to Kanchi as I am completely bed-ridden. Aditya must come here to see us. I will have a letter prepared in reply.'

Vandiyathevan, hearing the noise of several people coming down the corridor decided to quickly disclose to the Emperor all that was on his mind. 'My Majesty! I seek your grace to listen to my petition. Danger surrounds you here. You have to leave Tanjore immediately. Danger! Danger!' hurriedly said Vandiyathevan.

As he was speaking these words Junior Paluvettarayar entered the chamber. The bards and poets followed him.

The last few words uttered by Vandiyathevan angered the commander of Tanjore, Junior Paluvettarayar.

25

Court Poets and Bards

The great poets and bards entered the Emperor's chambers hailing the Emperor, 'Long live! Long live Emperor Sundara Chola.'

Sundara Chola, though not cheered by their words, tried to rise and welcome them, unmindful of his ailment.

'I am happy to see you all. Please be seated, I will be glad to hear some of your verses!' said the Emperor.

The poets recited the verses one after the other.

One poet started reciting a poem from a book in his hand describing the generosity of the Emperor who donated elephants, horses and palanquins even to the gods—Indra, Surya and Siva.

'Who else is there in this wide world who can be compared with your benevolence?' rose several voices from the group.

The Emperor wanted to know the name of the poet who had written that poem. No one knew who had written it and suggested to the Emperor to find out and give him an award.

Sundara Chola who was listening to all this, burst out laughing. The ailing Emperor had not laughed like that for a long time. On seeing his mirth, even Empress Vanama Devi smiled; the maids, the doctors in the chamber and all the poets and bards also laughed. Vandiyathevan laughed the loudest.

Sundara Chola addressed the poets.

'Dear poets! A long time ago some poets and bards had come to see me in Palayarai. Some of you might have been in that group. Each of them sang verses in praise of the benevolence of the Chola kings including myself. They praised me by saying that I gave this and that to this person and that person. My young daughter, Kundavai, who was with me, praised the beauty of those songs. I challenged her saying that I could compose much better verse and I playfully composed a verse at that time and asked her for a reward. My darling daughter clinging to my back pinched my cheeks saying, "Here is your reward". I remember that incident as if it was yesterday. But it is more than eight or nine years now. Perhaps she recited it to her teacher, and he has spread it all over the nation.'

'Great! Astounding!' rose several voices from the group.

As soon as he heard the name Kundavai, Vandiyathevan became attentive. He had already heard much about the princess of the Chola clan, her beauty, her intelligence, her ability and knowledge. The Emperor is very fortunate to have such a daughter. When the Emperor was speaking of his daughter with such pride, Vandiyathevan's hand was searching for his pouch in his waistband. The letter he was carrying for Kundavai was in that pouch. But he was shocked to find that the pouch was missing.

Where could it have fallen? In the audience chamber or elsewhere...If it reaches Junior Paluvettarayar I will be in peril. Oh! What a blunder!

He became restless.

The Emperor asked the poets, 'Can any one of you recollect the poem sung by a Tamil saint "We Shall Not Fear Death"?' A poet rose up to recite that verse:

No slaves to here
No fear of death
No horrors of hell
No pain of ill health...

Sundara Chola was touched by that poetic verse on death and everybody around him became very emotional. Junior Paluvettarayar, who remained unshaken said, 'My King! I am ready to wage a war even with death.'

'I have no doubt about that, Commander! No human has the power to fight death. We merely have the power to pray to God to give us strength to not fear death.'

The Emperor concluded the meeting of the poets with an appeal to gather all those important devotional songs into one anthology. The whole group left showering their blessings on the Emperor.

Vandiyathevan who was restless at not finding the letter brought for Kundavai, tried to mingle with that group and escape. But he did not succeed as intended. An iron-like grip shook him from head to toe and he looked up to see Junior Paluvettarayar holding him tightly.

26

Our Honourable Guest

When all the poets had left, Vandiyathevan was retained. Meanwhile, the Queen administered a new medicine to the Emperor which had been concocted by the palace doctor.

Junior Paluvettarayar asked the Emperor, 'My King! Do you find any improvement after this new medicine?'

'The doctor says that there is some benefit but I find no improvement. My fate is beckoning me. God of death will come soon. How long can I be in bed like this, burdening all?'

'My Majesty! Our palace doctors and astrologers say that there is no danger to your life. But this youth was talking to you about some danger...'

'Ah! That young man who came from Kanchi City? Yes, he was saying about some danger… Oh youth! What did you say? Did you mean to say something about my current condition?'

Vandiyathevan's mind was working at lightning speed. He unhesitatingly replied, 'My Majesty! Who am I to warn about danger! What danger can approach you when you have the brave Commander, Junior Paluvettarayar, the palace doctor and the Empress. I gave a petition to your majesty saying that I am a stranger to this Chola Kingdom. I am an ignorant youth, from the ancient clan of Vaanars serving the Chola Empire to the satisfaction of Crown Prince Aditya Karikalan. I beg your grace to return me at least a tiny portion of the lands of my ancient kingdom. This poor man needs protection of our Emperor, the King of Kings!'

On hearing this, the commander started frowning at Vandiyathevan.

But the faces of the Emperor and the Empress brightened.

'The goddess of learning is with him and his command over words is remarkable!' said the Empress.

Making use of the opportunity, Vandiyathevan turned towards her and said, 'I beg your grace to put in a word on my behalf! I am an orphan.'

The Emperor called his commander and said, 'Commander, I am very fond of this youth! Let us fulfil his wish. Young man, don't worry. We will do the needful. Commander, this youth has brought a letter from the Prince. Aditya wants me to go to Kanchi to stay in his new golden palace for sometime.'

'We shall act according to your wishes,' said the Commander.

'Ah! You may act according to my wishes! But my legs refuse. It is impossible to travel, let us ask Aditya Karikalan to come here...'

'Is it advisable to ask the Prince to leave Kanchi and come here? Our enemies in the north continue to be strong!'

'Parthiban and Malayaman can stay back and take care of that. Something in my heart tells me that I must have the Prince here beside me. And that is not enough; we must send a message to the younger Prince who is in Lanka—ask him to come back here immediately. I wish to consult both of them and come to a conclusion about an important matter. When Arulmoli is here we can talk to him about your objection in sending rice and foodstuffs to the Lankan campaign.'

'We can write the letter to Kanchi also tomorrow. Can we send this young man back with that letter?'

'This youth has travelled from Kanchi without any rest or stops. Let him stay here and relax for a few days before he returns. We can send the letter with some other messenger.'

'Do that. Perhaps he can remain here itself till Karikalan arrives.'

27

Palace Art Gallery

Junior Paluvettarayar dragged Vandiyathevan to the audience chamber. The explanation given by the youth about his conversation with the Emperor did not satisfy him.

However, he distinctly remembered the words of the youth *Danger! Danger! Perhaps the words Stranger! Stranger! had sounded like Danger! Danger! in his ears.*

He wanted to detain the youth till the senior returned.

He appears to be suitable for the secret spy service. I can even get him a part of his ancient lands to keep him loyal. But if he is proved to be an enemy he will be dealt with severely.

On reaching the audience chamber, Vandiyathevan started looking around here and there very anxiously searching for his missing waist pouch.

If that letter is lost, I will be in peril and I won't be able to meet the renowned Princess Kundavai. I will not be able to complete the task assigned to me by Prince Aditya Karikalan.

Junior Paluvettarayar, looking towards one of his servants, said, 'Take this young man to our palace and put him in our guest house, provide him with all facilities and wait till I get back.'

Vandiyathevan and the servant left.

Another servant came to Junior Paluvettarayar and bowingly handed over a letter in the palm leaf roll which he had found lying in the corridor, on the way to the Emperor's bed chamber, saying,

'It might have fallen from the waist-belt of that youth.' The Commander eagerly examined it. His eyebrows shot up in a frown!

'Ah ha! It is a letter written to Princess Kundavai by Aditya Karikalan in his own hand with a message:

> You had asked for a young retainer with capacity and courage for confidential matters. I am sending him to you for that purpose. You can trust him and assign him. He will hand over the letter personally to you.

Ah! There is some mystery in this! I wonder if my elder brother knows about this letter. I must be very careful in handling this youth!

The Commander of the Fort said these words to himself as he was reading some parts of the letter. He called the servant who had handed him the letter and whispered in his ear. The man immediately left the audience chamber.

All courtesies were shown to Vandiyathevan in the palace. He had a luxurious bath and got himself dressed up well with the new garments presented by the servants. He was served a very tasty breakfast. He almost forgot about the lost letter. Later, they led him to the exquisite art gallery in the palace. He was enjoying the beautiful art works on display in the gallery.

He was so enthralled by the numerous exquisite pictures on the walls of the gallery that he forgot the task for which he had come.

The portrait gallery depicting the glory, of the ancient rulers of the Chola Kingdom and the important events in their history, attracted his attention.

The guards were playing a game of dice outside the chambers.

28

Thieves! Thieves!

Vandiyathevan was amazed to see the paintings of the Chola monarchs.

How great the Chola kings have been! What a powerful dynasty with all territories under one rule.

All Chola emperors received considerable help from all the chieftains of the Paluvoor clan, especially Senior Paluvettarayar. There was enough justification in the present Paluvettarayars, enjoying such prestige and authority in the Chola Empire. No doubt, Sundara Chola reposed absolute confidence in them for all political matters.

The commander, Junior Paluvettarayar, suspects me for some reason and his suspicion will be confirmed once Senior Paluvettarayar returns.

The truth about the signet ring would be out and Vandiyathevan would be defenseless. He could be thrown into the infamous underground prisons. He could never escape from there. He decided to concoct some hoax to get away from the fort immediately.

He saw the commander, Junior Paluvettarayar, coming down the street seated on a horse surrounded by his retinue. This became the perfect opportunity for him to play a trick upon the three guards playing dice. He asked the guards to return his old clothes, to which the guards mockingly told him that they had already thrown them into the river. But when Vandiyathevan demanded his belongings to be returned at once, a quarrel erupted amongst them.

'Thieves, Thieves! Are you playing tricks with me? I will report you to your master!'

Saying this Vandiyathevan tried to cross the doorstep but he was blocked. He punched the nose of a guard. All of them fell down roaring with pain!

But all the three men recovered almost instantly and came towards Vandiyathevan more carefully and slowly. By now, Commander Junior Paluvettarayar arrived and Vandiyathevan shouted loudly,

'Thieves! Thieves!'

The Commander, Junior Paluvettarayar came upon the commotion. Vandiyatheven shouted,

'Commander, you have come back at the right time. These thieves have stolen my clothes and they are trying to kill me. Is this the way to treat guests? I am a guest of the Emperor and the Crown Prince. I wonder how you keep such thieves as servants. In my country, we would first hang such fellows and do other things later!'

The Commander was wonderstruck to see Vandiyathevan single-handedly tackling three of his strong men. His eagerness to recruit such a youth in his personal team increased. He quietly replied, 'Oh, young man, be patient. I will enquire and arrange for the return of your clothes and belongings.'

Then he shouted at his men, 'What the hell are you doing?'

'Master, we followed your orders explicitly. We took him to the luxurious bath and gave him the silken robes and ornaments. We also served him a sumptuous meal and took him to the art gallery. For some time, he was enjoying the paintings but suddenly he came out demanding his old clothes and began attacking us,' the servants replied.

'You stout fellows were beaten up by a single youth!' said the Commander angrily.

His old clothes were returned to Vandiyathevan on the orders of the Commander. Vandiyathevan searched carefully. He found more gold coins than he had had. The letter meant for Kundavai was also there.

How did these extra gold coins come here? How did the letter which was not found on his previous search turn up? The Commander must have already read it and put it back in the waist pouch now. Why has

he done this? Why has he placed the extra gold coins? He is a dangerous fellow. I must be very careful in dealing with him!

'Is everything alright? The gold and other items you had?'

Vandiyathevan separated the extra coins and placed them in front of the Commander. 'Sir, I am a messenger from Prince Karikalan. I am born in the noble Vaanar clan. I do not covet the possessions of others,' spoke the youth.

'I congratulate you on your integrity. When are you leaving? Or, would you like to stay tonight and meet my elder brother and then proceed?' asked the Commander.

'I will stay tonight and meet Senior before I go. Please warn your men not to touch me or my belongings.'

'Ask for whatever you wish.'

'Sir, I want to go around the Tanjore Fort for sightseeing.'

'Sure, these two men of mine will come with you and take you around. Don't leave the fort as the doors will be closed after sunset. You cannot re-enter if you go out.'

Then the Commander whispered some more instructions to his men. Vandiyathevan was able to guess the instructions given by him.

29

A Vampire on the Tree

Vandiyathevan left for sightseeing. The men sent by the Commander closely followed him to prevent his escape.

Vandiyathevan's mind was scheming a plan to escape before the return of Senior Paluvettarayar. While he was sightseeing, Vandiyathevan was able to assess the locations convenient for escape. He noticed the busy main streets and empty bylanes. He could use these bylanes and reach one of the thickly wooded parks and hide there. But he must get rid of the men, sent by Junior Paluvettarayar, accompanying him.

Suddenly a loud noise was heard followed by a huge commotion. It was the Velakkara Padai returning after meeting the Emperor. This was an opportunity to escape. He enthusiastically told the guards,

'One day I will enroll in this battalion and serve our beloved Emperor.'

So saying, he joined the marching soldiers cheering along with them. The guards were reluctant to enter the march and stop him. Soon they lost sight of him.

Vandiyathevan ran into a bylane which came to a dead end. He dashed against a towering wall in the darkness.

I have the whole night to come up with some sort of a plan to escape.

He sat down, leaned against the wall and was soon asleep.

Hearing a sudden noise, Vandiyathevan woke up with a shock. Did someone call him? Was it human or was it the call of some beast? He looked up at the wall and saw the sight of a vampire-like figure on top of the wall. Vandiyathevan froze in fright. Was it a ghost or a vampire? The vampire started whispering, 'What, Sir! I called you many times but you have fallen asleep. The Young Queen has been waiting for you for a long time.'

Vandiyathevan spoke to himself.

Which young queen wants to see me? Is it the Young Queen of Paluvoor? Have I been mistaken for someone else?

The vampire on the wall threw down a ladder for Vandiyathevan to climb up. He decided to go up and face the consequences. It was a girl and not a vampire, and she lent him her hand to pull him up onto the wall.

The girl then asked him to pull up the ladder and jump. Giving out such quick orders, the girl climbed down the tree.

Vandiyathevan followed her instructions and reached a large fragrant garden in front of a palace with lighted windows, turrets and balconies, as if in some dream world. He cleared his throat to ask whose mansion it was. Immediately the girl placed her index finger upon her sealed lips and shushed, 'Ushh!' She walked ahead down a garden path. Vandiyathevan followed her.

30

The Fragrant Garden

The maid was walking briskly down the garden through a thick grove of mango trees. Vandiyathevan followed with difficulty in the utter darkness. He almost collided against a flowering bush and stopped. The girl turned to look at him, 'Forgotten the way? Are you not the same magician fellow who can see in darkness?'

In reply, Vandiyathevan placed a finger upon his lips saying, 'Ushh!'

Vandiyathevan now guessed that he had been mistaken for a magician and continued his walk, deep in thought, without further talk. They neared a large mansion and walked towards a creeper-laden pathway leading to a fragrant garden gazebo.

What aroma! What a nice fragrance! They had entered the bower when heard a pleasant voice.

'Ask him to come in immediately! I have been waiting here for so long.'

The words filled him with dizziness! It was the voice of the young queen of Paluvoor. No doubt about it; it was Nandini. The flowers, the smell of the incense and the enchanting face of the Young Queen intoxicated Vandiyathevan.

'Don't lose your intellect to the mesmerizing power of the Young Queen which is more intoxicating than liquor!' warned his mind.

Upon seeing Vandiyathevan, the young queen, Nandini, stared at him in surprise and parted her coral lips revealing her pearl-like teeth.

He laughed lightly and said, 'My Queen, your maid had a sudden doubt! Whether I was the magician or not!' Vandiyathevan laughed.

Nandini smiled and lightning flashed showering honey and nectar.

'She gets such sudden doubts quite often! Vasuki! Wait outside. If you hear any footsteps, call me,' said Nandini.

'Yes, My Queen!' said Vasuki and left for the doorway.

Nandini lowered her voice as she spoke, 'Half the fellows who declare themselves as magicians are fools and liars. You are a true magician! What magic did you employ to arrive here now?'

'My Queen, I did not employ any magic to come here. I climbed a ladder leaning against a wall; it brought me here,' said Vandiyathevan.

'That is obvious. I asked about the magic you employed to fool my maid.'

'I smiled at her in the moonlight. That's all! If she had not been charmed, I was planning to use the signet ring presented by you.'

'Oh! You have it safe? You could have come here openly in broad daylight when you have that. Why come in darkness?'

'My Queen! The men of Junior Paluvettarayar are thieves. First, they tried to steal my possessions. Then they followed my shadow without parting even for a second. With great difficulty I escaped from them. When I saw the ladder leaning against the garden wall, I thought of you and your kindness.'

'You mentioned about a message sent by Alvarkkadiyan Nambi...'

'Yes, My Queen. At first, I wished to meet you mainly to deliver his message. But after meeting you just that one time, all those old reasons flew away.'

'What is his message?'

31

A Sorcerer

Suddenly Nandini heard the sounds of large drums, cymbals, men's cheers, hoof-beats of horses and elephants.

She told Vandiyathevan, 'The senior Paluvettarayar is back. So please go away before he comes here, but first, convey the message of Alvarkkadiyan.'

'Queen, that fellow told me you were his sister. Is it true?'

'Why doubt it?'

'Very difficult to believe that beauty and beast are from the same mother!'

Nandini laughed, 'Of course, we grew up together. He loved me deeply as his own sister. But I disappointed him. What is the message from him?'

'King Krishna is waiting for you. All the ardent Vaishnavite devotees are anxiously waiting to see your wedding with King Krishna!'

Nandini laughed. 'Ah! He has not yet forgotten those childish dreams. Ask him to forget me and I don't deserve to be like saint Andal.'

'I don't agree with you. You are greater than Andal.'

'Sir! Don't flatter me.'

'Madam, what is flattery?'

'Praising someone to their face.'

'If so, please turn around to show me your back.'

'Why?'

'To flatter you, without looking at your face.'

Upon hearing this, Nandini laughed loudly. 'You are surely a magician. It has been a long time since I laughed like this.'

'But Queen, it is very dangerous to make you laugh, your laughter will make the lotus in the pool bloom and the honey bee will swoon!' said Vandiyathevan.

'You are not only a magician but also a poet!'

'You have not yet told me your name?' asked Nandini with laughter.

'My name is Vandiyathevan Vallavarayan. I come from the ancient and famous Vaanar clan.'

'Your kingdom...?'

'The sky above me and the earth below my feet now, I am its sole Emperor.'

Nandini examined Vandiyathevan from head to toe and said, 'You will get back your kingdom.'

'Anything swallowed by the tiger won't come out. I have no desire to rule a kingdom after I saw Emperor Sundara Chola.'

'Why are the Commander's men looking for you?'

'He suspects me!'

'What suspicion?'

'About how I came to posses the palm tree signet ring.'

Fear-stricken Nandini asked,

'Where is the ring?'

'Madam, it is with me.'

'How did he know that you posses this signet ring?' asked Nandini

'I wanted an audience with the Emperor. So, I showed him the ring and told him Senior Paluvettarayar gave it to me in Kadamboor.'

Now the fear on her face and voice disappeared, 'Did he believe you?' she asked.

'He didn't believe me. That's why they are searching for me. He is planning to take me to his elder brother and find the truth.'

Nandini replied with a smile, 'I will see that he does not chew you out.'

'Queen! The whole world knows your influence. I have some

urgent tasks outside the fort. I seek your help to escape.'

'What are those urgent tasks?'

'I have many. I have to meet Alvarkkadiyan and give him your reply. What shall I tell him?'

'Tell him to completely forget that he had a sister called Nandini.'

'I can tell him that but forgetting you may not be possible for him.'

'What?'

'Even I, who has casually met you twice, cannot forget you. How can he, who spent his lifetime with you, forget you?'

A trace of pride was on Nandini's face.

'I shall tell you one thing. Will you agree?'

'Tell me, Queen!'

'I need you to be my confidential messenger. Will you accept?' she asked.

'I have already agreed to serve another lady.'

'Who is she in competition with me?'

'Princess Kundavai.'

'Lies! Lies! It is not possible! Are you jesting...'

'Queen, many have already stealthily read this letter, no harm in you also reading this.'

Saying this, Vandiyathevan gave her the letter given by Aditya Karikalan for Kundavai.

After reading the letter, Nandini gave a threatening look and said, 'Sir! You want to escape from this fort? Isn't it?'

'Yes Queen, that is why I came here seeking your help.'

'Only on one condition will I help you escape from here.'

'Tell me your condition, Queen.'

'Whatever reply Kundavai gives, you must bring it here. I will reward you. Okay?'

'A dangerous condition! What will be the reward?'

'You will get a reward beyond your wildest dreams. You will get a reward for which, the all-powerful finance minister of this Chola Empire, Senior Paluvettarayar, has been yearning for years. Such a reward will be yours!'

Saying this, Nandini once again threw her weapons of enchantment at poor Vandiyathevan.

His head swam in dizziness. He muttered to himself:

'Dear heart be courageous, don't lose your reason.'

At that moment, as if to help him, the horrible screech of an owl was heard in the garden—once, twice, thrice.

'The real sorcerer has arrived,' said Nandini.

32

Do You Remember?

Nandini said to Vandiyathevan, 'Let me meet the real sorcerer. Please hide yourself and wait.'

The sorcerer entered the gazebo, it was Ravidasa, one of the conspirators at the midnight meeting at the enemy's memorial in Thirupurambiyam who had urged the others to kill Alvarkkadiyan on sight instantly.

Ravidasa was full of anger on seeing Nandini. He sat down on the wooden bench in front of the couch and stared at Nandini lisping, 'Hoom, kreem, hareem, haraam!'

'Enough! Stop it! Say what you want to say and leave quickly. My husband has returned,' Nandini spoke with authority

'You woman! You have forgotten the past.'

'Why bring up those old stories, now?' asked Nandini.

'You ask why? I will first remind you of those incidents and then tell you...' Ravidasa spoke with fury.

Realizing that there would be no way of stopping him, Nandini sighed and turned her face away.

'Hey! Lady, listen, three years ago, one midnight, a dead body was burnt in the cremation ground beside the Vaigai River. Some men dragged you out of hiding in the forest to throw you in that burning pyre. They took a terrible oath individually. You were making some signs with your ravishing eyes conveying the meaning that you too wanted to be a part of that oath taking. You swore that you had more reasons to take revenge than those men. You also promised to use your beauty and intelligence for that plot and once that was fulfilled you would end your life. Nobody believed you except me. I saved your life. Do you remember all that?' asked Ravidasa.

Nandini remarked, 'Those incidents have been burnt with fire upon my heart.'

'After that night, one day we were all walking along the banks of the wide river Cauvery and suddenly we heard the noise of horses coming down the path. We all hid ourselves in the forest. But you forsook us and stood on the road. Senior Paluvattarayar fell victim to your charms. Later, he married you. All my men yelled at me, at your betrayal. One day I managed to see you and tried to kill you. But you begged for your life, saying that you had come here, mainly to fulfil our oath. You also promised all help to me and my men.'

Ravidasa finally stopped.

'Why didn't you send your maid to receive me in the usual place today?'

'Some other fellow came up the ladder meant for you. My stupid maid thought it was you and brought him here.'

'I was about to be caught by the soldiers searching for that youth.'

'You suspected me and you deserve it!'

'I escaped by hiding myself in the pond near this garden, immersing myself in the water by holding my breath, till those men left.'

'Why did that young stranger come here? You showed your true colours by disclosing our secrets to him...'

'I didn't tell him anything. I discovered his secrets.'

'What did you discover?'

'He is a messenger taking letters from Kanchi to Palayarai. He is carrying the letter for the tigress at Palayarai. I requested him to bring her reply to show to me. You came in at that time.'

'What is the use of all that to us?'

'That's your stupid brain. We have sworn an oath to destroy the tiger clan and its very roots. But you men think only of the male tigers forgetting the female tigresses. Who is really ruling this Chola Empire when the Emporor is sick and the princes are in Kanchi and Lanka...'

'It is Senior Paluvettarayar.'

'The world thinks so. In reality, that female tiger-cub at Palayarai is ruling this nation. That arrogant female sits in her palace and pulls the wires to make all dance. I will use this youth to put an end to her exploits.'

Surprise and respect replaced the rage on Ravidasa's face.

'You are truly capable! But how am I to believe all this as truth?'

'Take the youth with you and find out. You have not yet told me the purpose of your visit: do you need more money? There's just no end to your demands.'

'We need Lankan coins for our men.'

'You took all this time to say this! I have made arrangements even before you could ask.'

Nandini gave him a bagful of Lankan gold coins.

'Take it and leave quickly. My husband will be here any time now.'

As Ravidasa was about to leave, Nandini called out to him,

'Take the young man also out of the fort. Let him fend for himself thereafter.'

She then looked at the direction in which Vandiyathevan had gone and clapped her hands to call him. But no response.

Vandiyathevan could not be seen. Ravidasa left.

33

Battle of Roaring Lions

The two brothers of Paluvoor were compared to the ideal brothers of Rama and Bharatha of the epic Ramayana or best brothers Arjuna and Bhima of the epic Mahabharata. They had very close understanding and affinity. Normally, when the elder brother entered the fort, the younger brother would welcome him back. But today when the senior Paluvattarayar entered Tanjore, the usual enthusiasm and his younger brother were both missing. But he did not mind it.

The Commander stepped outside his mansion to meet his elder brother and they went directly to their private chamber. The elder brother asked,

'Brother, any special news? How is the Emperor's health?'

The brother replied, 'His health remains as usual.'

'Then why do you look dull today? Why didn't you come to the gates to receive me?'

'Brother! A minor incident happened; I'll tell you about it later. How about the affairs for which you travelled?' asked Kalanthaka the Commander.

'Oh! All the invitees unanimously agreed to Prince Madurandakan ascending the throne after the Emperor.'

'What if the people dissent?' asked Kalanthaka.

'Ah! Who is going to ask the people? If the people object, let us deal with them.'

'What about the Velakkara Padai? How do we handle them?'

'The Velakkara Padai has sworn blood oaths to protect the person of Sundara Chola, not his sons! Let us round up their leaders and throw them in the dungeons?'

'Brother, the main opposition will be from those two women in Palayarai...'

'Let us not be worried about those two women.'

'You mentioned that there was some incident here: what was it?'

'A youth came here from Kanchi. He brought a letter for the Emperor and another for Kundavai.'

'What did you do with him? Hope you have confiscated the letters and thrown him in prison?'

'No, brother! He said that he had met you at Kadamboor and you asked him to see the Emperor and deliver the letter. Is it true?'

'Oh! Utter lie! An unknown youth calling himself Kandamaran's friend, arrived at Kadamboor. But he did not tell me anything about bringing letters! I suspected him when I saw him. I hope you have not been duped by him?'

'I have been duped by him because he mentioned your name.'

'You fool! What did you do after that? Did you give the letter to the Emperor? Did you at least read it?'

'Yes, there was nothing in it except an invitation for the Emperor to visit the golden palace at Kanchi. After delivering the letter to the Emperor the youth was saying something about danger...'

'Did you not suspect him at least after that and have him thrown in the dungeons?'

'I suspected him but did not arrest him.'

'I was a fool to have given you the name Kalanthaka and making you the commander of this fort. Don't you feel ashamed to admit that a young fellow has fooled you in my name?'

'He didn't merely mention your name, he showed me your signet ring. Did you give it to him?'

'Never! Am I foolish like you to be deceived like that?'

'He had the signet ring. He showed it to me and also to the gatekeeper before entering the fort. If you didn't give it to him, he could have obtained it only from one other source.'

'Whom do you mean?'

'I mean the Young Queen...'

'Damn you! Be careful! I will cut off your tongue!'

'Cut off my tongue and chop off my head but I will tell you what I have to tell you. She is a dangerous snake. One day it will surely strike. Avoid that! Throw her out before that!'

'Kalanthaka! I, too, will tell you something that I have been intending to say for a while now. You can bravely criticize my activities if you don't like them. But if you utter even one word against the Young Queen who is wedded to me, I will kill you with these very same hands that raised you!'

That wordy duel between the brothers was like a battle of roaring lions clashing against each other.

34

Nandini's Drama

When Senior Paluvattarayar returned to his palace, it was well past midnight. His mind was brooding over his brother's failure.

Why must he unnecessarily find fault with Nandini? It is natural for anyone to easily escape the consequences of one's own mistakes by throwing the blame on someone else.

But now his mind became suspicious of Nandini.

I am enslaved by my madness for her at this old age. I picked her up at the wayside without knowing her lineage. Her words and deeds have aroused my suspicion. My brother's words have confused me.

I must confirm from her directly. She often borrows the signet ring. She goes and sits alone in the gazebo for hours. Some sorcerer is also visiting her often. Why? I can let all that go. But why does she not share her bed with me? Why does she make me wait so long after marriage? She talks of some penance and worship. But she is never specific. What prevents her from sleeping with her lawfully wedded husband? Tonight, I must talk firmly about it and decide once for all.

He returned to his mansion with these thoughts lingering in his mind. Nandini was still in the garden gazebo.

What is she doing there at midnight? Why is she so indifferent?

He walked towards the garden with anger and saw Nandini and her maid walking towards him. She stopped on seeing him and turned her face away in the darkness. She did not look up at him, even after he came very close to her. He forgot all his intentions of scolding Nandini. Instead, he consoled her.

'My darling! Why this anger? Please look at me?'

Saying this, he placed his iron-hard hand on her soft shoulders.

But Nandini pushed his sturdy hand away with her flower-like hands.

'You pushed me away with your silken hands! That itself is my good fortune. You accomplished what could not be accomplished by warriors. Why are you angry? My ears thirst for your nectar sweet voice.'

That great warrior was begging her.

'How many days since you parted from me? Hasn't it been a full four days?' Nandini sobbed, melting Senior Paluvettarayar's heart, which could withstand the assault of several swords.

'Oh! All this anger for that? Can't you bear my parting even for four days? This parting of four days is difficult for me too. Come and sit on your flower laden couch! Let me see your face and satisfy my hunger.'

He took Nandini to her couch, wiping away her tears.

His earlier plans to admonish her disappeared into thin air. He remained at her feet to obey the slightest of her whims. Any kind of slavery is bad but slavery to the beauty of women is the worst.

'You were away on important government business, agreed, but then why visit your brother first and come here next? Is your brother more important than I am?'

She cast an angry glance at her hapless husband who replied, 'It's not like that, darling. I had to discuss some urgent official matters and ensure that fool Madurandakan reached his palace safely.'

'My King, I am interested in all your undertakings. But I feel uncomfortable at the thought of you taking a young man in a palanquin meant for me. People think that you are taking me along with you wherever you go.'

'I am also not happy. I tolerate this for the sake of the important undertaking. It was you who suggested this idea of taking Madurandakan in your closed palanquin.'

'I merely did my duty. As a wife I am bound to help you.'

'We tried several times to bring Madurandakan into political life but we could not shake him. But you spoke to him twice and changed him completely! He is more restless to ascend the Chola throne! What magic did you cast on him? You being a sorceress, why seek the counsel of other sorcerers? People talk about it unnecessarily…'

'My King! You men confront men in the battlefield and never fight with women's cunningness. Only a snake knows its kind. I have told you earlier why I consult a sorcerer. You know nothing about the cunningness of Kundavai. You have forgotten how she humiliated both of us. She asked me in the midst of a hundred women, "That old fool on his death-bed has gone woman-mad losing all his senses. Why did you marry an old buffalo?" How can I forget those words?' Nandini sobbingly spoke these passionate words with tears in her eyes, wetting her heaving breasts.

35

Paluvettarayar's Infatuation for Nandini

Senior Paluvettarayar was aware of the criticism of the people, including Kundavai, about his marrying a young girl in his old age. But none told him what exactly Kundavai had said about him till Nandini revealed it. His heart was burning like a furnace fuelled by Nandini's tears.

'My dearest! Did she call me an old buffalo? Just you see what I will do to her! I will trample her and throw her out just like the water-buffalo trampling a lotus vine!'

He spat venom. Nandini tried to pacify him.

The Senior continued,

'Darling, I know you can't bear her insulting me. But remember the lion in the forest that can effortlessly break the neck of an elephant but will never pounce on a cat.'

'Yes, Kundavai is a cat but she controls the mighty Chola Empire with magic. We have to break her magic with more powerful magic. But if you don't like me doing that, please let me know. I will move out of this palace.'

Nandini sobbed.

'No dear! Never do that. You can even bring in a thousand magicians and make them live here but never leave me. You are dearer to me than my own life... How will this body survive without life?'

'My King! There is no need for magic spells when you have the sword and spear in your hands. Leave the magic spells and sorcery to me.'

'Darling! When you open your coral lips and call me "Dearest", my very being is filled with joy and your golden face makes my head swim. I have no arrows against Cupid's darts! You have them! This fire of passion consumes my very life. Let me embrace your flower like body and rejoice. Save my life, darling! It is more than two-and-a-half years since we were married. But till now no wedded bliss for me. You put me away with excuses of vows and penances. You may as well poison me to death with your own hands.'

Nandini covered her ears and said,

'My King! Don't utter such cruel words! I will drink poison and die.'

'No, no! I won't say anything like that again. Forgive me! How can I be at peace if you drink poison and die? Already I am half mad. Soon I will become totally mad.'

'Dear King, why should you become mad? On the very day we married, we became one in two: heart and heart mingled. Why bother about mere bodies? This body is made of mere dust. One day it will go to dust again.'

'Stop! Stop! My ears burn with your harsh words. Brahma, the creator, has fashioned your divine form, collecting delicate divine flowers from the gardens of heaven.'

'My King! You talk as if you stood beside the creator and watched all this!'

'Nandini, when I first saw you in the middle of a forest path, I had a strong feeling we were together in the past several births—you as Ahalya married to Sage Gauthama, I was Indra coveting you—so we were cursed by your husband in the epic Ramayana. Then you were Kannagi and I was Kovalan, wrongfully put to death in the epic Silappadikaram.'

'My King! Call yourself Manmatha (god of beauty) and me Rathi (goddess of beauty) only that will be befitting!'

Senior Paluvettarayar's face brightened with pride and joy.

'My dearest, you are Rathi but am I Manmatha? You call me so because of your love for me.'

'You are Manmatha for me! Bravery is beauty for menfolk. There is no warrior who is your match in this land. You gave sanctuary to this orphan, without looking into my past and showering all your love on me. I will not make you wait for long. The time for ending my penance and fulfilling my vow is drawing close,' spoke Nandini.

'Dearest, tell me clearly what your vow and penance is about. I will complete it for you as quickly as possible.'

'None of the descendants of this Sundara Chola should ascend the Chola throne and the pride of that arrogant female, Kundavai must be pricked.'

'Nandini! The job is done. Aditya and Arulmoli will not get the throne. Chieftains of all the territories, barring two, have agreed to crown Madurandakan as the next crown prince.'

'We must be careful till the deed is done.'

'No doubt about it. Mistakes may occur because of the foolishness of others. Even today such a mistake occurred. A young messenger from Kanchi duped Commander Junior Paluvettarayar and met the Emperor.'

'You are always praising your younger brother. Didn't I tell you he is not smart enough?'

'Leave it dear, he has acted foolishly in this matter. That youth had our signet ring.'

'Losers find some silly excuses for their failure. But is he making an effort to find him?'

'Yes. The search for him has begun. They will find him soon. After the Emperor, the throne is surely for Madurandakan.'

'My King, the time has come now to reveal the aim of my penance...'

'Dearest, I have been asking you to tell me that...'

'My vows will not be fulfilled by crowning that idiot, Madurandakan, who shows his teeth to every woman.'

'What will fulfil your vows, tell me. I will accomplish it.'

'My King! A famous astrologer read my horoscope when I was

very young. I would achieve an envious position of prestige and pride after the age of eighteen and the man who takes my hand will rule a large empire and kings will salute him. Can you fulfil this?'

When the senior Paluvettarayar heard these words, everything began to swing before his eyes. The flower laden gazebo revolved; its pillars revolved. The dark garden in front began revolving. Treetops bathed in the moonlight began revolving. The mansions on both sides revolved. The world revolved!

36

Dark Underground Passage

Let us now see what was happening with Vandhiyathevan.
Vandiyathevan hid himself to avoid the sorcerer. He tried to listen to the conversation between Nandini and the sorcerer, but he could hear nothing. He decided to quit the garden to escape from the seductive net of Nandini.

In the presence of the palace guards, his brain was sharp and his arms were strong. But, before Nandini, his intelligence failed.

He also realized Nandini's flaming hatred towards Kundavai during his interaction with her.

He wanted to escape from that place. But how? His brain started working diabolically.

Let me also use my eyes and look all around here. There is a mansion in utter darkness. Can I escape through this dark mansion?

He came near the mansion to find a huge door with a large lock. Luckily there was a tiny door in that huge door and he could easily enter the mansion through that door. It was pitch dark inside. Somehow his eyes spotted huge pillars. He groped with his hands and started walking forward in the darkness but could not find any escape route.

Maybe I should go back to the gazebo. It is better to face Nandini. I can overcome her wiles better than grope about in this utter darkness. I can promise her whatever she wants for now and manage later. This must be the infamous underground dungeons of Tanjore.

The usually cool Vandiyathevan started sweating in anxiety.

He suddenly heard a noise.

Are those bats beating their wings? No, it sounds like footsteps.

Suddenly he heard the footsteps becoming louder and coming closer. His eyes were staring into the direction from which the sound of the footsteps came. A light was becoming brighter and coming closer. Someone was bringing a lighted torch. He saw three persons coming. As soon as he saw their faces, all traces of fear vanished. It was his dear friend Kandamaran, the next one was Prince Madurandakan. He could not identify the third one holding the torch. Now, the three men had ascended the steps and had gone up. The light became dimmer and dimmer.

Vandiyatheevan was wondering if he could follow them but abandoned that idea. He started walking down the steps to escape.

Vandiyathevan walked along the underground passage carefully placing each foot ahead of him. He found it difficult to grope in the utter darkness as the passage was wide and long. Suddenly, he saw a dim light. Some sort of glow was emanating from the objects stored there—gold crowns, ornaments, diamonds, rubies, etc. It was the treasury of the great Chola Empire!

The goddess of wealth had brought him there! He was amidst all these riches collected by the Chola armies in their campaigns over hundreds of years.

Vandiyathevan touched everything and rejoiced. He dipped his hands into the pots of pearls to feel them trickle through his fingers.

Today, I have experienced all the three types of greed—greed for women (Nandini)), land (her promise of regaining his ancestral land) and wealth (treasury). I have escaped from the first two temptations and must overcome this also. The earth with the sky as roof is my palace. Why complicate it by desiring for wealth? Why give up this pleasant life for a life of danger? I must get out of this treasury and this fort!

All of a sudden, he heard doors open and shut somewhere at a distance and footsteps approaching him from two different directions.

Soon he was able to see that Kandamaran and Madurandakan were coming from one direction, Senior Paluvattarayar and Nandini were coming from another.

Vandiyathevan became breathless. The two parties met each other. Kandamaran asked Senior Paluvettarayar something, pointing towards Nandini and when Senior Paluvettarayar replied he acknowledged it with reverence and walked away. Senior Paluvettarayar again made some sort of a sign to the palace guard; the guard also acknowledged it, bowing with his palm covering his lips, and followed Kandamaran. Senior Paluvettarayar and his young queen walked in the opposite direction.

Then Vandiyathevan began to follow Kandamaran in the hope of finding an exit from that maze. He was even prepared to seek the help of Kandamaran by concocting a story.

Vandiyathevan walked silently and quickly followed the torch light, neither too far nor too close, through the twisting, turning, narrow passage.

The passage came to an abrupt end at a thick, roof-high wall. None could guess that there was an exit in that wall. The guard placed the palm of his right hand on a handle on the wall. The wall had an opening big enough for a person to exit. Kandamaran stepped into the opening with one leg inside and the other outside.

Ah! What is this? What is the guard doing?

The guard removed his palm from the handle on the wall and stabbed Kandamaran on the back with his dagger. Vandiyathevan ran up from his hiding place and pounced upon the guard. The torch fell down and the servant saw the furious Vandiyathevan.

37

Is This Friendship?

Vandiyathevan pounced on the guard, twisted his neck and then tied his hands behind him with a cloth. He ran towards Kandamaran, who was lying with a knife stuck to his back and lifted him. He stepped outside the passage carrying his friend on his shoulder. He felt the breeze and smelled the water from the river Vadavar encircling the fort. He could see the rapid flow of water down, deep below, with swirls and whirlpools, in the dim moonlight.

He walked along the bank and found a huge tree fallen across the river. He used that as a bridge to cross the river and placed his friend under a mango tree. He remembered Amudan's house was nearby and decided to take him there for help.

At the moment he was concerned about Kandamaran's condition and tapped his face asking,

'Kandamara, can you hear me? Do you know me?'

Kandamaran slowly opened his eyes and whispered,

'Oh yes! How can I forget my dear most friend Vandiyathevan? After all, you stabbed me in my back!'

His words fell like whiplashes on Vandiyathevan.

'Kandamara, do you think it was me who stabbed you!'

Thinking of something he stopped suddenly.

'You didn't stab me. Your knife gently caressed my back! You thankless sinner! It was for your sake I came rushing through the secret passage at midnight to save you from the Paluvettarayars. How many times have we sworn loyalty to each other? You have forgotten all that! I wanted to inform you about some important changes taking place in Chola politics. Oh dear! Whom to trust in this world anymore?' He groaned and fainted.

'When there are so many trustworthy people in the world why did you trust the Paluvettarayars?' mumbled Vandiyathevan, his eyes brimming with tears. He lifted his friend once again onto his shoulders and started walking.

He smelt the fragrance of the blooming night flowers and reached Amudan's garden house. But alas! What a difference between yesterday and today. The garden had been totally devastated.

Oh! Paluvoor soldiers who have come here in search of me have committed these atrocities!

However, his horse was still there, tied to the tree in front of Amudan's house. Perhaps they had left it there to lure him. He wanted to leave his friend in the safe custody of Amudan and his mother and go to Palayarai.

He walked as silently as possible and reached the front door of the house and tapped Amudan's shoulder as he lay asleep on the front porch. He sat up, startled; Vandiyathevan covered his mouth and spoke softly,

'Brother! Help me. I am in danger. This man is my dear most friend Kandamaran, son of Kadamboor Sambuvarayar. Someone stabbed him in the back.'

Amudan replied, 'I will look after him. Late last evening, several groups of soldiers came in search of you and totally destroyed my garden! But it's all right as long as you are safe. Luckily, they did not take away your horse. Go away immediately.'

'That is my intention too. But please, save my friend.'

'Don't worry my mother is good at such matters.'

Amudan opened the door and woke up his mother. They carried Kandamaran to the inner room of the house. Amudan's mother examined Kandamaran and went into the kitchen and came back with a bunch of herbs and some clean pieces of cloth.

Vandiyathevan was not familiar with the route to reach Palayarai.

He had to carry a message to Kundavai. Therefore, he asked his friend Amudan to accompany him. Both of them mounted the horse and silently left the place. Once they were out, it galloped quickly down the road.

By now five or six soldiers had reached Amudan's house. They banged loudly on the door and Amudan's mother opened the door. The soldiers entered, roughly pushing her down.

'The man is here,' shouted one of the soldiers

'Hey this fellow seems to be somebody else,' said, another.

'Never mind let us carry him to the Commander.'

Four men lifted Kandamaran. Just then the sound of a galloping horse was heard. The soldiers dropped Kandamaran and ran after the horse.

38

Palayarai—Chola's Old Capital

Vandiyathevan reached Palayarai after overcoming several hurdles and dangers. Palayarai was the original capital of the great Cholas situated on the banks of river Arasalar.

Palayarai is the gem-encrusted head-jewel of Mother Tamil. Studded with rubies, pearls, emeralds and sapphires such as the surrounding rivers, streams, creeks and fields, always brimming with fresh water and coconut palms, punnai trees spreading cool shadows on its banks. Amidst this lush green sylvan setting, the tall towers and turrets of temples, crowned with golden cupolas touching the sky, were a breathtaking sight to see and rejoice.

Huge army encampments in the Palayarai neighbourhood provided housing for the various battalions of Chola armies and their families. The Chola Palace stood shining in all its splendour, rising majestically in their midst. The Chola Palace was a huge complex with several mansions designed and built by every prince and princess of the Chola dynasty during their lifetimes. A thousand eyes would not suffice to take in its beauty and magnificence. It is simply the imagination of ten thousand bards and poets.

After the emperor, Sundara Chola, became bedridden, the Chola capital was moved to Tanjore. The regional chieftains, provincial kings, councilors and ambassadors from foreign lands stopped coming to Palayarai; their supporting staff and other top dignitaries (ministers, judges, government officials, etc.) had also moved to Tanjore along with their families. The soldiers who used to live in the army cantonments were now engaged in the Lankan war and were part of the peace-keeping forces in Madurai and Kanchi.

However, architects, religious ascetics, spiritual singers, priests and pilgrims thronged the streets of Palayarai. All important occasions were celebrated with the same spirit.

Today was a special day of carnival, celebrating Krishna Jayanthi (Birth of King Krishna). Men, women and children were dressed in beautiful clothes and jewels. People gathered in groups here and there at street crossings, witnessing colourful street plays performed by various artists in vivid costumes. They were enacting various leelas of King Krishna dressed up like Krishna, his maids and his cowherds.

There was much activity around the Vishnu temple at Nandipuram. The familiar voice of Alvarkkadiyan Nambi was heard singing in praise of Lord Vishnu. Chariots and palanquins were parked in front of the temple. All the women members of the royal family living in the palace visited the temple on the occasion of Krishna Jayanthi.

Sembiyan Madevi, revered by one and all as the Queen Mother, came walking followed by other queens and all the princesses including Kundavai and Vanathi. Even in her old age Sembiyan Madevi was stunningly beautiful and majestic, spreading radiance and dignity all around.

Just as the Queen Mother was about to get into her palanquin, Alvarkkadiyan's singing caught her attention. She sent for him. Alvarkkadiyan came up with reverence and bowed before her.

'Nambi, I have not seen you for some time. Were you on some journey or pilgrimage?' asked the Queen Mother.

'Yes, My Majesty! I was on a pilgrimage. I saw several astonishing things wherever I went!'

'Come and see me this evening.'

'I am at your service, My Majesty.'

All the palanquins and chariots now moved down the street towards the Chola Palace. Kundavai's eyes conveyed a secret message to Alvarkkadiyan. He nodded his head, understanding the message.

Queen Mother was deeply religious. She was always dressed in simple white silk, with sacred ashes on her forehead and holy rudraksha beads around her neck, amidst all the riches and splendour of the palace. Though she wore neither a crown nor any other rich adornment, her very posture and radiant face proclaimed her royalty. There was nothing surprising about the fact that each and every member of the Chola clan, without any exception, worshipped her as a goddess and did nothing against her wishes.

But, her son, Prince Madurandakan, acted against her wishes. Disobeying her orders, he married a daughter of the Paluvoor family and he was also coveting the Chola throne. All these had given rise to a wrinkle of worry on her radiant face.

The courtyards of her palace were always teeming with visitors of various kinds—musicians, spiritual singers, religious savants, poets, artists, sculptors, temple architects, priests and doctors.

That day there were delegations of various temple trustees and architects from many townships. She had agreed to provide funds to all their requests.

Alvarkkadiyan and his cousin brother, Esana Bhattar, entered the chamber as invited by the Queen Mother.

39

Queen Mother

A renowned architect had brought a model for a large granite temple complex which he had created using all his fantastic imagination. Queen Mother was greatly impressed by the model, she turned towards the gentleman standing next to Alvarkkadiyan and said,

'All Siva temples in this kingdom can be renovated in this new fashion. Some people say, "Why so many temples for Siva…".'

While the Queen Mother was talking, Alvarkkadiyan interrupted,

'I am one of those persons who objects to so many Siva temples being built and Vishnu temples being ignored.'

Esana Bhattar, standing close to the Queen Mother, hurriedly offered his apologies for his cousin impetuousness.

In those days members of a family followed the faith of their choice. Though Esana Bhattar and Alvarkkadiyan were cousins, Bhattar was very broad-minded, accepting both Saiva and Vaishnava faiths, while Alvarkkadiyan was a fanatic of Vaishnavism. Which is why Bhattar begged pardon on his brother's behalf.

After a while all others left except Alvarkkadiyan. The Queen Mother lowered her voice and asked Alvarkkadiyan,

'Any other important news?'

'Yes, my Mother. I have brought some important news. I was waiting for the others to leave. Who knows if there was a spy among the visitors? All sorts of discords are rampant in our nation. Aditya Karikalan, Malayaman and Partiban feel that the Paluvettarayars have imprisoned the Emperor in Tanjore Fort. A letter was sent through a messenger to the Emperor, inviting him to Kanchi.

I also found out who the messenger is. He is not an ordinary man. He is very capable and courageous. Besides being a messenger, he is also a spy. I tried talking to him. If I try to jump across the stream, he leaps across the river! Without disclosing anything, he tried to pry secrets from me. Even the Kumbakonam astrologer tried his tricks on him. But nothing worked. Now, I heard that he had somehow entered Tanjore Fort and delivered the letter to the Emperor.'

'What was the Emperor's reply?'

'Apparently, the Emperor promised to send a reply the next day. However, Junior Paluvettarayar became suspicious about the messenger and ordered him to be arrested. Meanwhile, that fellow has escaped from Tanjore.'

'He really must be very capable. Then what did you do? Where did you go from Kanchi?'

The Queen Mother enquired anxiously.

Alavarkkadiyan briefed the Queen Mother about the midnight meeting at Kadamboor Palace and the conspiracy to make Madurandakan the Emperor.

'Alvarkkadiyan, all this is her doing! All these dangers surrounding this Chola Empire are caused by her, your sister, the junior queen, Nandini. Were you able to meet her?'

'No, my Majesty, I could not do so. I raised and nourished that snake as my own sister for several years. After she became the queen of Senior Paluvettarayar, she refused to even see me.'

Queen Mother was in utter shock. Then she muttered to herself, 'Oh God! Such a huge punishment for an offense I committed!'

Finally, wiping away her tears, she spoke,

'Alvarkkadiyan, come back here again before you leave. By then I will consult Kundavai and think of some solution to overcome this danger!'

Alvarkkadiyan spoke hesitantly,

'Mother, it may be better if you do not disclose this information even to Kundavai.'

'Do you also suspect her?'

'Yes.'

'Nambi, I will believe you even if you say that the sun rises in the west and sets in the east. But I won't accept if you blame Kundavai. Do you know this? On the day she was born, the palace midwife picked her up and brought her to my arms before showing the baby to others. From that day, I have been raising her with love and affection. She reveres me more than her own father or even mother and loves me deeply.'

'My Majesty, let me ask you one thing. Did Kundavai tell you about her visit to the Kumbakonam astrologer's house?'

'No. So, what?'

'Did she mention about her meeting with that youth of the Vaanar clan in the astrologer's house and subsequently on the banks of the river Arasalar?'

'No. But if she has not mentioned it to me, there must be a reason for her not having done so.'

40

The Young Spy

There was a beautiful lake behind the Palayarai Palace complex. Apart from its scenic beauty, the lake provided a perfect security cover for the royal members in the palace complex. Only the commanders, ministers and other important dignitaries were allowed to use that lake.

After the Emperor moved to Tanjore, Kundavai became the sole mistress of his majestic palace with the beautiful garden behind it full of rare flowering shrubs and trees with branches touching the sky. In the midst of these pleasant groves, there was a beautifully carved marble gazebo. Kundavai and her friends would spend most of their evenings there, teasing each other, telling stories, recounting titbits, singing and dancing.

That evening, Kundavai and Vanathi were rejoicing. They were enjoying their time together, swinging on the long swings hanging from the banyan tree, listening to the songs of birds amidst their chatter and laughter.

Kundavai posed a question to Vanathi.

'Sister, what did you say?' asked Vanathi.

'What did I say! Where is your mind?'

'Nowhere. It's right here.'

'You thief! I know pretty well. It has gone to the battlefield in Lanka. Your mind is trying to play tricks on my blameless brother!'

'If only I had wings, I would fly to Lanka at once...' Vanathi said shyly.

'Fly away! What will you do there in Lanka? You will only be a hindrance to him. Chola men never take their women to the battlefield.'

'Why, Sister?'

'Chola men are not concerned about their wounds. They are more concerned about their women.'

At that very moment, thoughts of Vandiyathevan entered Kundavai's mind and she became preoccupied.

'Do you remember how he stood spellbound when he saw all of us?'

'Whom are you talking about?'

'That youth in Kumbakonam astrologer's house...'

'Sister, I remember... But you are wrong in saying "All of us". He stood spellbound looking only at you. In fact, he noticed none but you!'

'Vanathi, let us not allow our mind to wander like that. Oh! listen... What is that sound? It sounds like the drummers proclaiming something. Let us listen.'

An announcer was declaring in a loud voice:

'An enemy spy who entered Tanjore Fort by showing a false signet ring escaped after wounding two soldiers. He is young and well-built, capable and intelligent like a magician. His name is Vandiyathevan. Anyone who gives asylum to him will be sentenced to death. Thousand gold coins will be given as reward for anyone who finds him. This is by order of Commander Junior Paluvattarayar.'

After the announcement, the drums rolled like thunder, once again. Kundavai felt upset.

A maid reported to Kundavai, 'Princess! A Vaishnavite gentleman has come to see you. His name is Alvarkkadiyan Nambi. He says it is urgent.'

'Please send him in,' said Kundavai.

41

People Grumbled

Alvarkkadiyan left the Queen Mother to meet Kundavai. On the way, he was thrilled to witness Sri Krishna Jayanthi celebrations in the town. His heart rejoiced to watch a play about King Krishna. Several actors were enacting the story of Krishna. The actor playing the role of Kamsa with a masked face, attracted Alvarkkadiyan's attention. He had heard that voice somewhere.

There was a sudden change in the joyous mood of the people. The festive mood became more subdued and the crowd started dispersing… Drumbeats were heard and the sounds of dancing stopped!

The cause for the change was the drummers's proclamation about the spy, which had upset Princess Kundavai as well as the people. Unknown faces were questioned. Some even looked at Alvarkkadiyan with suspicion.

The people were also talking about the unjust rule of the Paluvettarayar brothers at Tanjore.

The Paluvettarayar brothers were refusing food and supplies to the soldiers in Lanka who were accompanying their darling Prince Arulmoli even though the granary in Tanjore was full with overflowing grains.

Which foreign king was so powerful to send a spy into the vast Chola heartland? If these wretched fellows from Paluvoor disliked someone, they would go to any extent to charge him and dub him as a spy and finally end his life. Or they may have him thrown into the dungeons of Tanjore!

Alvarkkadiyan heard all these murmurings of people and

understood the unrest. He was worried about the consequences as he neared Kundavai's palace.

Alvarkkadiyan entered Princess Kundavai's palace with these thoughts.

The young princess was fond of chatting with Alvarkkadiyan on political affairs of the state. She always welcomed him with pleasantness. But today, Alvarkkadiyan noticed a change in her mood. Her face indicated that her mind was preoccupied with something else.

'Nambi! What is new? Why have you come?' Asked Kundavai.

'I wanted to share with you the happenings in the country. Forgive me if I have come at a wrong time. Shall I take leave of you?'

'No! No! Wait a while, it was me who asked you to come... Where have you been on this journey? Tell me!'

'I travelled from Cape Comorin in the south to Tirupati in the north.'

'What do the people talk about?'

'People are surprised about the changes in young Prince Madurandakan, his marriage and his sudden interest for the throne.'

'Nambi! How is your darling sister singing devotional songs?'

'What does she lack for, she has everything and rules like an empress in the mansions of the Senior Paluvattarayar.'

'Only in his mansions? She is all powerful in the entire Chola Empire...!'

'Some even talk about it, dear Princess! But why talk of her on this festive day?'

Kundavai remarked,

'I heard a drum beat today. What was that about Nambi?'

Alvarkkadiyan Nambi who was waiting for this question replied,

'It is about some spy who escaped! They even announced a reward for anyone who captures him.'

'Do you suspect anybody?' asked Kundavai.

'Princess, I'm not sure. But I met a brave young man at Veeranarayanapuram. He said that he was going to Tanjore but did not reveal his purpose. In fact, he questioned me about many things...'

Kundavai interrupted,

'Tell me about him!'

'He appeared to be from a noble family. He was handsome with sharp features. He looked very strong, brave and energetic.'

'What did he ask you?'

'He enquired about the Emperor's health. Then he asked about the successor to the Chola throne. He asked about our Junior Prince in Lanka. He has also asked the same questions to the Kumbakonam astrologer.'

'Did he visit the astrologer?'

'Apparently he created a big commotion and entered the house even while you were inside. Fortunately, he did not recognize you.'

'Oh, I see. If you happen to see that youth anywhere bring him here to me. I have something important to discuss with him!'

Alvarkkadiyan bowingly said,

'No need for that, Princess. I need not go in search of him. He himself will come to you.'

With these mysterious words, Alvarkkadiyan took his leave.

42

Romantic Moment

After visiting Princess Kundavai, Alvarkkadiyan Nambi went to his elder brother, Esanya Bhattar's house in the Siva temple near the Chola palace complex.

There he came to know that Vandiyathevan had entered Palayarai with a group of stage play actors who enacted the story of Krishna in the Krishna Jayanthi celebrations. The actor donning the role of Kamsa with a face mask was none other than Vandiyathevan.

Alvarkkadiyan's brother Enanya Bhattar had helped Vandiyathevan to hide in the Jain caves behind the Siva temple and was taking him to Princess Kundavai's palace through the lake in a boat.

Alvarkkadiyan closely followed them to observe the happenings between Vandiyathevan and the Princess from a hiding place in the garden.

A scene, dramatized by the great romantic poets like Kalidasa and Keats, took place there.

Kundavai was seated on a marble garden seat atop the steps.

Vandiyathevan looked up to gaze into the Princess's face and stood there, stunned. Only the tendril of a flowering creeper stretched its gentle arm between the two of them. A beautiful multicoloured butterfly flew in to sit on a flower on that creeper. Kundavai gently looked at that butterfly. Vandiyathevan kept looking at her unblinkingly.

The soft waves of the lake became still. Birds stopped singing. The whole universe came to a standstill. They forgot themselves.

Early man freely lived in a forest near the mountains just like the birds in the sky. Yet, in his heart of hearts, he was pining for the constant companion of his dreams.

At the same time God created early woman near the same forest on the other side of the mountain. She had food to satisfy hunger, spring waters to quench her thirst and mountain caves to shelter her. She was also longing for a companion.

Once, during a hot summer, there was a wild forest fire in the mountain that separated man and woman. Sensing danger, they began climbing the mountain. They met at the peak and stared at each other without blinking. The forest fire was forgotten. Hunger and thirst were forgotten. They forgot why they had climbed the mountain. Finally, they realized that they had been living their life only for that moment.

God the Creator watched this romantic moment and was happy to see that his wonderful task of creation was progressing well. Only after Bhattar cleared his throat did they come to their senses.

'I think you wanted to see me in private? You could not have anticipated meeting me once again so soon,' said Kundavai to Vandiyathevan.

'You can say that only if we had parted... You have not left my thoughts, even for a moment, ever since our first meeting...' said Vandiyathevan without taking his eyes off the Princess.

'Careful warrior! The lances and swords of Chola men are very dangerous weapons. Strangers crossing our borders should be careful, particularly spies...'

'The swirling whirlpools in the fresh floods of the Chola rivers are more dangerous than the Chola men. They made me struggle.'

'How did you get caught in the whirlpool?'

'I came as a messenger carrying letters from your dear brother, but the commander of Tanjore Fort, Junior Paluvettarayar, accused me of being a spy and sent his men to capture me. A youth named Chendan Amudan in Tanjore came with me to show me the way to Palayarai.

Meanwhile, some of the soldiers chasing us came very close to us.

I decided to travel alone from there. I told him to tell the soldiers that I drowned in the river. Amudan refused to lie. So, I had to tie him with the horse and jump into the river.

Oh God! What swirling whirlpools in the rapids of these Chola rivers! My Princess, do you know what I recalled when I was struggling in those swirling whirlpools?'

'How would I know?'

'In those swirls of water, I saw some beautiful fish caught just like me. Those darting fish reminded me of the swirling eyes of the Chola women.'

Vandiyathevan said this looking deep into Princess Kundavai's eyes.

The melodious notes of a flute were floating down from the palace. The tinkle of ankle bells, the booming resonance of hand drums and the soft voice of young maids singing were floating in the air delighting Vandiyathevan and Kundavai. They were lost in each other.

'Now what task has brought you to me?' asked Kundavai who came out of the magic moment first.

'I have brought a letter from your beloved brother after combating several dangers,' said Vandiyathevan handing over the letter.

43

Surprise of Surprises

Princess Kundavai took the letter from Vandiyathevan and started reading it. Her face brightened up and she asked Vandiyathevan, 'Warrior, you have delivered the letter. What do you plan to do next?'

'My assignment is over after delivering this letter. I must go back.'

'Your assignment is not yet over; it has just begun. The Prince has written that I can entrust any confidential assignment to you. Looks like you are hesitating. Don't you like womenfolk? Or don't you like me?' asked the Princess with a smile.

What a beautiful question! Can the blue sky dislike this divine earth? Can the cloudburst dislike a flash of lightning? Can the bees dislike flowers? If I dislike you, why am I speechless when I see you? Why does the smile on your coral lips drive me crazy?

All these thoughts crowded Vandiyathevan's mind. But he said nothing.

'How long since you left Kanchi? Tell me all that happened till you reached here.'

'It's been ten days since I left Kanchi and how I reached here is a long story, my Princess.'

'Doesn't matter! Please tell me. Only after hearing your story, I will give you my next assignment. Let us proceed in this boat for some time. I want to listen to you fully.'

Vandiyathevan was thrilled to ride in the same boat in the company of the Chola Princess.

I must have done penance in the previous birth to gain this golden opportunity.

He began his narration of the incidents that took place at Kadamboor Sambuvarayar's mansion. Kundavai became more agitated and restless.

'Finally, I jumped into the river after tying Amudan to the horse. I somehow managed to escape the swirls and rapids and came out of the river and was resting in a wayside pavilion. Nandini's sorcerer Ravidasa had followed me there and tried to kill me. I escaped that too and entered Palayarai disguised as a stage-play actor and reached here.'

By then, the boat had returned to the shore. As they walked back to the garden, they heard ankle bells and drum beats indicating the dance practice in the palace.

After hearing all the details, Kundavai looked at Vandiyathevan with eyes full of surprise.

'The good wishes of the goddess of victory is in favour of the Cholas! That's why you have safely reached this place. Now, I will send you on a mission which is even more dangerous.'

Vandiyathevan stood with keen enthusiasm to accomplish the task to be assigned by her; if needed he would swim across the seven seas, battle a thousand lions without any weapons, climb the tallest mountain to pluck the heavenly stars from the skies.

Princess Kundavai took a palm-leaf and a writing instrument made of gold and wrote:

'Ponniyin Selva! Please come soon. The valiant warrior bringing this will give you all the details. You can trust him completely.'

At the end, she drew a tiny symbol of a fig leaf. Giving the letter to Vandiyathevan, she said,

'You may proceed to Lanka immediately and give it to Prince Arulmolivarman and bring him back.'

Vandiyathevan was overjoyed. One of his life-long ambitions had already been fulfilled after meeting the famous Chola Princess, Kundavai. Through her, his second ambition of meeting Prince Arulmoli was about to be fulfilled!

'My Majesty! You have given me a pleasant duty. I will leave immediately.'

Kundavai placed the letter on his palm, softly touching his lucky hand with her flower-like fingers. His joy knew no bounds. Thousands and millions of colorful butterflies fluttered around him! A million nightingales sang for him! Mountains showered fragrant flowers on him! He looked into Kundavai's eyes. His heart brimmed with eagerness to say many things. But mere words couldn't express his emotions.

His eyes conveyed whatever he intended to convey. Even Kalidasa the Great or the ancient Tamil bards could not compete with Vandiyathevan in his flight of imagination. Somewhere outside, the winds were whistling through some dry leaves.

44

Paranthaka Hospital

Using her savings, Princess Kundavai had established a government hospital for the welfare of the womenfolk and elderly people of the men who had gone to the war field. The hospital was named after Kundavai's greatgrandfather, Paranthaka I, the most distinguished Chola monarch. She had asked for Vandiyathevan to travel to Kodikarai and from there to Lanka in the guise of a doctor going in search for herbs to treat the Emperor's sickness. She had also asked the chief doctor's son, Pinakapani, to accompany him. She came to the hospital to see him off.

Two swift horses from the palace were waiting, restlessly, to carry Vandiyathevan and the doctor's son.

Kundavai stayed back to see them off as they were embarking on a long journey. Vandiyathevan turned to Kundavai and spoke in a secret language, then he reluctantly mounted his horse, looked at the Princess eagerly once more and set his horse galloping.

Kundavai was immersed in deep thought.

Why am I, who rejected kings and princes, so concerned about the welfare of this youth? Why am I so anxious about his safe return?

'Sister! What are you brooding over?'

Vanathi's voice brought her back to earth.

'Nothing! Vanathi. I was thinking about the courage of that young man.'

'Yes, Sister! He is quite artful! A clever bandit.'

'Why do you call him a bandit?'

'An ordinary thief will burgle things like silver and gold. But this young warrior has stolen the very guardian deity of the Chola Empire—your heart!' said Vanathi, mischievously.

45

A Dream City

About 300 years before this story, the famous Pallava kings had designed and built a beautiful port city like a dream world with spectacular sculptures, rock-cut temples, with shiploads of wealth from far lands. It had a natural harbour at Mamallapuram, near Chennai.

Tamil land was always known for war heroes comparable to the epic warriors like Bhima, Arjuna, Bhishma, Drona, Gatotgaja and Abhimanyu. Their deeds of bravery stunned the world. Even old men had the strength to move mountains and the youth had the capability to fly across the skies and bring even the stars down from the heavens.

In the temple city of Mamallapuram, three such brave noblemen were on a chariot, heading towards the seashore, discussing the crisis in the Chola Kingdom. Of the three noblemen, one was the bravest of the brave, Crown Prince Aditya Karikalan, the eldest son of Emperor Sundara Chola; the other was his dear friend, the Pallava prince, Parthibendran, and the third was Aditya's maternal grandfather, King Malayaman.

Prince Aditya Karikalan, known for his valour, had performed heroic deeds in several battlefields. In the final battle at Madurai, he defeated the Pandiya king, Veerapandiya. Soon after that, he was coronated as the Crown Prince in honour of his victories. He was stationed in Kanchi to strengthen his army with more arms and supplies against futher invasions.

The Paluvettarayars did not cherish his domination and they started giving troubles indirectly in various ways. They stopped the supplies and food from the Tanjore granary to the Lankan forces headed by Karikalan's younger brother, Prince Arulmolivarman. This enraged Prince Karikalan enormously.

The other nobleman in the chariot was the maternal grandfather of Karikalan, King Malayaman of Thirukovilur. Sundara Chola's wife, Empress Vanama Devi, was his daughter. In age and experience, he was comparable to Bhishma of the epic Mahabharata. Karikalan had great regard for his grandfather and sought his advice on important matters.

The other man in the chariot was Parthibendran of the ancient Pallava dynasty. He had gained the confidence and friendship of Aditya Karikalan through his heroic deeds and remarkable service.

Aditya Karikalan told his grandfather Malayaman,

'I cannot tolerate the arrogance of these Paluvettarayars anymore. Day by day, they are crossing their limit. How dare they accuse my messenger Vandiyathevan of being a spy? They have announced a reward for his capture. The sword in my arms shrinks with shame! Yet grandpa, you advise me to be patient!'

'Prince, I cautioned you not to send Vandiyathevan on important missions. He is an impatient youth though he is proficient in the use of his sword and spear,' said Parthiban

Parthiban never liked Prince Karikalan's enormous affection towards Vandiyathevan. He wouldn't ever miss any opportunity to find fault with him.

'Parthiba, you have started your story again! No fault lies with Vandiyathevan. He has perfectly fulfilled the assignment given by me! Those Paluvettarayar brothers are angry because of this,' said Karikalan and turned to his grandfather.

'Grandfather, why are you silent? What is wrong if we take a large army and invade Tanjore to free the Emperor and bring him here to Kanchi? How long are we to tolerate these Paluvettarayar brothers guarding the Emperor like a prisoner?'

King Malayaman who had the experience of over sixty battles, cleared his throat and said,

'My dear boy, let us first get off from this chariot and sit down in our usual place on the shore and chat.'

The three noblemen reached the shore and continued their discussion.

'I am pained to see the supplies collected for the northern invasion being diverted to Lanka,' said Parthiban.

'I am also pained. I wonder what those wretched fellows intend to do. How long am I to tolerate this grandpa! Why are you still keeping quiet?' asked Karikalan.

'Karikala! Their intention is to separate you and your brother and weaken both of you. That's why they are not sending the supplies from Tanjore granary through Nagapattinam; instead they are forcing you to send what you have stored for your northern invasion from here. Which will, in turn, irritate you. They want your brother to lose the battle in Lanka and face disgrace.'

As Malayaman was speaking passionately, Karikalan intervened.

'Their intention will never succeed, Grandpa! None can separate us. I will give up my very life for Arulmoli. I should sail to Lanka and help my brother.'

'Karikala, you and Parthiban are brave heroes. But both of you are rash.'

'Grandpa, you have said this several times. Now, tell me what must be done.'

'You must somehow bring your brother Arulmoli here, immediately.'

'Grandpa, if Arulmoli comes here what will happen to the war in Lanka?'

'Oh! The Lankan war is now at a standstill. Our soldiers have captured Anuradapura. Now the rainy season begins in Lanka and nothing will happen for four months, all we can do is safeguard the positions captured through our generals. Arulmoli can come back here immediately to resolve the current crisis.'

'Why are you frightening me?'

'My boy, don't I know your courage? Remember these lines of Thiruvalluvar:

Not to fear what to be feared is absolutely folly
To fear what to be feared is wise men's duty.

When you confront an enemy there should be no fear. But we must fear the secret enemies and take adequate precautions.'

'Grandfather! Why can't you be specific?'

'A few days ago, a secret meeting took place at midnight in Kadamboor Sambuvaraya's palace in the presence of Senior Paluvettarayar and other chieftains of the Chola Empire.'

'Let them have their meeting! So, what? All of them must have dined till their stomachs burst, watched fun and frolic till midnight. Why should we be concerned about it?'

'Their Chief, the oldest among them, got married recently to a young lady.'

When the conversation turned to a discussion on the old man's wedding, Aditya Karikalan's face darkened and his eyes turned bloodshot. Malayaman did not notice these changes in Karikalan but Parthiban did.

Parthiban intervened to say,

'Why talk of that wedding now, Grandpa? Tell us what happened at Sambuvarayar's palace after that.'

'That midnight meeting was not convened merely by old men. Some young men were also there. One youth was Sambuvarayar's son, Kandamaran. Another was your elder grandmother Sembiyan Madevi's divine son—your uncle Madurandakan. Till recently, he was saying, "I'll become a saint following the path of devotion". Now he has entered into matrimony not once or twice but thrice.'

'Let him get married many more times! So what?' said Parthiban.

'My boy, Madurandakan's marriages are not ordinary marriages. They are political alliances organized by the treacherous Paluvettarayar brothers.'

'Grandfather, what is the use of their secret meetings?' asked

Aditya with some impatience.

'They are trying to announce that you and your brother have no rights to the Empire and thus place Madurandakan on the Chola throne. They are trying to get your father's consent for this. That is why they guard him in Tanjore Fort like a prisoner,' said King Malayaman.

46

Agitated Crown Prince

Prince Aditya Karikalan was agitated when he heard the news that the Paluvettarayars were conspiring to make Madurandakan the next Emperor. Parthiban was also speechless. Even the roaring sea became quiet.

Karikalan sought his grandfather's opinion.

'What is your opinion, Grandfather?'

'Of course, your elder grandfather, Kandaraditya, ruled this Chola Kingdom before your grandfather, Arinjaya. Don't you think his son has more rights to this empire than you two brothers?' asked King Malayaman.

'Never! That fool can't even utter four words clearly. He has never touched a sword in his lifetime. He should have been a woman but by accident he was born a man. How could such a man have a right to the throne? What about our Prince Karikalan who entered warfront at the tender age of twelve and never met with any defeat?' screamed Parthiban.

Karikalan silenced him and spoke to King Malayaman,

'This empire is not a big thing for me. I can establish an empire ten times bigger than this. I would not have cared if they had declared right in the beginning itself that the kingdom was for Madurandakan. With the consent of countrymen, citizens and chieftains, they coronated me as crown prince. How can they change it now? How can you support that?'

'I won't support it even if you agree to give up the throne!' roared King Malayaman.

Karikalan who was gazing at the sea for some time asked, 'Grandpa, if this is your opinion, why not send our armies immediately and capture Tanjore Fort and free the Emperor after imprisoning Madurandakan?'

'Yes! None can win against you in warfare. But what can you both do against conspiracy and treachery? They will announce that the son has declared war on his father. They will also announce that your father, the Emperor gave up his life in shock.'

Covering his ears Aditya Karikalan said,

'This is disgusting even to hear!'

'That is why I've been cautioning you from the very beginning that grave danger surrounds us.'

'What is the solution, Grandfather?'

'First we must send a trustworthy and capable messenger to Lanka to convince and bring back Arulmoli,' said Malayaman.

Parthiban said,

'If it is agreeable to you, I may be sent to Lanka.'

'That depends on you and Karikalan.'

Karikalan asked, 'Grandfather, any news of Vandiyathevan?'

'I have just got news that he stabbed his intimate friend, with whom he was in our army camp, Kandamaran, in the back.'

'Grandpa, Vandiyathevan will never stab anyone in the back, that too his own dear friend. If my good friend Vandiyathevan were to join sides with my enemies, the earth will shake, the deep ocean will dry up, the sky will shatter and the sun will rise at night,' spoke Karikalan with conviction.

'I agree with the Prince. Vandiyathevan will never betray us. The only fault I find with him is he will fall before beautiful women.'

King Malayaman now asked with surprise,

'Any information from Princess Kundavai?'

'No news till now.'

'Once Prince Arulmoli comes here, we must bring your sister also here. We can leave everything to her and follow her orders. Your sister has mastered the art of governance. She made us dance to her wishes even as a child. Even now her word is the law for me! Karikala, I am not undermining you by praising your sister. It is an added merit for you to have such a sister. None can match her intelligence. Even our prime minister consults her on important issues.'

The jealous Parthiban said,

'All that is fine but we will become helpless if Vandiyathevan falls prey to that enchantress—the young queen of Paluvoor.'

On hearing these words, Karikalan looked at Parthiban with eyes full of fire. At this juncture, King Malayaman left for a story-telling show, asking them to continue their discussions.

Parthiban looked at Karikalan and spoke passionately, 'My dear Prince! There is some commotion in your mind. Perhaps, it has something to do with the young queen of Paluvoor. Your very face is transformed if there is any mention about the old man, Senior Paluvettarayar, marrying the young queen. You call me your dearest friend but you don't share your secrets with me. Why don't you tell me? Give me a chance to wipe away your tears.'

Aditya Karikalan sighed deeply, 'My friend! My ailing heart has no cure. Only death will cure it. Anyhow, I'll tell you tonight. Let us go back to the palace.'

47

Poison of Passion

After King Malayaman left for the story-telling show, Aditya Karikalan and Parthiban went up to the terrace of one of the Pallava palaces in Mamallapuram for a long chat.

Silence prevailed in the streets. The sound of the storyteller narrating the tale of Aravan, a valiant hero of the epic Mahabhrata, could be heard at a distance. The roar of the ocean was like a lullaby.

'Look at my grandfather! Even at this age he goes for the story-telling show late at night. I have no words to commend the enthusiasm of these old timers!'

'Prince! What have the old timers achieved that we have not? I have not heard of anyone even in the epics performing such daring deeds like you at young age,' said Parthiban.

'Parthiba! You are a pure-hearted person concealing nothing in your mind. But at times you flatter.'

'Prince! If someone makes up untrue stories about a person and recounts them with a selfish motive, such tales are flattery. If I praise Madurandakan, the slave of the Paluvettarayar brothers saying—You are the bravest among the brave—it is flattery. But in my praise for you I said nothing untrue. Which warrior of ancient times has achieved as much as you have, barring a few?'

'Real achievement does not lie in our victories, beheading so many people. Can anyone in our times or after us, create a dream-world like this magnificent Mamallapuram? Look around you in all directions. See the beauty of the stone carvings speaking so eloquently. We must be proud of those Pallava kings to have established a city like this beholding their glory eternally.'

'My Prince, some time ago, you accused me of flattering you. But I also fault you on a few occasions. After several victories in the north, the Pallavas lost interest in battles and focused on immortal art and sculpture. As a result, their enemies gained power and came back to destroy them.'

'Your ancestors created this world of sculpture which has withstood thousands of years and will withstand for thousands of years more proclaiming their glory to the world.

What have we done, comparable to their creations? We killed thousands of men in battlefields and raised mounds of dead bodies with blood flowing like a river. What else have we done to establish our fame in history?' asked Karikalan with some despair.

Parthiban was stunned to hear these words spoken by Aditya Karikalan as he himself had won several battles since his younger days. He spoke, 'Prince, your mind is agitated today. Why don't you share your grief with me?'

'Parthiba! If I open up my heart and show it to you, what will you find inside?'

'That is what I would like to know, my Prince!'

'My mother and father who gave life to me won't be there. My sister and brother dearer than my life won't be there. My closest friends, you and Vandiyathevan won't be there. A woman, the embodiment of all wiles, will be there. The young queen of Paluvoor, the evil incarnate, will be there. All these days, I have not spoken to anyone about the torture that venomous woman, Nandini, is giving me.'

Aditya Karikalan spoke with the fiery heat of a furnace,

'Prince, how did this undeserving love take hold of your heart? You are born in a tradition which worships every alien woman as a mother. Senior Paluvettarayar is old in age and is primarily responsible for the victories of the Cholas.

Today he may be a conspirator. Your father and grandfather regarded him so much. How can you even think of Nandini, who is now legally wedded to that great man, however wretched and sinful she may be?'

'I shouldn't think of her now! This poison of passion for her gripped my heart long before she became the young queen of Paluvoor. I am unable to get rid of this unworthy obsession however hard I try. I speak as if everything is her fault. Only God knows whose mistake it is. Perhaps the blame lies on the Creator who brought us to this world or I must blame my fate, which united us to separate us!'

'My Prince, when did you meet her?'

'That is a long tale. I will tell you soon. Will you be able to comfort me? No solace for me in this birth or even in my next birth. Anyway, I will tell you for your peace. I don't want you to go to Lanka with a restless mind.'

He, then, began recounting his tale.

48

My Lover

'I met Nandini for the first time at the young age of twelve. I, my younger brother Arulmoli and sister Kundavai were returning after playing around behind our palace. We saw our grandmother talking with three people in our palace garden. One of those three was a young girl about my age. The other two appeared to be her parents. They were saying something about that girl to my grandmother. When the three of us walked in, they stopped and all of them turned to look at us. All that I can remember now is that the young girl's beautiful eyes opened wide in surprise and she was staring at me me keenly.'

After saying these words, Karikalan started gazing at the stars in the sky perhaps to catch a glimpse of the face of that young girl in the floating clouds.

'Prince! What happened next?' asked Parthiban.

'Queen Mother introduced that smart girl to us as Nandini, saying, "They have come from the Pandiya country to the house of our Esanya Bhattar. They will be here for a while. Why don't you make friends with her and play with her? She will be a good companion to you." The three of us left the garden and walked towards the palace. But I soon found that my sister didn't like her.

My sister Kundavai was jealous of her beauty like any other woman. Among all the women of my clan, my sister is renowned for her beauty. She could not stand the sight of another attractive girl! Otherwise, why should she make such a comment? So, I did not let my sister off easily. I teased her often, praising the comeliness of the new girl. Arulmoli was too young to understand this bickering. Soon after this, I left with my father to the war in the Pandiya Kingdom. We engaged in several combats against the Pandiya forces as well as their allies from Lanka which came to support them. We won the battle. The defeated Pandiya king, Veerapandiya, escaped to the mountain caves. I returned to Palayarai after two-and-a-half years.

I had almost forgotten that beautiful daughter of the priest, Nandini. When I came back to Palayarai, I found that both my sister Kundavai and that girl Nandini had grown beyond recognition. Both had become great friends. Nandini was stunningly beautiful, shining with silken garments and jewels gifted by my generous sister. Nandini, feeling shy, hesitated to see me or talk to me. I tried to make her overcome her shyness. I found incomparable pleasure in talking to her and spending time in her company. Like the fresh floods of the Cauvery, a new emotion, an inexplicable enthusiasm, overpowered me. But none of my dear ones liked this new interest of mine in her. Kundavai started disliking that girl. One day, Queen Mother advised me, "You both are no longer kids. Your intimacy with her is not appropriate." Disregarding her advice, I began meeting Nandini secretly. But that did not last long. Then, one day, Nandini and her parents left to their village in the Pandiya Kingdom. Sadness, anger and disappointment gripped my mind and I let out my anger upon my sister. Fortunately, I had to leave soon for the north, along with the battalion, to fight the Rashtrakuta forces.

We won that battle but lost in Lanka, which was led by the elder chieftain of Kodumbalur. On hearing this, Veerapandiya, who had been hiding in the mountain caves came out and captured Madurai to raise his fish flag over that city. I swore that I would not return home without Veerapandiya's head. My father agreed to send us on that campaign.

We defeated the Pandiya forces and captured Madurai. But we were not satisfied with that. We wanted to capture King Veerapandiya and his retreating battalions and kill them mercilessly so that they could never regroup again.

You and some men went swiftly along the banks of river Vaigai. I stepped into the riverbed and went southward to find the marks of a single horse's hoof-print and blood stains on the sandy riverbed. Following the clue, I entered a grove in the middle of the riverbed surrounded by a few cottages with flowering bushes and a Vishnu temple.

Dear friend, earlier I had ordered all of you not to enter it, even accidentally. The reason for my strict orders was not merely to safeguard the temple, but also because the queen of my heart was living in that grove. Previously, when I had come this side, I had seen her in a new appearance—like that of Saint Andal—with a garland around her shoulders and tresses bound over her forehead. When questioned, she said that after she was forced to leave the palace, she had vowed not to marry any man except Divine Lord Krishna, just like Saint Andal! I thought of resolving the issue after the war to restore my love. I asked her if she needed any help. She asked me not to send any of our soldiers into this garden as her aged father and half-blind mother were living there with her. I met her again, later, two or three times. My passion for her grew manifold. But I restrained myself. The assignment on hand must be completed first and I must go back to Palayarai with Veerapandiya's head. As a reward for that, I thought of asking my father for Nandini's hand.

When I was so resolved, I saw the single horse's hoof prints going towards that garden and I was enraged. I entered Nandini's house to see Veerapandiya lying on an old cot with Nandini giving him water and nursing his wounds. I was enormously enraged. Nandini who was nursing his wounds, stopped upon seeing me and came towards me. She fell at my feet with folded hands swearing in the name of the love we had for each other once, begging me to save that mortally wounded man.

Hesitantly, I asked, "What is your relationship with this man?" Nandini replied, "He is my lover, my god."

Even the little pity I had for Veerapandiya on seeing his wounds now vanished. I would not have minded if he had captured my kingdom but now, he had abducted the queen of my heart! How could I show him mercy?

I pushed Nandini aside and chopped off Veerapandiya's head with one swift blow of my sword. I feel ashamed of it now. As I was about to step out of the house, I looked at Nandini once more. She was staring at me with anger and anguish. I have never seen such a look on this earth with such emotions.

By then, you and several of our men came there in pursuit of me. Upon seeing Veerapandiya's headless body and bleeding head, you all raised cheers of victory. Yet, my heart remained shattered.'

49

Unexpected Incident

The story-telling session was coming to an end at the distance.

'Aravaan's story is over. But your story is not yet over. It is said that Senior Paluvettarayar saw her somewhere along the wayside and dragged her to the palace, making her his ninth wife!' said Parthiban.

'I am astonished by that, my friend!'

'Astonished? About how that old man was trapped in her wiles?'

'No! About, how she, who once swore love for me and then for King Veerapandiya, has now married that old man! This is what astounds me.'

'Prince, I am not surprised by that. What surprises me is your attitude. How could you spare her, when she begged for the life of your sworn enemy—that greatest coward, King Veerapandiya? You could have chopped her head if you didn't like that, or at least brought her here as a prisoner.

Now I remember, you brought Veerapandiya's dead body and threw it outside the cottage. We heard sobs from inside the house; you prevented us from going inside saying, "Some woman of a priest's family! She is already terrified." We all left that place with Veerapandiya's head. You were apathetic. I was wondering if you were wounded or something,' said Parthiban.

'There was no wound on my body, Parthiba! But a wound in my heart is pestering me! That sight of her falling at my feet before Veerapandiya's bed and pleading for his life with folded hands is still paining my mind. Even now I tremble to think of not having heeded her request. I curse myself now.'

'What happened after that, my Prince? Did you ever meet Nandini after that? Did you ever ask her why she married that old man, Paluvettarayar?'

'That night after the death of Veerapandiya, after all of you went to sleep in our camp, I went to see her, console her and beg her forgiveness.

With an agitated mind, I dismounted and walked towards the grove to find the burnt cottages. That old man and woman were wailing. I identified them as the same two persons who had brought Nandini to Palayarai long ago. Upon seeing me, their sorrow increased. Then I came to know that they had gone to visit their elder daughter as it was time for her childbirth. As usual, an adamant Nandini didn't go with them. On the way back, they saw some rogues trying to throw a woman into a funeral pyre, binding her hands and legs. They thought that such atrocities were natural in times of war and had hurried away from the scene with fear. On coming back home, they could not see Nandini there. After disclosing all this, the priest and his wife started wailing louder, asking for their daughter. Then I returned to the camp, unnoticed, before daybreak.'

'Yes Prince! We never knew that you have locked up all your agonies in your heart for so many years. If I had been you, I would have shared all my feelings as a true friend.'

'But you were not like me, Parthiban! No one in the world should be in my position.'

'Why worry about the past? What happened after that? When did you see Nandini again? Was it before or after she became the Young Queen of Paluvoor?'

'If I had met her before, she would not have become Paluvoor's queen. When Senior Paluvettarayar got married, you and I were not in Tanjore. Remember how disgusted we felt on hearing that news. Some months later, I was coronated as the crown prince.

All the citizens, people, ministers, generals and chieftains upheld it and raised cheers of joy.

In those celebrations, I had forgotten Nandini. An incident which took place a few hours after the coronation proved that I could never forget her. My father took me to the inner courtyard of the palace to seek the blessings of my elder grandmother, mother and other elderly women of our clan. My younger brother, the prime minister and the Paluvettarayar brothers followed us. Along with the older women, my sister Kundavai, her friends and several other young noblewomen were waiting in the courtyard to greet me. They welcomed me with cheerful faces. But, among all of them only one face caught my attention: it was Nandini's enchanting face with her dark eyes, coral lips, lustrous tresses and robust appearance. The angel of my heart, Nandini, whom I thought had burned to ashes had now appeared in the court. She was stunningly beautiful, dressed in those wonderful clothes and jewels shining like an empress among all those queens!

Within a few seconds, my heart built castles in the air and I was wondering if it was a dream or real. I felt it was the luckiest day as I had found my Nandini again on the day of my coronation. As I daydreamed, my mother Vanamadevi hugged me with a kiss. Suddenly, an unexpected incident happened. My father screamed loudly and swooned. There was confusion everywhere. We tried to revive the Emperor. All those women except my mother and the Queen Mother left the chamber. My father regained his senses soon. I led my sister Kundavai a little way away and asked her, "How did Nandini come here?" My sister said that Nandini married Senior Paluvettarayar and was now the young queen of Paluvoor. Sharp lances pierced my heart!

My friend, I have been wounded several times in battlefields. But the wound caused by my sister's words, "Nandini is the young queen of Paluvoor", has not healed till this day.'

Aditya Karikalan finished his story, holding his chest with both his hands as if the pain was still lingering in him.

50

No Peace on Earth

Parthiban who was listening to the story of Karikalan with no sympathy in the beginning now felt moved.

'My Prince, I never dreamt that the love for a woman could cause so much damage.'

'After that, Nandini called me to her palace, I visited her palace when Senior Paluvettarayar was not in town.

Parthiba, when I stood before Nandini that day, I was like one of those sailing ships caught in a strong ocean current. My body, heart and soul were all shattered into a thousand formless pieces.

Nandini expressed her joy about my becoming the Crown Prince. "I have no pleasure in it," said I. "Why?" she asked. "What question is this? How can I feel happy, when you have betrayed me like this?" I questioned. She pretended innocence.

I accused her of deserting me to join Veerapandiya as her lover. I spoke sarcastically about her marriage to an old man.

"Prince, first, you killed my love for you; later you killed my lover before my own eyes; you won't be content till you kill me also. Please kill me and satisfy your desire!" Saying this she pulled out a sharp knife from her waistband.

"Why should I kill you? You are the one torturing me to death!" I told her.

In the end, I spoke words which I am now too ashamed to even think about.

"Nothing is lost even now. You leave this old man and come with me! I will renounce my kingdom and elope with you to faraway lands across the seas," I told her.

Nandini laughed horribly. Even now, my hairs stand up to think of that laughter.

"What are we to do by going away to faraway lands? Shall we chop wood for a living? Or shall we raise a plantain garden?" she asked with sarcasm.

"From being the daughter of a priest to becoming the Paluvoor Queen now: you won't give up these new found riches."

"I won't be satisfied with this. I want to sit on the throne of this Chola Empire as an empress. If you accept this, please kill both these Paluvettarayar brothers, throw the Emperor in prison, become the emperor and make me your consort!" she demanded.

"Oh! What horrible words you speak!"

"Was it not horrible to kill my lover Verapandiya right in front of my eyes?"

This enraged me further. I rose to leave. She didn't let me go easily.

"Prince! If you ever change your mind, when you decide to make me your empress, come back to me!"

I left her that day and have never seen her again,' finished Aditya Karikalan.

Parthiban, was shocked to hear all this. 'My Prince, can there be another monster like her?'

'She occupies my thoughts throughout the day; fills up my dreams at night. Sometimes she comes to me with an enchanting smile hugging me, kissing me or she comes with a sharpened knife, ready to kill me. Either she is screaming in horror or laughs at me, like a mad person tormenting me!

Our grandfather has asked me not to go to Tanjore for several reasons. The real reason for me not going to Tanjore to bring my father to Kanchi is Nandini.'

'Prince! Are you avoiding Tanjore just because you are afraid of a mere woman? What can she do?'

'No, Parthiba! You have not understood me even now! Are you afraid that she will treacherously kill me? I am afraid she will make me follow her commands. "Throw your father in prison! Chase your sister out of this country! Kill this old man and place me on your throne!" If that enchantress orders me once more, I am afraid that I would feel like doing all those things. My friend, either Nandini should die or I should die or both of us should die. Otherwise, there is no peace for me on this earth.'

'Why do you speak like this? Why should you die? Allow me to go to Tanjore and kill her before proceeding to Lanka.'

'If you ever dare to do anything like that, you will become my first enemy. If Nandini has to be killed, I will kill her myself and end my life too. I will allow none to harm even the tiny nail of her little finger. Parthiba, you forget Nandini, forget everything I said about her. As advised by Grandfather, leave for Lanka tomorrow itself and bring back Arulmoli here. Let him stay in Kanchi. We both can leave for Lanka in ships with large armies. Later, we can go to Java, Sumatra, Burma and Malaya and install our victorious tiger flag in all those countries. From there we can go to Egypt, Persia, Arab worlds and Yavana kingdoms to spread the fame of Tamils everywhere.'

Before Parthiban could reply, King Malayaman returned from the story-telling session and said,

'Why are you both up this late? Parthiba, don't you know that you have to leave for Lanka tomorrow?'

'That is what we have been discussing,' replied Parthiban.

51
Kodikkarai Lighthouse

Kodikkarai is a small fishing hamlet with a lighthouse, near the town of Nagapattinam. The sun was setting down on the horizon of Kodikkarai. Catamarans and boats were returning to the shore. Trees in the dense forest were quiet with no rustling of leaves and silence ruled in all directions.

A small boat was gently floating on the sea near the shore; a young girl was leaning backwards on it, singing melodiously. She was stunningly beautiful with dark curls dancing on her rounded shoulders and a necklace of seashells around her neck.

The sea, the wind, the sky and the earth became quiet to listen to her melodious song. There was some sweet sorrow in her voice.

'When the sea is still and so is the sea
Why should the inner sea rant and rave?
When the earth maid is asleep
Why should the heart be restless and weep?...'

On reaching the shore near the lighthouse she decided to go to the Siva temple in the forest. On the way, she saw a group of spotted deer crossing the sand dunes to reach the forest. A baby deer was caught in a mud trap. She set it free saying,

'Animals are far better than humans!'

She reached the Kulagar temple amidst flowering trees and blooming bushes; the priest welcomed her happily giving her sacred offerings and a coconut after the evening pooja.

Suddenly she heard the gallop of horses. She wondered:

Who could be coming? These days many people come and go, even

yesterday, two men had come. Their sight was very repulsive. My brother took them in his boat to Lanka for a sizeable amount of money to satisfy his greedy wife.'

The hoof-beats came closer and closer. Two men arrived, worn out after a very long journey. The fellow on the first horse was young and handsome with a well-built body and dignified posture. It was Vandiyathevan. Behind him was Pinakapani, the doctor's son, with a clumsy posture.

Vandiyathevan's face brightened on seeing the beautiful young girl and his drooping spirits revived. Upon seeing strange men, the girl started running towards the shore. Vandiyathevan also ran behind her.

Vandiyatheven identified the girl as Poonkulali described by Chendan Amudan.

Vandiyathevan found it very tough to run behind her as she was running like the elusive golden magic deer of Ramayana. He wanted to befriend her to seek her help in his mission.

At one stage, he thought of abandoning his chase as the girl was too swift.

'I had better go back!' he decided.

But, how could he accept defeat while competing with a girl? He used all his remaining energy and sprinted forward. Suddenly he couldn't move any farther; he wondered what had happened. He was caught in a mud trap! First his knee caps were buried and next his waist was buried; these mud traps could swallow horses and elephants also. For him the only recourse lay in that peculiar girl, Poonkulali. Vandiyathevan started screaming loudly.

'Oh dear! Save me! I am drowning.'

Poonkulali stopped running and came back.

She looked around and pulled a thick log and gave it to Vandiyathevan. After a great struggle, she used her monstrous strength and dragged him out of that mud trap.

'Oh God! What strength in her tender arms! Her arms are as strong as an iron grip.'

Once he was out of the mud trap, Vandiyathevan laughed although his legs were shivering.

'Do you think that you saved me by pulling me out?' he asked.

'Then why did you scream for help?' asked Poonkulali.

'Only to make you stop running.'

'Then, I'll push you back into this mudrap. Get out yourself!'

She took a step to push him in.

'Oh! No!'

Vandiyathevan stepped back.

'Then why did you yell?'

'I am not afraid for my life. I fear only mud! Already my clothes are soiled!'

Poonkulali smiled. 'Go to the sea and wash up.'

They walked towards the seashore avoiding mud traps.

'Why did you run away on seeing me? Am I a ghost?' asked Vandiyathevan.

'All men are wicked. I never like men!'

'Even Chendan Amudan?' asked Vandiyathevan softly.

'Who? What did you say?'

'I mentioned Chendan Amudan of Tanjore.'

'What do you know about him?'

'I know that he is your beloved lover.'

'What?'

'Are you not Poonkulali?'

'Yes...'

'Is he not your beloved?'

Poonkulali laughed. 'Who said that?' she asked.

'Who else? Amudan told me.'

'Tanjore is very far away. That is why he could say that and get away with it. If not...'

'If not?'

'If he had said that here, before me, I would have thrown him into that mud trap!'

'So what? There is plenty of water in the ocean to wash off the mud. He also said you are a good singer.'

'You can find that out for yourself! Here comes the sea.'

They were standing on the seashore.

52

Is She Mad?

Stars were twinkling up in the sky with the crescent moon strolling and the wind becoming louder amidst the roaring sea.

'What are you waiting for? Wash away the mud quickly. I have to go home soon, or else I won't get any food,' said Poonkulali.

'Ok, but you have to help me reach Lanka.'

Vandiyathevan stepped into the water and washed away the mud. A while later, the doctor's son, Pinakapani, also reached there bringing along Vandiyathevan's horse.

'Dear Poonkulali, what if the horse steps into the mud trap?' asked Vandiyathevan.

'It won't. Animals are more intelligent than human beings,' said Poonkulali.

Poonkulalai caressed Vandiyathevan's horse and it neighed to show its joy.

'My horse also likes you. That is good.'

'Why is that good?'

'I have to go to Lanka leaving this horse in your care.'

'I will look after him. All animals are my friends but not humans.'

'This man and I have come here to collect medicinal plants to treat our Emperor's illness.'

'You said that you were going to Lanka, just now?'

'Any herb that is not available here has to be brought from Lanka. Don't you know that Hanuman's medicinal mountain is still in Lanka?'

'Two fellows came here two days ago. They too said something like this.'

'Who were they?'

'They claimed that some sorcerer had sent them to find tiger claws and elephant hair for making a bracelet to guard the Emperor against evil. My brother has taken them to Lanka in his rowboat.'

'Oh! Is that so!' thought Vandiyathevan.

Who are those two who have gone to Lanka before me? She seems to be innocent. I can trust her and become friendly with her.

'Poonkulali, I want to tell you the truth. I told you that I had come here to collect herbs; that is false! I am going to Lanka on a very important and secret mission. I can tell you if...'

'No need. Don't you know that one should not share important secrets with women?'

'That is for ordinary women, not for you.'

'How do you know that I am not an ordinary girl? It has not been even half an hour since you met me.'

'Poonkulali, I studied you the moment I saw you. I will ask you something. Will you answer truthfully?'

'Try me.'

'Is it true that Amudan is not your beloved? Won't you marry him?'

'I do not love Amudan. But I have several other lovers!'

'Dear me! Other lovers! Who are they?'

'I will leave my house at midnight. You may follow me to see them!'

After saying this, Poonkulali roared aloud with laughter.

Her laughter disturbed Vandiyathevan. Poor thing! This girl must be mad! It is foolish to expect any help from her on my mission. Better not to discuss my affairs with her.

They approached the house near the lighthouse. An elderly man and a woman came out of the house.

'Poonkulali, who are these men? Where did you find them?' The man asked.

'I didn't find them, Father! Rather, they found me!'

'It's all the same. How many times have I told you not to come late? You never listen! You brought two men the day before yesterday. Now you have brought another two. Why have these men come here?' asked the woman.

'They have come here to collect medicinal plants for the Emperor,' said Poonkulali looking at her father.

'Why Sir? Is that true?' asked Poonkulali's father.

'Yes, Sir. Here is the official letter.'

Vandiyathevan handed over the palm leaf roll which Princess Kundavai had given to the elderly man. Poonkulali's father began reading the letter and his face cheered up, he said to his wife,

'Princess Kundavai has sent this letter. Let us feed these men before our daughter-in-law empties the rice pot!'

53

Poonkulali's Midnight Lovers

Vandiyathevan met the lighthouse keeper and sought his help to reach Lanka on an urgent mission. The lighthouse keeper expressed his inability to arrange for a boat as the existing ones had already been diverted as supply vessels for the armed forces in Lanka. One of his personal boats had already been taken by his son to carry two newcomers to Lanka.

'Who are those men? Your daughter mentioned that they were not good people.'

'Yes, of course. But I don't know them and their purpose of going to Lanka. They had the palmtree signet of Paluvoor. Otherwise, I would not have permitted my son to go with them. But my greedy daughter-in-law insisted that her husband go with them in return for a bag of gold coins.'

Knowing Vandiyathevan's friendship with Amudan at Tanjore, the lighthouse keeper decided to help him. Moreover, he knew about the important letter sent by Princess Kundavai to Prince Arulmoli.

'There is another boat but there is none to row it. You can take it if you can handle it.'

'I don't know how to row.'

'There is only one other way. You can try it if you are feeling lucky,' said the lighthouse keeper.

'What should I do?'

'There is none comparable to Poonkulali in handling boats. She has crossed the sea to Lanka several times. I can tell her, you can also ask her,' said the lighthouse keeper.

'Please call her. We can request her,' said Vandiyathevan without patience.

'No. She is very stubborn. If we ask her now, she may refuse. We cannot change her mind later. We will talk to her tomorrow when she is in a better mood.'

Vandiyathevan went to sleep on the porch. Suddenly his sleep was disturbed. Somebody emerged out from inside the house. It was Poonkulali.

Vandiyathevan recollected what had she said earlier: 'Follow me at midnight. I'll show you my lovers!'

I thought it was a joke. Now, she really is walking out at midnight. Following her now might be useful to befriend her and convince her to take me to Lanka in her boat.

Vandiyathevan followed Poonkulali and reached the edge of the forest full of overgrown dunes and valleys. She walked further towards a marshy seaside and suddenly she vanished as if by magic.

He found the traces of her footsteps and climbed over it. It was pitch dark. The moving shadows of bushy shrubs and trees turned into ghosts. Even the movement of leaves sent a shiver through Vandiyathevan. Poisonous reptiles and horrible beasts could pounce on him. He felt that it had been a blunder to have come behind her and get lost.

As he was about to turn back, he heard Poonkulali's voice, sobbing and singing.

Vandiyathevan abandoned the idea of going back. Poonkulali also noticed Vandiyathevan and said,

'You have come! I thought you might be sleeping like Kumbakarnan. Why did you follow me?'

'You had asked me to follow you! Have you forgotten?'

'Why did I ask you to follow me?'

'You promised to show me your lovers!'

'Over there! Look behind you!' said Poonkulali.

54

Poonkulali Is Peculiar

Vandiyathevan looked behind him. His intestines rose from his stomach blocking his chest and then his throat. He had never experienced such terror, not even in the underground passage of Tanjore. Such a horrifying sight appeared before his eyes. A hundred fiery furnaces of fire rose from the ground and stood upright like a monster's mouth without a head, suddenly disappearing and reappearing.

He heard demonic laughter behind him and turned around to find Poonkulali.

'Did you see my lovers?!' asked Poonkulali. 'These fiery ghosts are my lovers. I come here at midnight to make love with them! Can your friend Amudan compete with these lovers of mine?'

No doubt, Poonkulali was deranged!

Such apparitions are natural in marshy lands formed by constant water stagnation over soil rich in sulphur! Ignorant country folk fear this natural phenomenon thinking it to be ghosts and phantoms.

'Girl! Your lovers won't go anywhere else. They will be there only. We can come back tomorrow. Now let us go home.'

Poonkulali agreed to go back with him. They walked towards the house.

'I have to go to Lanka urgently to bring some medicinal plants. Can you row your boat and take me to the island?'

'Why do you need me? Don't you feel ashamed in asking a girl to row the boat for you?'

'Your father said that there was no one else as your brother had already left yesterday.'

'So what if he is gone? Don't you have two hands?'

'I know nothing about boats...'

'There is nothing magical about boats. If you pull on the oars it will glide by itself.'

'Shouldn't I know how to navigate? What if I get lost in the mid seas?'

'If you are lost, drown in the deep sea!'

They reached the lighthouse. Vandiyathevan did not want to provoke her further and confirm her refusal. Even though she appeared to have refused, her tone and words gave him some hope.

Vandiyathevan got up cheerfully at daybreak but he could not see Poonkulali at home. So, he went in search of her.

Vandiyathevan walked into the forest but there was no sign of Poonkulali anywhere. Impetuously, he decided to bathe in the cool waters of the sea to get rid of his fear of water. He placed his waistband and pouch on the ground and waded into the shallow waters. As he was enjoying the coolness of the water, he looked back towards the shore. He spotted Poonkulali picking up his waist pouch.

He shouted 'Hey girl! Don't touch that!'

She can't hear me...

'Poonkulali don't take my pouch!'

She started walking away.

'Stop! Stop!' Screamed Vandiyathevan and began running towards the shore. Poonkulali also began running towards the forest.

She is a wretched girl or else insane! How do I recover my pouch from her? I must do it somehow.

He reached the shore and ran after her. They reached a dense forest. But he could not see her anywhere.

Suddenly something fell from the tree top. Yes, it was his waistband and pouch. He eagerly opened his pouch. The palm-leaf letter, gold coins—everything was intact in the bag.

'Is the money safe?' asked a voice from above. He looked up to see Poonkulali sitting on the tree.

'Why did you run away with my pouch?' asked Vandiyathevan angrily.

'If I hadn't done so, you wouldn't have followed me into this forest. You might have gone back to my house.'

'What if I had returned to your house?'

'Climb up this tree and find out for yourself.'

'What will I see?'

'Ten or fifteen horses with shining swords and spears.'

Vandiyathevan climbed the tree and looked towards the lighthouse. There were several horsemen searching for him.

Poonkulali had saved him from immediate danger. Both climbed down.

'Poonkulali, you have saved me from great danger. My sincere thanks to you. How did you know that those soldiers had come in search of me?'

'This morning your friend, that doctor's son, asked for my help to find herbs in the forest. I brought him here. In the course of our conversation, he revealed his love for me. I said, "Don't we have to ask the elders?"

Your dear friend replied, "Let us follow the ancient custom and consummate our relationship in secrecy!" How is this story?'

'That rogue, sinner!' said Vandiyathevan.

'By then we heard the sound of galloping horses.'

'What happened afterwards?'

'I also told him to hide since the soldiers would arrest him too for accompanying a culprit but he ran directly into their midst.'

'Poor fellow!'

'Reserve your sympathy.'

'Why do you say that?'

'This fellow said, "I know you have all come in search of Vandiyathevan. Will you let off me if I expose him to you?"'

'Traitor! Sinner!'

'After those horsemen left, I came in search of you. You were bathing in the sea.'

'Why did you not tell me all this on the shore itself? Why did you run away with my waist-belt?'

'You would not have followed me if I had not done what I did. By the time I had explained all this, those soldiers might have spotted you and arrested you.'

Vandiyathevan felt ashamed for having thought her insane.

I must trust her completely. I cannot cross the sea and reach Lanka. All my efforts will be wasted.

'Girl! You have helped me a lot. You must help me some more...'

'What do you want me to do?' she asked.

'You must row your boat and take me to Lanka.'

Poonkulali was silent.

'Dear girl! Believe me I won't do any wrong! I'm going to Lanka on an important mission. I need your help...'

'If I help you, what will you do for me in return?'

For the first time, he noticed some signs of shyness in her. Cheeks dimpled and a playful smile added radiance to her face.

'If you help me now, I will never forget you for all of my life.'

Hesitantly, Poonkulalai replied, 'Then I'll tell you when the time comes. You should not forget.'

'Never. I will remain beholden to you.'

'Fine! I shall now take you to a place in this forest. You must remain there till dusk,' said Poonkulali

Poonkulali took Vandiyathevan to a sand dune covered with shrubs and creepers in the middle of the forest. There was an old ruined building there, a pavilion covered with overgrown trees and sand dunes.

'A leopard used to live in this place. So, I call it leopard pavilion. Now it is my personal hideout to avoid human beings. Don't come out even if you hear voices. Come out when I make a call like a cuckoo. Let us be ready to leave at nightfall in the boat,' said Poonkulali.

'I'll wait for the call of the cuckoo.'

'No tigers or leopards here anymore. Only jackals and wild boars might come here. Are you afraid of them?'

'No, I am not!' replied Vandiyathevan.

'You have come without your weapon here take this weapon,' said Poonkulali handing over a curious instrument studded with sharp thorns on both sides, made from the tail-bone of a fish.

'Earlier I used it to kill the leopard that lived here,' said Poonkulali.

55

Ocean Princess

Vandiyathevan spent the day in the hideout sleeping most of the time and thinking about the peculiar character of Poonkulali while awake.

What a wonderful girl with such a severe attitude! She killed a leopard with a fishtail bone! Why is she so concerned with my affairs and why did she save me from those soldiers?

Darkness enveloped in all directions with a wonderful sun setting in the western sea at Kodikkarai. He could not remain in the hideout anymore. He came out and saw the lighthouse. All sorts of curious and mysterious sounds in the forest created terror in his heart. If anyone were to come face to face with a tiger in daylight, reason would overcome fear; at night, even if a mouse moved underneath, horror grips the heart!

Then he heard the melodious voice of Poonkulali signaling him to come to the shore. The boat was ready on the beach and they started sailing towards Lanka.

'When will we reach Lanka?' asked Vandiyathevan.

'If two persons row, we can reach by daybreak.'

'I will pull the oars and help you.'

Vandiyathevan picked up the oars and pulled at them. The boat swirled and stopped completely.

'What is this? When you pull on the oars, the boat glides. When I pull on them the boat stops?' asked Vandiyathevan.

'I am the Ocean Princess,' laughed Poonkulali

'What a wonderful name!'

'Just like how the Emperor's son is called "Ponniyin Selvan".'

On hearing this, Vandiyathevan touched his waistband to make sure of his waist-pouch.

Poonkulali noticed this and asked,

'Hope it is safe?'

'What are you asking about?'

'I am talking about that letter in your waist-pouch.'

Vandiyathevan was shocked; a tiny suspicion crept into his mind. Poonkulali was pulling at the oars as she talked. The boat was gliding forward. The sight of poles and logs in the boat caught his attention. He asked,

'What are these poles used for?'

'To keep the boat stable and sail without rocking.'

'Oh! Will the boat rock more than this? Even now it is dancing and I feel uneasy.'

'You call this rocking? You must see it in the rainy season when the wind blows harder. If a whirlwind blows and the boat capsizes, we can unbind these logs from the boat and float by holding onto them to save ourselves.'

'Oh dear! Can this boat capsize in a big wind?'

'Even huge sailing ships can break into pieces if caught in a whirlwind.'

Suddenly, terror struck Vandiyathevan's heart.

'Oh dear! I won't come! Take me back to the shore!' he shouted. 'If you don't turn back, I'll jump into the water!'

'You are welcome to! But, before jumping out, hand over that letter you are carrying for Ponniyin Selvan.'

'Oh! How do you know about that letter?'

'Would I agree to take you to Lanka without ensuring who you are and why you are going to Lanka? I opened your pouch and examined its contents this morning while sitting on the tree.'

'You deceiver! I trusted you and came here!'

He began shouting in panic,

'Turn back! Turn back! Or I will jump.'

'You are free to jump!' said Poonkulali in disgust.

Crazed with fear, Vandiyathevan jumped into the sea thinking that the water would be shallow. But he realized the depth only after jumping into the water. He started shouting in fear. His fear of water made him weak. When the waves pulled him deep down, he cried for help. His tongue refused to cooperate. The face of Kundavai floated into his mind.

Poonkulali remained indifferent for a few minutes. She thought he would somehow manage and come out. Thinking of teasing him, she moved the boat away. Soon she realized her mistake.

He is not joking when he shouts for help; he is really frightened. If delayed he will drown. I have made a mistake; my teasing has turned into a disaster. I should not have disclosed the content of the letter. I never knew this fool would do such a thing.

She quickly moved the boat close to him and called, 'Come, come! Get into the boat.' But he did not hear her.

She immediately jumped into the water. A drowning man is bound to pull down anyone coming to rescue him. She swam closer to him and punched him hard with her fist. Her hand, strengthened by several years of rowing boats, landed on his face like a thunderbolt. His felt as though his head had split into a thousand pieces and he lost consciousness. She then dragged him onto the boat using all her strength.

56

Ghost Island

When Vandiyathevan regained his senses, he was staring at the twinkling stars. He was lying down and his clothes were wet and a rope was wound around his waist. A cool breeze and a melodious song comforted his mind and body.

He sat up and looked around to see Poonkulali rowing the boat and singing a melancholic song. He was recollecting all the earlier incidents in a flash—his drowning and struggling and Poonkulali coming towards him. He could not recollect anything beyond that.

Poonkulali must have rescued me by pulling me into the boat and has bound me to the floorboards with a rope to prevent further mishap.

He touched his waist-pouch and made sure that it was intact with the money and roll of letters.

Ah! How foolish of me to doubt this girl? If her intentions were not right, she would not have saved my life. She must have struggled to pull me into this tiny boat. How did she manage? What an extraordinary girl she is!

'Poonkulali, Poonkulali!'

'Oh! You are awake?'

'Free me from these ropes, I'll help you.'

'It will be a great help if you just keep quiet. You can unbind yourself; the rope is just wound around your waist. But, please don't jump into the sea again.'

Vandiyathevan sat up and unwound the rope around him.

The boat sailed on swiftly.

'Ocean Princess! I am thirsty.'

'You swallowed a lot of salt water, naturally you will feel thirsty!' She picked up a gourd and came closer.

'I had brought some food for you but when you jumped out the food bag fell into the sea.' Saying this, she gave him the gourd. He took it and drank the water in it.

Vandiyathevan cleared his throat and said,

'I mistook your intentions. I am sorry.'

'Doesn't matter.'

'The wind has changed and we can reach Snake Island by sunrise.'

'Snake Island?' quizzed Vandiyathevan.

'Yes. There are several islands along the coast of Lanka. One of those is Snake Island. If you land there, you need not cross water again. You can reach the main island crossing over a land bridge.'

There seems to be some other mysterious reason in this peculiar girl helping me. I must talk to her and find out.

'People say that Lanka is full of forests and mountains. I must explore these forests. Where can I find the Prince in this vast land? It may take many days to travel through all those forests and find the Prince. I have to deliver this letter to him immediately. You saw the seals on the letter, you know how urgent it is.'

'There is a way,' said Poonkulali.

'Please tell me.'

'Near Snake Island, there is Ghost Island. Only those who are not afraid of the ghost, go there. If you wait for half an hour on the beach of Ghost Island, I will find the whereabouts of Ponniyin Selvan.'

'Whom will you ask on Ghost Island?'

'I will ask the ghost,' Poonkulali said with a smile.

'Can I meet that ghost?'

'That is impossible.'

Vandiyathevan and Poonkulali were approaching a tiny emerald-like island. It really was like paradise on earth. Indeed, it must be the hand of a divine artist.

'That island, in front, is Ghost Island. The land on the right is

Snake Island. Where shall we go? Shall I leave you on Snake Island? Can you find your way?'

'No Poonkulali, let us go to Ghost Island. Even if there is a delay, it is better to go on after ascertaining the whereabouts of the Prince.'

The boat came ashore on the sandy beach of the tiny Ghost Island. After requesting Vandiyathevan to guard the boat, Poonkulali walked into the island. Vandiyathevan was gazing at her, till she disappeared into the woods.

He wondered how the name of the island had changed over the course of time from Gautama Island to Ghost Island. He also wondered about the secret in the heart of this peculiar boat-girl. Poonkulali returned quickly and got into the boat and they sailed towards the Snake Island.

'Did you find the whereabouts of the Prince?'

'I understand that our prime minister, Aniruddha Brahmarayar, has reached Mathotam to meet the Prince. Don't assume that it will be like the forest of Kodikkarai. It is a dense jungle full of sky-high tall trees with darkness all around. Be careful when you go out as elephant herds and wild beasts are aplenty here.'

The boat was nearing the snake island. Poonkulali was immersed in deep thought till Vandiyathevan addressed her, 'Oh! Ocean Princess!'

'What?'

'You said that you expect a favour from me. Tell me now, we may not get another chance.'

She did not reply for some time. She seemed to be mentally grappling with some conflicting thoughts.

Vandiyathevan continued to talk,

'You have not merely helped me; you have rendered immense service to this great Chola Empire. I won't be satisfied unless I repay my debt in some form.'

'The first time I saw you, I felt that you were a good man. So, I'll tell you this...'

'First impression is always the best impression.'

'When you meet Prince Ponniyin Selvan, after delivering all the messages, when he is relaxed, ask him "Do you remember the Ocean Princess?" If he replies, "Yes, I remember!", tell him, "She was the one who brought me to Lanka!"'

'Poonkulali! I will surely tell him. Even if he does not remember, I will tell him.'

'No. You must not tell him anything if he does not remember.'

'I'll definitely tell him everything.'

'What will you say?'

'I will tell him everything just the way it happened. "Prince, Ponniyin Selva! Do you remember the Ocean Princess? If you don't, please recall. It was she who saved me from all the troubles. It was she, who brought me safely to Lanka. But for her help I won't be alive to deliver these letters today". That is what I will tell him. Is it alright?'

'So far it is correct. Don't add anything more to it. And don't tell him that I told you to say all this. If the Prince says anything in reply, you must come back and repeat it to me exactly without changing a syllable of what he says.'

'Where can I see you again?'

'I can be found at Kodikkarai or on this Ghost Island or in my boat on the sea.'

'On my way back, can I look for you on this Ghost Island?'

'Ghost Island is a very dangerous place. You must never enter that island for any reason. Please call out to me with some sort of signal before you enter. You know how I called you like a cuckoo last night? You can call like that?'

'I cannot call like you. But I can call like a peacock!' He covered his face with his hands and made a call like a peacock! The sound made Poonkulali laugh. Meanwhile, the boat had neared the shores of Snake Island.

57

Honourable Prime Minister

Alvarkkadiyan Nambi landed on the coastal town of Rameswaram enroute to Lanka on the same day that Vandhiyathevan landed on Snake Island.

Alvarkkadiyan got into an argument with the Saivite priests near the temple which peaked into a fistfight.

'Catch him!'

'Finish him off!'

The crowd shouted with hostility; suddenly, their attention was diverted by the announcements of a herald.

'Emperor Sundara Chola Paranthaka's most trusted prime minister, Honourable Aniruddha Brahmarayar is coming. Make way! Make way!'

The prime minister of the Chola Empire, Honourable Anbil Aniruddha Brahmarayar, was seated with dignity on a barge, surrounded by guards. He noticed the commotion beside the temple wall and Alvarkkadiyan standing most innocently in the midst of the crowd, with folded hands and staff tucked away.

The Prime Minister instructed his guards to bring Alvarkkadiyan to his chambers and left.

The Prime Minster's barge moved on. Nambi, encircled by the guards, followed.

Prime Minister Aniruddha Brahmarayar was conducting his court in one of the ancient mansions on a tiny island next to Rameswaram. Accountants, writers, clerks, messengers, guards and other servants were waiting for his orders. The Prime Minister called for his visitors.

Five prosperous merchants from the Guild of Sea Merchants

entered and presented a gem-encrusted jewel on a platter to the Prime Minister. He accepted it gracefully and ordered,

'Enter this into the temple accounts meant for Queen Mother Sembiyan Madevi's charities.'

Then he enquired about their welfare and asked what he could do for them.

Their representative spoke, 'We represent the Merchant Guild that has its trading activities in the island kingdoms of Southeast Asia, Bay of Bengal, Arabian Sea and South India for several centuries.'

'How is your trade in the Pandiya territories?'

'It improves day by day.'

'How is trade these days, in the countries of the Southeast Sea?'

'Nothing lacks under the just rule of Emperor Sundara Chola.'

'Any problems with pirates?'

'No problems at all this year.'

'Good. What about your support for Lankan campaign?'

'We have collected a thousand sacks of rice, millets, beans, etc. and brought them to this island.'

'I am very glad. Please send food supplies just like this to Lanka till the war ends. Now you may leave.'

After the representatives of the guild left, a courtier came up to announce,

'The commanders of the well-known Kaikola Regiment are awaiting your audience.'

'Please send them!' ordered the Prime Minister.

Three distinguished men entered. The goddess of valour dwelt on their faces. They were brave and fearless. The Prime Minister enquired,

'Are you from the Sundara Chola's Popular Kaikola Battalion?'

'Yes, Sir. We are a company of three batallions. All our men in the regiment are wasting their time eating and sleeping without work for the past six months.'

The Prime Minister smiled as he asked,

'What is your petition?'

'We wish to join the army under the leadership of Prince Arulmoli, and engage in the war in Lanka.'

'Fine, when I return to Tanjore, I will obtain the Emperor's permission and inform you. Till then continue your assignment as peace-keeping forces in Pandiya territories.'

All three commanders stood up and raised cheers hailing the Emperor and Prince Arulmoli and left after bidding farewell to the Prime Minister.

The Prime Minister was lost in deep thought for some time and murmured,

'What great power of attraction our Prince Ponniyin Selvan possesses! Even those who meet him only once become crazy!'

Meanwhile his man came to inform him of the arrival of Alvarkkadiyan.

'Ask him to come in.'

Alvarkkadiyan Nambi entered the chamber of the Prime Minister with humility and greeted his master.

Prime Minister smiled and said, 'Nambi, why this commotion wherever you go?'

'I had to teach those Saiva fellows a lesson. People say that you have forgotten all loyalty to Vaishnava faith because the Emperor has rewarded you with a land grant of ten villages and confirmed it by a copper plate edict.'

'You should not heed such jealous gossip. Yes, the Emperor did reward me with a land grant. But I had become his prime minister many years before that. Did you not know that?'

Alvarkkadiyan was silent.

'Do you know how the Emperor and I became friends? We had both studied under the same guru in our boyhood days. We studied the literatures of Tamil and Sanskrit; we learnt the intricacies of mathematics, logic, astronomy and grammar. Neither he nor I even dreamt that he would become the Emperor. The unexpected turn of events forced Sundara Chola to accept the throne. At that time, he anticipated several complications. He asked me to stand by him, help him govern the disorganized nation. He was ready to forsake the throne if I was not willing to help him. Then I accepted his request to help him administer this vast nation. I have kept my promise to him. I thought you knew all this?'

'I know all this, Sir! But what is the point in my knowing it? The people don't know it.'

'You need not worry about such people. I did not come to Rameswaram on a pilgrimage, but on official visit. I went to Mathotam in Lanka to meet our Prince Arulmoli Varman.'

'Did you meet the Prince?' asked Alvarkkadiyan eagerly.

'Yes, I met the Prince and talked to him. King Mahinda of Lanka had a huge army. There is no trace of it now. Mahinda's army included several units of Tamil forces from the Pandiya and Chera kingdoms. When those men came to know that Arulmoli was the Commander of the Cholas, they dropped their weapons and crossed over to our army. Mahinda disappeared in the mountains of Rohana. Now our armies have no enemies to fight.'

'Well! Then why can't our Prince return to our homeland with our army? Why all this conflict about sending food-supplies for our men?'

'We should make Mahinda and his people accept the rule of our tiger flag. Our Prince is trying to achieve this objective. Our men are engaged in renovating all those structures—ancient mansions, palaces, mausoleums, temples and spires that were damaged in the war; they have been ordered to do so by Prince Arulmoli.'

'Fantastic!'

'If anyone on this earth has the qualification to rule as absolute emperor, it is Arulmoli. He is born with such divine favour. Did you overhear any of my conversations with the merchants and Kaikola Regiment commanders? Those merchants, who are so tight-fisted about money, become quite generous upon hearing the name of our Prince Arulmoli. All our soldiers are eager to fight under his leadership!'

Alvarkkadiyan spoke hesitantly, 'Sir! You are building castles! Here, they are trying to topple the very foundations of this empire. If you were to see all that I saw and heard, you wouldn't be so enthusiastic. You will realize the danger surrounding this Chola Empire.'

'Nambi! I have been distracted by my enthusiasm. Let me hear the news, however horrifying. There is a secret chamber in an underground cave on this island. Let us go there and discuss.'

58

Beloved Son of Ponni

Kundavai and her dear friend Vanathi were mounted on an elephant heading towards Tanjore.

The young princess had not visited Tanjore in the recent past for certain reasons. Women of the royal household preferred to live in the old capital of the Chola Empire, Palayarai, since it was comfortable with the freedom to go around as per their liking. But in Tanjore, there were too many protocols imposed by the Paluvettarayar brothers in the name of security. Apart from protocols, Kundavai did not relish Nandini's arrogant behaviour.

My brothers are far away in Kanchi and Lanka. My elder brother, Karikalan, has asked me to periodically send him news through secret messengers about the activities in Tanjore. How can I gather information about Tanjore while I am staying at Palayarai? Till now, I disliked the noblemen of Paluvoor merely because they were wielding enormous powers beyond their limit. Now they are conspiring against the Emperor using foolish Madurandakan to fulfil their wishes. They have absolute control over several chieftains and officials of this nation to support their cause. My father's life is also in danger! If something happens to the Emperor, these traitors can easily crown Madurandakan and declare him as the new ruler. They will do anything to achieve their goals. Even if they don't have such diabolic thoughts, this sorceress Nandini will misguide them! Considering all this, I must be in Tanjore.

If Madurandakan is crowned, he will be a puppet in their hands, fulfilling their whims and fancies. Nandini's word will become the law of the land. I will never allow all this.

Moreover, she too was eager to find out the news about Vandiyathevan, who was facing threat from the Paluvettarayar brothers.

They will have to accuse him of some major crime and give him a fair trial. That is why they have charged him with attempt to murder.

While Kundavai's heart was confused by such complications and conspiracies, Vanathi's mind was engrossed with something else. Dreaming about Prince Arulmoli!

'Sister! You have asked him to return immediately. When he returns from Lanka, where will he go? Palayarai or Tanjore?' asked Vanathi.

Vanathi was concerned about Prince Arulmoli. Kundavai, who was thinking of something else turned to her and asked,

'Whom are you asking about? Is it about Ponniyin Selvan?'

'Yes sister! You never told how he got that title. Sister! Tell me the story about the title—Ponniyin Selvan. Tanjore Fort seems far away and this elephant is walking like a tortoise!'

Kundavai smiled, 'If this elephant walks any faster than this, we will fall down. All the time you are thinking of my brother. Fine, listen to this tale.'

Kundavai retold the old story.

In those early years after Sundara Chola had ascended the Chola throne, his family life was filled with happiness. One day the Emperor was on a cruise on the river Ponni (Cauvery) with his queen and children and suddenly a cry came, 'Where is the baby? Where is Arulmoli?' It was Kundavai's voice. It was Kundavai who first noticed the missing child. Everyone was stunned. And they searched all over—in the cabin and below deck. Kundavai and Karikalan began crying. Footmen had already jumped into the water, looking for the baby prince. Sundara Chola had also jumped into the river, swimming across the currents looking for his dear son.

Suddenly, an astonishing vision appeared. It was in the middle of the river, a little beyond the royal boat. A female form was wading in the floods holding a child in her arms, raising him high above the water level. Sundara Chola was the first to see her. He swam across to reach for his son. And the child was brought back. As soon as the Emperor climbed back on deck, he swooned. All were comforting the child and reviving the Emperor. They forgot the woman who had saved the little prince. None had seen her clearly to give a proper description.

They unanimously decided that the river goddess, Mother Cauvery, must have saved the darling prince. The royal household made arrangements to worship Goddess Cauvery called river Ponni on that day every year. From that day onwards, Arulmoli was known as 'Ponniyin Selvan'—beloved son of river Ponni.

59

Two Full Moons

Tanjore City bustled with excitement to see two full moons at the same time.

After a long time, their beloved Princess Kundavai was visiting Tanjore. There was not a single soul in the Chola land who had not heard of Princess Kundavai's beauty, intelligence, culture and generosity. Her name was a mantra in the minds of all the people. They were also curious to see the young queen of Paluvoor participating in Navaratri celebrations along with Princess Kundavai. A sea of humanity had gathered outside the Fort to see both of them. Just like the ocean, during high tide, reaches for the full moon, this sea of people was thrilled with excitement.

Two full moons appeared at the same time. Princess Kundavai and her retinue reached Tanjore Fort; its massive doors were open with a thunderous roar amidst shouting cheers of the public and parade of the palace guards.

The Paluvettarayar brothers were at the gate to receive the Princess. Behind them was an ivory palanquin, embellished with pearls, carrying another full moon, Junior Queen Nandini.

Both the ladies descended, Kundavai from the elephant and Nandini from her palanquin. Nandini received the Princess and Kundavai acknowledged her reception with a gracious smile. When people saw these two stunning beauties of the Chola Empire side by side, the massive crowd began cheering again, their enthusiasm breaking all bounds.

Nandini was golden in colour while Kundavai was like a soft pink lotus. Nandini's golden face was round like the shining full moon of summer. Kundavai's divine face was like that of an exquisite bronze statue, chiseled by a master sculptor. Nandini's large jet-black eyes were like buzzing bees. Kundavai's large blue-black eyes were like the curved petals of a beautiful blue lily. Nandini's nose was smooth like polished ivory. Kundavai's nose was longer, resembling a healthy rose bud. Nandini's lips were like coral-red shells filled with intoxicating liquor. Kundavai's slender honeyed lips were like delicate pomegranate buds. Kundavai's majestic appearance proclaimed her as the beauty queen.

Womenfolk of the city were unhappy with Nandini for some reason. Every one of them was very fond of Kundavai, as if she was their family deity.

The conversation between the two women was like flashes of lightning trying to cut across one another.

'Welcome, my Princess! Welcome! We wondered if you had completely forgotten us. But today we are happy to see you here,' spoke Nandini.

'Queen, what is this? Does living at a distance mean that one has forgotten? You have not visited Palayarai. Does it mean you have forgotten us?' replied Kundavai.

'Everyone will visit beautiful Palayarai City, like honey bees find fragrant flowers without invitation. It is your kindness that has brought you to ordinary Tanjore City.'

'How can you say that Tanjore is ordinary, when beauty itself is imprisoned here?' said Kundavai sarcastically.

'The handsome Emperor is imprisoned in this fort. Now there is no cause for concern as you have arrived,' spoke Nandini with flashing eyes.

'Fantastic! Even gods in heaven cannot imprison Emperor Sundara Chola. I was talking about Nandini, the angel who is the personification of beauty imprisoned inside the fort...'

'Well said, Princess! Well said! Please repeat it so that my husband can hear it. He keeps me here in this city like a prisoner. If you could speak on my behalf and recommend...'

'Why my recommendation? You are not an ordinary prisoner. You are a prisoner of love that too, the love of an...'

'Yes, Princess! If the prison of love is that of an old man, there is no escape. Some people talk of Tanjore's dungeons. Perhaps one could escape from those underground dungeons of Tanjore but not...'

'Very true, Young Queen, very true! Especially, if the prison is of one's own making, escape is difficult,' replied Kundavai.

There was a big roar from the groups of women gathered outside the Fort gate. Kundavai and Nandini walked towards that group. The women in the crowd called loudly in chorus.

'We want to visit our favourite Princess Kundavai freely at the palace with no restrictions at least for the nine days of the Navaratri festival.'

Kundavai turned to Nandini and said, 'Young Queen, why don't you submit their representation to your husband or your brother-in-law and recommend? What danger can befall this Empire because of these simple womenfolk?'

For the next few days, Tanjore was immersed in endless festivity. It became special because the Navaratri festival coincided with Kundavai's visit. Commoners were permitted to enter and leave the Fort without any restrictions for the nine days of the festival. Several celebrations and competitions were held in the fort and the city as well as in the townships around the city.

There was constant competition between the young queen of Paluvoor and Princess Kundavai. Their fierce duels were fought with arrow-sharp words and darting lance-like eyes. Two tigresses possessing beauty were wrestling with each other.

Princess Vanathi found it difficult to even get a chance to talk to Princess Kundavai those days and she did not care about anything that happened outside. She created a secret dream-world of her own thinking of Prince Arulmoli.

60

Distressed Midnight Call

Chola monarchs developed art and culture through dance and drama. Tanjore was well-known for several famous theatres and actors.

During the Navaratri celebrations, a historical play on the glorious history of Chola dynasty was enacted for three days in the Emperor's beautiful auditorium inside the palace. During these shows, young queen of Paluvoor, Nandini came to sit beside Princess Kundavai.

Of the three plays, the third one highlighting the story of Paranthaka Chola was the best. There was some commotion among the viewers on the third day.

Among the Chola kings, Sundara Chola's grandfather Paranthaka I was famous for his bravery. The Chola Empire had grown extensive during his forty-six years of golden rule. He had fought in several victorious battles. His last battle at Takkolam against the huge army of the Rashtrakutas of the north was a great victory. The eldest son of Paranthaka I, Prince Rajaditya, died atop an elephant. His body, pierced with enemy arrows, was brought back to the palace in the capital. All the queens embraced the dead body of the valiant Prince who sacrificed his life for the country and shed uncontrollable tears. Finally, a voice from the skies spoke:

'Don't weep! The Prince is not dead for he lives in the heart of all men and women of this brave Chola nation.'

The play concluded with this final scene

The audience immensely enjoyed this play. The cause for commotion during the show was that in all the big wars fought during the rule of Paranthaka I, he was ably assisted by two chieftains—one was the Kodumbalur and the other Paluvoor. They were bound to the ruling Chola clan with a string of marriage alliances. They were like two hands to the Emperor. The Emperor treasured them both as his two eyes.

The actors of today's play were very careful in their portrayal of both these chieftains, giving equal prominence to each. The viewers belonging to both the groups raised cheers whenever the bravery of their nobles was highlighted. Initially this rivalry was mild. Later, it turned more hostile. Both factions raised loud cheers and shouts.

Princess Kundavai became enthusiastic on hearing the cheers coming from both factions.

When the cheers from the Kodumbalur faction was loudest, she would turn to Vanathi saying, 'Look Vanathi, your party is winning now!' Innocent Vanathi would smile happily.

Princess Kundavai would look at Nandini when the Paluvoor faction was cheering, and say, 'Young Queen, your party is winning now!'

Queen Nandini was not happy with Kundavai's mischief and encouraging the rivalry between the two factions. She didn't like being treated at par with Vanathi. She bit her tongue and gnashed her teeth to sit quietly till the end.

Princess Kundavai observed everything. The expressions on Nandini's face were crystal clear like reflections on a mirror, except at one time. One scene in the play depicted the following incident:

The Pandiya king lost the battle and sought asylum with the Lankan king. When the Lankan king did not come forth with the expected support, Pandiya left his crown and other royal jewels with the Lankans for safe custody and escaped to the Chera Kingdom. Everybody in the audience expressed happiness during this scene. But Nandini's face showed extreme bitterness and sorrow. This was mysterious to Princess Kundavai.

Princess Kundavai, trying to pry into Nandini's mind, said,

'It's sad that our Emperor could not enjoy this wonderful play because of ill health.'

Nandini replied softly, 'His beloved daughter is with him now. He will surely recover when the medicines from Lanka arrive.'

'Medicines from Lanka?' asked Kundavai.

'You ask as if you don't know! I believe the doctor from Palayarai has sent a man to collect herbal plants. In fact, I heard that you had assigned a retainer for the job. Isn't it true?'

Princess Kundavai bit her lip revealing her beautiful teeth like jasmine buds. Cries of cheers from the audience interrupted their conversation.

With a final cheer of praise for the health of Sundara Chola, the play ended. The crowd cheerfully dispersed.

Empress Vanamadevi and some other noblewomen of the palace made preparations to go to the temple of Durga, the family deity of the Cholas. The temple had special midnight poojas on all nine days of the Navaratri.

Though it was not the practice to allow young ladies to attend the midnight poojas at the Durga temple, Princess Kundavai accompanied her mother on all nine nights and offered prayers for her father's well-being. Vanathi was left alone in the big palace.

On a particular night, Vanathi went for a walk on the upper terraces of the palace. The panoramic view of Tanjore at night can be seen from the terrace. As she was new to the palace, she lost her way in spite of the brightly lit lamps.

Suddenly she heard a wailing voice filled with sorrow. Vanathi was frightened and stood rooted to the spot. Again, came that anguished cry.

'Is there no one to help me?'

Ah! This sounds like the Emperor's voice! What danger is this? Is there no one with him?

She took a few steps further into that balcony. Cautiously, she moved further. The voice came from down below. She looked down into a large, wide chamber.

Isn't this the bed chamber of the Emperor? Yes, there he is, lying on his bed! All alone! He is moaning and wailing. What is he saying?

'You wretch! It is true that I killed you. Why do you still haunt me even after twenty-five years? Won't you leave me in peace? Help me! Go! Go away! No! Don't move, stop!'

These words fell into Vanathi's ears like molten lead.

A figure stood before the Emperor, a little away, towards one side in the shadows of a large pillar: a female, half visible, half hidden by shadows and the smoke from the incense burner.

It seems like the Young Queen of Paluvoor? One more person! Senior Paluvattarayar! I'm not mistaken, it is them! Is the Emperor crying in fear on seeing her? What is the meaning of his cry, 'It is true that I killed you?'

Suddenly, Vanathi felt faint but she managed to move away.

When Princess Kundavai returned from the temple with her maids, she found an unconscious Vanathi in the passage way close to her bed chamber.

61

Emperor's Hallucination

Next day Princess Kundavai was with her father Emperor Sundara Chola, by his bedside.

'I disobeyed your orders and came to Tanjore,' said Kundavai

'Yes, darling you shouldn't have come here. This palace in Tanjore is not good for young girls. There is a ghost wandering about this palace.'

Saying this Sundara Chola started shivering and his craze-filled eyes were looking into the distance.

'Father, let us all go back to Palayarai. I see no improvement in your health here. The Palayarai doctor says that he can cure your illness.'

'I am fortunate to have such an affectionate daughter. No medicine can cure me in this birth. What cure is there for mental illness?'

'Father, why do you fear when you have two lion cubs as sons?'

'Both your brothers are incomparable warriors. But I do them no good by leaving this cursed kingdom.'

'What curse can this kingdom have? You are hallucinating about something. If you leave this fort...'

'Ah! I am preventing the ruin of this ancient kingdom by remaining here. Last night, I was watching the play from the terrace. At one point, I even wondered if I should order to stop it after seeing the behaviour of those men watching and shouting in rivalry. If they behave like this when I am here, what will happen if I am not here? They will fight amongst themselves and kill each other, paving the way for the destruction of this empire.'

'Father, the nobles of Paluvoor as well as Kodumbalur are duty bound to obey your orders. If you come to know that one among those two clans is committing treason...' Kundavai spoke hesitantly.

Sundara Chola looked at her with surprise,

'What are you saying, child? Treason against me? Who instigates it?'

'Father, some who pretend devout service to you are secretly conspiring against you by declaring both your sons ineligible to ascend this throne; they are secretly planning to crown another...'

'Who? Crown whom?' Sundara Chola asked.

Kundavai spoke softly, 'Uncle Madurandakan.'

Sundara Chola sat up a little, 'Ah! If only their efforts are successful...!'

Kundavai was shocked. 'What is this, Father? Are you an enemy to your own sons?'

'No, I am not! I wish them well; they do not need this curse-ridden empire. If only Madurandakan agrees...'

'He is very willing, ready to be crowned even today! Should you not consult my brother, the Crown Prince?'

'Yes, we must also convince your grandmother, Sembiyan Madevi, to agree. Your grandmother has great affection for you. You must convince her to give the throne to Madurandakan.'

Kundavai was too stunned to say anything. The Emperor continued,

'Go to Kanchi after that. Convince your brother also, let us be free from the curse.'

'Father, what is tormenting you?' asked Kundavai.

'The time has come for me to reveal the deepest secrets of my life. I am going to tell you something which no father would tell his daughter.

It seems like my previous birth. I have not talked about it to anyone till now. Please listen to my story,' said the Emperor.

'My grandfather, Paranthaka, was very fond of me since my infant days and personally raised me in his palace. I had no rights to the kingdom. There were three brothers elder to me, eligible to ascend the throne. He permitted me to command the battalion sent to Lanka as desired by me.

But my army lost that war and countless men were dead. The remaining army of men gathered on the beach to sail back to our homeland. I did not like the idea of going back as I had lost all my men on the battlefield. But I was forced to leave. While the ship was sailing, halfway, I saw a tiny island at a distance, jumped into the sea unnoticed and swam to the island.

I was sitting on a low tree branch enjoying the beauty of the place and lost in thoughts. Suddenly, I heard a female voice and turned back to see a young girl running as she screamed. A bear was chasing her. I killed it with my spear. When I tried to talk to her, she ran away.

She returned after some time with her father. She was stunningly beautiful. Her father informed me that the girl was mute and she screamed and ran only to distract a bear which was about to attack me. I felt pity for her which eventually turned to love.

We made garlands of the wild flowers and exchanged it. Several years passed on that paradise of an island in the company of her divine love. Those were the happiest days of my life.

Soon a shipload of men from my homeland came in search of me. The great Chola Empire awaited me. I had to leave. I made up my mind to come back after fulfilling my duties. I promised a thousand times. When I climbed into the boat, she was staring at me with tear-filled eyes. I controlled myself, putting duty ahead of my love and left.

Kundavai, the sight of that mute girl, gazing at me with tear laden-eyes, has never left my memory however hard I try.

I came to Tanjore to see Emperor Paranthaka, my grandfather, on his deathbed. Rajaditya, the crown prince, had died in the battlefields of Takkolam and my father Arinjaya also had been badly wounded in the same battle with little chance of survival. My other uncle, Kandaraditya, eligible for the throne, did not have children. The great Chola Empire was heirless. In such a situation, when the Emperor saw me, his face brightened with happiness.

"Our clan is sure to regain its greatness during your times!"

He spoke such words for a while. He even made me promise to uphold the greatness of the Chola Empire.

My promise became my life's mission. But I had no peace of mind, thinking of the fate of that mute girl on the island who saved my life from that bear. How could a mute island girl with no social background become the queen of the great Chola Empire?

My uncle, Kandaraditya, was coronated after Emperor Paranthaka's death, I was also coronated as the crown prince on the same day.

My dear daughter! The people of this country were obsessively fond of me those days, just as they are fond of your brother, Arulmoli, now. During the coronation ceremony several thousands of people had gathered outside the palace, patiently waiting for the newly crowned King and Prince to appear before them. My uncle and I stepped into the viewing gallery to accept the roaring greetings of the people.

Suddenly, I saw the face of that young island girl filled with sadness looking at me piteously in the midst of that vast multitude. I lost consciousness…

I sent my friend, Prime Minister Aniruddha, to search for her. She was found in Kodikkarai. She had become insane and refused to come to Tanjore.

I went to Kodikkarai with Aniruddha only to learn that she had jumped from the lighthouse. She could not be found anywhere, even after an intense search. We decided that she had been swallowed by the ocean.

I returned and became involved with the affairs of the empire. I married your mother and you children were born.

Do you remember that incident when Arulmoli had fallen into the river Cauvery when he was a baby? Everyone decided that Goddess Cauvery had saved the child. But, do you know what I saw? That island girl saving the child. She gave the baby to me and vanished. Everyone thought I fainted because of the mishap. But it is not so.

It is because I saw her ghost saving the child.

Over the years, with the passing of time, those nightmares left me and she faded from my memory.

Suddenly she reappeared and started tormenting me.

My daughter! Do you remember the coronation day of your brother? I once again saw the island girl's ghost standing amidst all those women and staring angrily at Karikalan. I fainted on that occasion too. I wondered why she stared angrily at Karikalan. Maybe it was my imagination. Later she came before me four or five times at midnight to warn me. "You killed me even that I forgive. But, don't sin again. Don't covet an empire which belongs to another and give it to your son!"

Daughter! You must help me in this matter. My sons do not need this cursed kingdom! Let us give it to Madurandakan.'

'Father, how can you talk like this? Why should we change a decision already approved by all the citizenry and nobility? Will the world agree to this?' Kundavai spoke with shock.

'My uncle, Kandaraditya, did not have any children when I was coronated as the crown prince. Subsequently, he married Sembiyan Madevi and Madurandakan was born. It is not lawful that I, the son of a younger brother, should ascend the throne when a son of the elder brother is alive. Now, I suffer for such sins. Why should my sons commit a similar sin? We must crown Madurandakan before I die. After crowning him, I will go to Kanchi to live with Karikalan. You first go to Palayarai and convince the Queen Mother, then go to Kanchi and convince your brother.'

Then, Kundavai firmly said,

'Father, you have been harbouring all these haunting memories in your heart for so long. Now that you have told me everything, you will soon feel better.'

After this, father and daughter talked for a while. Kundavai then left for her chambers. On the way, she met her mother and said, 'Mother! Never leave father even for a moment!'

Certain doubts that had been worrying Kundavai were now clearer. A twinkle of light began to appear in the pitch darkness. Her intellect warned her that some huge conspiracy fuelled by sorcery and cunningness was taking shape against her brothers. But she was not sure about the details of that conspiracy—who was really behind it or how it was being organized. Kundavai felt it was her duty to protect them from such danger.

62

Which Is the Worst Betrayal?

Women folk in ancient Tamil land were at the forefront of social life, doing a lot of charities.

Kundavai utilized her wealth in a different manner. She undertook the establishment of free medical facilities all over the kingdom. Currently, she was involved in founding a trust to run a hospital in the name of her father at Tanjore. A grand ceremony was organized to inaugurate the free hospital on the occasion of Navaratri festival.

People in large numbers—men and women, children and the aged—all well-dressed, gathered in a jubilant mood. The ministers, senior and junior officers, stone masons, architects and members of various guilds also assembled. A contingent of the Velakkara Battalion was playing on drums, cymbals and trumpets. Another contingent (Tanjore's Guard Corps) came displaying spears and lances.

The ceremony began with the singing of mesmerizing spiritual songs. Nandini moved closer to Kundavai as she softly spoke, 'Princess! It is said that long ago, Saint Sambandar sang this hymn and anointed the Pandiya King with holy ashes to cure the ailing monarch. Even holy songs and ashes have no healing powers nowadays!'

'Very true, Young Queen! In those days justice prevailed; these days, the world is full of liars and sinners. That is why the powers of chants have decreased.' Kundavai peered into the face of Paluvoor's young queen.

Nandini's face revealed no change. 'Is that so? Are there traitors who conspire against their kings these days? Who are they?' she asked calmly.

'That is what I am not sure about! I intend to remain here for some more time till I find out the truth,' Kundavai spoke softly.

'A good decision, my Princess! I will also help you as much as I can. Also, we have a guest in our mansion; he also may be able to help you,' Nandini replied with a slight sarcasm.

'Who is the guest?' asked Kundavai.

'Kandamaran, Kadamboor Sambuvarayar's son. Have you met him? He is tall and well-built! He keeps babbling constantly about spies and traitors. You mentioned about treason just now; can you say what is worse than betrayal of one's king?'

'Sure. If a woman betrays her husband, it is worse than treason!' Kundavai once again peered into Nandini's face after saying these words. But there was no expected change. Nandini continued with the same enchanting smile.

'You are, of course, correct. But, Kandamaran won't agree! He will say that the worst sin is betrayal of friendship! I believe that Kandamaran's best friend not only became a spy but also stabbed him in his back. Since then, Kandamaran has been babbling like this.'

'Who is he? Who committed such an evil deed?' asked Kundavai.

'Apparently it is someone named Vandiyathevan. Have you heard of him?'

Kundavai bit her coral lips with pearly teeth,

'The name sounds familiar. What happened after that?'

'My brother-in-law has sent men to arrest that spy!'

'Is he a spy? How will you know he is a spy or not?'

'All I know is what Sambuvarayar's son says. Perhaps you may talk to him in person to find out.'

'Yes, I should meet him. I heard that it was a miracle that he is alive!'

'Yes. Somehow he survived; his wound has not healed completely.'

'I am surprised that he is not fully cured with you by his bedside nursing him! Anyway, I'll visit him.'

Nandini replied, 'I will be honoured.'

Finally, the royal permit from Sundara Chola was read out, giving tax exemption to the related villages, which would be financing Kundavai's hospital.

63

The Spy Is Caught!

The incidents of the day had immensely irritated Senior Paluvettarayar. It had become an occasion for the people to display their love and loyalty to the Emperor and the royal family.

'Commoners! These mindless cattle will walk if four lead the way to an abyss!' He muttered, expressing his anguish.

'The Emperor will ruin this empire before he leaves the world! He orders, "Remove taxes for this town and that village"! Soon there will be no towns or villages paying taxes. How to send food supplies and monies for countless battle campaigns.' He shouted so loudly that all around him were frightened.

Finally, his younger brother, Kalanthaka, had to come to preach patience, 'Brother! No use of shouting. Let us be patient till the time comes.'

When Senior Paluvettarayar heard about Kundavai's impending visit to his mansion, his anger knew no bounds. He walked up to Nandini and asked,

'What is this? Why is she coming here? Did you invite her? Have you forgotten her insults?'

'I won't forget the good and the bad done to me,' said Nandini.

'Then, why is she coming here?'

'She wishes to therefore she is coming. Her arrogance in being the Emperor's daughter brings her here.'

'Why did you invite her?'

'I didn't, she is coming of her own accord, to visit ailing Kandamaran. How could I ask her not to come? A time will come when I can say it.'

'I can't be in the mansion when she visits! In fact, I can't remain in this city also. I will go to Malapadi for some work.'

'Yes! My Lord! Leave that snake to me. I know how to control her. Don't be surprised if you hear some astonishing news when you come back.'

'What astonishing news?'

'You may perhaps hear that Kundavai plans to wed Kandamaran, or Aditya Karikalan plans to marry Kandamaran's sister Manimekalai.'

'What nonsense is this? If anything like that happens, what will happen to our plans?'

'Mere talk does not mean that an act has taken place. You have been saying that Madurandakan is the next king. Is that really going to happen? Are we striving like this to crown that fool?'

Nandini blinked her large eyes and looked at Senior Paluvettarayar.

He was no match for her beguiling looks. He sat down beside her and picked up her flowery hands, kissing them.

'Very soon, you will sit on this Chola throne as its all-powerful empress,' said he.

Kandamaran was very restless from the moment he came to know about Kundavai's impending visit to see him. He had always been enchanted by Kundavai's intelligence, beauty and greatness.

What a great honor to see her! I will willingly bear several more bruises and fall even more sick for such an honour! Oh dear! Why wasn't I wounded on my chest? I have to repeat my wretched friend's betrayal and his stabbing at my back.

All his resolve vanished the moment he saw Kundavai.

'It would have been better if Vandiyathevan, that ungrateful friend of mine, had struck me on my chest. I would have really forgiven him if he had done that.'

Kundavai felt that Kandamaran's emotional words had a ring of truth to them. She wondered if Vandiyathevan could have done the dastardly deed. She asked Kandamaran to describe the incident in detail. Even Nandini was thrown into a sea of surprise by the imaginative tale told by young Kandamaran!

'At midnight, I was walking along the banks of river Vadavaru encircling this fort searching for my friend Vandiyathevan. In the dim moonlight, I found him climbing down the outer wall of the fort. I asked him, "Friend, what are you doing?" That heinous friend stabbed my back and escaped, I found myself in a mute woman's house when I came to my senses.'

Nandini laughed to herself on hearing this story concocted by Kandamaran. Kundavai could not make up her mind about how much of it could be believed.

'How did you come to the mute woman's house? Who brought you there?' asked Kundavai.

'That is a mystery for me! That dumb woman could not say anything. Apparently, her son also was not there on that night. The truth may come out when that fellow returns. I have to be patient till the Paluvoor men arrest my friend Vandiyathevan.'

'Do you think that he will be arrested?'

'How can he escape? He cannot fly away! I am staying back here, in Tanjore, to see him. I am confident of earning a pardon for my friend.'

'Sir! You are to be commended for your large heartedness,' said Kundavai. But her heart said Vandiyathevan should not be arrested.

A servant maid came running into the chamber,

'Queen! The spy has been caught! They are bringing him down the street.'

Nandini and Kundavai were shocked. Nandini controlled herself instantly. Kundavai could not do so.

64

Tigress versus Tigress

When the servant maid informed them about the arrest of the spy, all three felt agitated. Kundavai was more agitated than the other two.

Nandini asked, 'Princess, shall we go and see what that cunning spy looks like?'

Kundavai hesitated, 'Why should we bother about that?'

'I want to see him, I'll go,' saying this Kandamaran tried to get up.

'Don't get up. You will fall...' said Nandini.

Kundavai also said, 'Let us find out who he is and what he looks like! Can we see the street from the balcony of this mansion?'

'We can see very clearly. Come with me.' Nandini took them.

'My Lady, if it is really my friend, please help me to meet uncle Paluvoor and get pardon for him,' Kandamaran requested Nandini.

'How will we know if he is your friend?'

Saying this Nandini glanced towards Kundavai.

'I will identify him!' Kandamaran walked with faltering steps.

The three of them stepped onto a balcony on the upper storey of the mansion. Seven or eight horses were coming down the street below, with soldiers bearing arms. A man with his hands bound with ropes was walking in the middle. Two horsemen on either side of him were holding the ends of the ropes that bound him. A curious mob was following. Initially, the face of the spy was not visible.

Kundavai's eyes were fixed on the procession. Kandamaran said, breaking the silence,

'No! That is not Vandiyathevan!'

Kundavai's face brightened. The fellow being dragged by the horsemen looked up. Kundavai recognized him as the doctor's son from Palayarai.

Without disclosing her happiness, Kundavai said,

'What foolishness is this? He is the son of the doctor in Palayarai.'

'Oh! Is that so? My brother-in-law's men are always like this. They will let the real culprit escape and arrest some innocent fellow.'

Kandamaran was speaking again, 'Ah! My friend Vandiyathevan won't be caught so easily. He is very clever.'

'Why do you still refer to him as your friend?' asked Nandini.

'He betrayed me. But, in my heart, my regard for him has not changed.'

'Perhaps these soldiers have killed your dear friend!' Saying this, Nandini looked at Kundavai. She found that the word 'killed' tortured the young princess.

You proud female! I have a weapon to avenge you! If I don't utilize it fully, my name is not Nandini, wait and see! Nandini thought to herself.

Kundavai burst out in rage, 'What spies?! Utter foolishness. These old men seem to lose all their senses. They suspect everyone! I had sent this man to Kodikkarai to collect medicinal herbs. Why did they arrest him? I must ask your brother-in-law immediately!'

'Oh! Is he the man sent by you, Princess? Did you send just this one man to collect medicinal herbs? Didn't you send another fellow as well?' asked Nandini

'Yes, I had sent another man with him. I had asked one of them to go to Lanka if necessary.'

'Aha! I understand everything now. My guess was correct.'

'I don't understand. What did you guess?'

'I have no more doubts, everything is clear, my Princess. Was the other man sent with this fellow known to you?'

Kundavai hesitated, 'He is the same fellow who brought me letters from Kanchi from my elder brother.'

'It's him! It's him!' said Nandini in glee.

'Who?'

'He ... the spy!'

'Why did they suspect him to be a spy?'

'How would I know that? It's an official secret. As a matter of fact, that spy acted suspiciously. He ran away in the night wounding Kandamaran on his back.'

'I cannot believe this. If he had stabbed him, why did he carry this gentleman to the mute's house?' asked Princess Kundavai.

'My Princess, you speak as if you witnessed the whole incident. Somehow, you seem to have a soft corner for that spy. He must be a magician. Look, this gentleman still calls him a friend! Whatever it may be, he is dead! If these soldiers have killed him... A lost life cannot be regained.'

Kundavai's eyes reddened, her throat choked up, her heart beat fast, 'It couldn't have happened. It cannot...' she mumbled under her breath.

'I am sure. Vandiyathevan could never be caught by these soldiers,' asserted Kandamaran.

'If not yet, he will be arrested soon,' retorted Nandini.

Kundavai gnashed her teeth, 'Who knows what happens tomorrow?' She continued with anger, 'Since the time the Emperor has fallen ill, the whole country is in turmoil! Who authorized these nobles to arrest men sent by me to collect medicinal plants? I will discuss this with my father at once.'

'My Princess, why should you disturb your ailing father on this petty matter? Why don't you ask my brother-in-law? Perhaps if he knew what was on your mind, he will obey your orders. Who in this great empire can go against the wishes of the Young Princess?' Nandini tried to soothe her rage.

In that conflict between the two tigresses that day, Nandini emerged victorious. Wounded Kundavai had to make tremendous efforts to conceal her emotions.

65

Infamous Tanjore Dungeons

Nothing is more enigmatic than life on earth. Skies remain clear for long and then, suddenly, dark clouds plunge the world into darkness; thunder rolls, lightning strikes and the rains drench everything. Even the leaves on the trees remain still. Unexpected storms from somewhere uproot all large trees. Luscious gardens turn into ruins by monkey hordes.

Such a whirlwind was now swirling in Kundavai's mind. Until recently life had been a bed of roses for Kundavai with no worries. Love and affection, song and dance, poetry and painting, jewels and adornments, garden parties and boating trips filled her days.

Everyone—her parents, brothers, ministers, gurus, friends and servants—treated her as their cherished darling. Emotions like sadness and worry were known to her only through poetry and drama. But she was deeply worried now.

Her father's illness coupled with the looming danger to the Empire deeply upset her. Her brothers were far away in distant lands. People were in the grip of unfamiliar fear. Kundavai, born in a clan of generations of brave warriors, had the strength to face all such obstacles. She was confident of solving all these problems with her sharp intellect. However, an unexpected incident disturbed her confidence.

When Kundavai met Vandiyathevan, her lotus bud–like heart opened its petals gently, blooming in full glory. But how unfortunate! A dark bee came to sit on that bloom to bruise its soft petals with its poisonous stings.

The mere thought of that gallant youth from Vaanar clan being arrested distressed her. Even when she had all her near and dear ones close by, her heart was agitated for some unknown youth whom she had met just twice or thrice.

She sent word to the commander of the fort, Junior Paluvettarayar, that she would visit him under the pretence of visiting the art gallery and would have a chat with him.

'Sir! Nobles of the Paluvoor clan have rendered incomparable service to the Chola family over several generations!'

'It is our good fortune, my Princess!' The Commander bowed very low.

'No doubt… that this Chola Empire is an apt reward for such service…'

'My Princess, what cruel words these are?!'

'But, wait till the Emperor's end. Why such impatience to grab the powers of this empire?'

Kalanthaka was sweating. Mopping his face with a scarf, he said,

'Princess! Why this rage with arrows of words? What have I done to receive such harsh words on me?'

'Is it wrong for me to send men to collect medicinal plants to heal my father?'

'Not at all, my Princess!'

'Then why have you arrested the doctor's son from Palayarai, whom I had sent to collect medicinal plants from Kodikkarai?'

'Princess, you may not be aware that he is an accomplice to a spy. He admitted that the other fellow with him did not go for collecting herbs, he was travelling with some letters for someone in Lanka.'

'He is a fool, blabbering nonsense. The other man who journeyed with him was also sent by me. I am sure you knew that.'

'Yes, I was aware of that, my Princess. That youth, named Vandiyathevan is really a spy.'

'Never. He is a messenger sent by my brother from Kanchi with letters for me.'

'Princess! He brought letters for the Emperor also from your brother in Kanchi. So what? Spies use all kinds of tricks to fulfil their mission.'

'Sir, what proof do you have to say that Vandiyathevan is a spy?'

'If he is not a spy, why did he travel along byways instead of taking the Royal Highway? Why did he enquire about the Emperor's health with the astrologer, entered Tanjore Fort clandestinely showing the Paluvoor signet ring? He lied, saying that Senior Paluvettarayar had given him that signet ring. He also stabbed Sambuvarayar's son.

He mingled with the stage actors and entered Palayarai covertly! He disguised himself as a doctor and travelled to Kodikkarai! If he is not a spy, why did he remain hidden for one whole day from my men? Why did he sail away to Lanka at night?'

'Oh! Did he escape to Lanka? Couldn't your men catch him?' Kundavai could not conceal the delight in her voice.

'Yes, my Princess. That magical spy fooled my men and escaped. These idiots let him go and arrested the doctor's son and not that spy.'

'Sir, forget that spy; I don't care about him. I sent the doctor's son and I am sure that he is innocent. You must free him immediately.'

'My Princess, even if he is not a spy, he has helped the real spy.'

'Reserve some room for locking up the real traitors. Sir, free the doctor's son immediately.'

'As I said, I cannot accept that responsibility, my Princess.'

'Will you obey the Emperor's orders?'

'Princess, I do not need the Emperor's orders for this. I am giving you these keys to the Dungeons of Tanjore. You are responsible for the consequences.'

Lord Kalanthaka presented the keys to the Princess. Kundavai controlled her rage and said, 'Fine! I shall bear the responsibility for the consequences!'

'If any grave danger threatens this Chola Empire, it is surely because of two women!' Lord Kalanthaka spoke with disgust.

'I am one, who is the other?' asked Kundavai.

'It is the young queen of Paluvoor, Nandini.'

Finally, Kundavai smiled wholeheartedly,

'You equate me with the all-powerful authority of this Chola Empire! If he comes to hear of it, your brother the Senior Paluvettarayar will banish you from this land!'

'No problem,' said Kalanthaka, the junior Paluvettarayar.

66

Royal Mint

The royal mint inside Tanjore Fort was like a mini-fortress, guarded well. Work for the day in the mint was over. Princess Kundavai and her friend Princess Vanathi arrived at the mint on the pretext of inspection. The guards and goldsmiths cheerfully greeted them.

The headman of the mint received them and took them inside. After inspecting the mint, they walked towards the underground dungeon entering through a small door in the farthest wall of the chamber in the dim light. They heard the frightening growls of tigers, lions and cheetahs walking to and fro inside their cages.

'Sister! Do they feed living human beings to these cats?' asked Princess Vanathi.

'No. But anyone trying to escape from these dungeons has to come through this chamber; then they will become prey to these beasts.'

'Oh God! What horror!'

'There will be mercy as well as horror in governance. Vanathi, a day may come when I myself may be thrown here...'

'That's absurd, Sister! No power in this universe can imprison you. If anybody tries to do anything like that, the very earth will split open and swallow this Tanjore City.'

'Who knows who will become a double-crosser?' said Kundavai bitterly.

As they walked, the growl of tigers became louder. Kundavai asked the soldier,

'The tigers seem very angry, why?'

The soldier replied cleverly,

'They are happily welcoming our beloved Emperor's gracious daughter.'

'Good reception!' laughed Kundavai.

'It is time to feed these tigers.'

'Oh! Let us finish and leave quickly. Where is the entrance?'

They entered a narrow passageway. The cells were all of different shapes. Some held only one man, some housed two and some were empty. Some prisoners were chained to the wall with very heavy metal bonds. Apart from the growling of the beasts they heard piteous wails and cries for help. In the midst of all those wails was heard a pleasant voice singing a song about the Lord with the golden-hued body, Lord Siva.

Vanathi asked, 'What horror is this? Why are these people shut up like this? Is there no fair trial for them?'

'Ordinary crimes are dealt with proper trial. But treason against king and those abetting spies are thrown into these cells.'

Now they came closer to the young man singing the divine lyric.

When the guard held up the torch to cast light in that cell, they could see a young man inside.

The Princess, touched by his innocent face, asked him,

'You seem happy.'

'Yes, my Princess. No dearth of joy here. The all-pervading God is here with me.'

'You speak like a philosopher. What was your occupation?'

'When I lived outside, I was stringing flower garlands for God. Here, I sing divine lyrics.'

'Do you know many other lyrics?'

'Yes, my Princess! But here I sing only this song.'

'Why?' asked Kundavai.

'When I saw the heaps of pure gold piled here in the mint, it reminded me of our Lord with the golden-hued body.'

'You are blessed. People are tempted when they see gold. But your mind is filled with thoughts of God. Any kith or kin for you?'

'Just my mother, living in the flower garden in Tanjore's suburbs.'

'Her name?'

'Vaani.'

'I will meet her and tell her that you are happy here.'

'It's of no use, my Princess. My mother is mute.'

Kundavai was astonished. She asked, 'Oh! Is your name Chendan Amudan?'

'Yes, Princess!' answered Amudan with surprise.

'Why did they bring you here?'

'I was imprisoned for the crime of helping a spy.'

'How is that? Which spy did you help?'

'Vandiyathevan. He said that he belonged to the ancient Vaanar clan.'

Kundavai and Vanathi looked at each other. Vanathi spoke, 'Please tell us all the details!'

Amudan started narrating everything, telling his tale from the moment he met Vandiyathevan outside Tanjore Fort till he was caught on the river bank by Paluvoor soldiers.

Vanathi asked, 'Why did you trust a stranger and help him so much?'

'Princess, sometimes we take a liking to people just by looking at them. Sometimes, when we meet some fellows, we feel like killing them immediately. Today, one man was imprisoned in this same cell with me. The anger I felt against him was limitless! Fortunately, he was freed a short while ago by retainers of the Young Queen of Paluvoor.'

'What? Who was that man released in such a hurry?'

'He is a son of the doctor in Palayarai.'

'What outrageous things did he say that you wished to kill him?'

'My uncle's daughter, Poonkulali, lives at Kodikkarai. This man uttered defaming words about her. That's why I was so angry with him. But he also gave me some good news, that's why I let him go free!'

'What was that good news, young man?' asked Kundavai.

'Apparently, this man had gone to Kodikkarai with my friend

Vandiyathevan. This traitor tried to betray my friend over there by trying to help Paluvoor soldiers in finding him. But he could not succeed.'

'Could not succeed? Did that spy escape?' Both Vanathi and Kundavai asked eagerly. They had come this far into the dungeons of Tanjore just to find out this news.

'Yes, Princess. My friend escaped. Poonkulali took him to Lanka in her boat. The searching soldiers were hoodwinked, this man was also fooled.'

Both women looked at each other, their faces reflecting their joy. Kundavai asked Amudan,

'Sir, how could you be so happy about a spy escaping from royal soldiers? Perhaps it is right that you have been thrown in this prison.'

'Princess! If it is correct to imprison me for that crime, both of you must also be placed in this cell next to me!'

The two women laughed.

'Very tricky! You will corrupt all in this prison with your songs. I will arrange for your release as soon as possible,' promised Kundavai.

'Please don't do that, my Princess! There is a man in the cell next to me. Every day he begs me to teach him to sing. He repeats a hundred times, "If you teach me one song, I'll tell you the secret of where the Pandiya crown jewels are hidden in Lanka". Let me remain here till I find out that secret,' said Amudan happily.

'Poor fellow! Are you ready to remain here till you go mad like him? What about the fate of your mother?'

With these words, Kundavai turned back.

Within half an hour, soldiers came to release Amudan from the prison.

67

Nandini's Letter

One evening, Nandini was seated in her garden gazebo on a swing. Her body was shivering and sweating even in the cool evening while she was writing a letter. The contents of the letter were such:

> O Prince! I pen this letter with much reluctance. When there are rumours of all kinds, you seem to be unconcerned about anything. Though your ailing father has asked you many a time, you are not visiting Tanjore. I doubt if I am the cause for it. If only I could meet you just once, I will be able to clear your doubts. Will you oblige me? If you dislike coming to Tanjore, we can meet at Kadamboor in Sambuvarayar's palace. By relationship I am your grandmother now. So, none can doubt our meeting. I will send this letter with Sambuvarayar's son, Kandamaran. You may send your reply through him. I, the most unfortunate Nandini, write these words to you.

She completed the letter with great difficulty. When her maid brought Kandamaran to the gazebo she asked him to sit down.

Unable to look at Nandini in the eye Kandamaran was looking elsewhere.

'You don't wish to look at me with your eyes that have gazed upon Kundavai's face!' Nandini said with a playful smile. Her words and smile dazzled him into dizziness.

'A thousand Kundavais are not comparable to one Nandini!' mumbled Kandamaran

'Still, if Kundavai moves her little finger, you will fly to the heavens and bring Lord Indra's throne! But you won't even sit down by my side even if I beg you.'

Kandamaran sat down quickly.

'If you order it, I will go to the abode of Lord Brahma and bring his head for you! My Queen, please don't mention Kundavai's name. My blood boils to think of her sympathy towards that treacherous Vandiyathevan.'

'In fact, you managed your conversation with Kundavai very well when you met her. What a fantastic description of the imaginary encounter you had with your friend!'

Kandamaran was embarrassed and said, 'I had to say something. That's why I said it. But it is true that he stabbed me.'

'Sir, please recollect all the details of that incident as to what really happened on that night. When you came back through that underground passage with Madurandakan, you met me and Senior Paluvettarayar. Do you remember that?' asked Nandini.

'Yes, I remember. I can never forget that meeting. I only remember that I was mesmerized on seeing you.'

'I remember your words. "Sir, I had heard a lot about the beauty of your daughter! Today I see that beauty now, here!"'

'Oh! Is that what I said? Perhaps that is why he was furious. He doesn't like me much...'

'Never mind! I like him. I must have performed several penances to have a husband like him.'

Kandamaran was confused by her words. He did not know what to say.

'Will you trust me and help me with something?'

'I am ever at your service.'

'You must go to Kanchi on my behalf. I'll give you a letter; you must deliver it to Prince Aditya Karikalan in Kanchi. You must also invite him to be your guest in your palace at Kadamboor. Your family, my family and some other important families in this country are facing some grave dangers. Do you know who is behind all this?'

'Tell me, my Queen!'

'She who came to visit you in my house. That witch.'

'Oh! You mean Princess Kundavai?' Kandamaran asked curiously.

'Yes. She has sent your friend Vandiyathevan to Lanka. Do you know why? Collecting medicines is just an excuse. She is not concerned about the Emperor's health. She is keen on crowning her beloved puppet brother Arulmoli and then your dear friend Vandiyathevan will be the real Emperor.'

'Oh! Is that possible? It must be stopped at all costs. We must inform my father and your husband immediately.'

'It's of no use telling them. They won't believe it. We must overcome Kundavai's tricks with tricks. If you help me, it is possible.'

'Order me, my Queen!'

'Carry this letter carefully and deliver it to the Prince in Kanchi.'

Saying this, she extended her hand and gave him the casket tube of letters. Kandamaran, ensnared in a net of passion, lost his mind, grabbed her hand instead of the casket tube.

'I will do anything for you!' He babbled.

At that moment, a loud noise was heard. Senior Paluvettarayar was hurrying down the path leading to the garden gazebo.

68

Wax in Fire

Kandamaran was terrified to think that Senior Paluvettarayar might misunderstand the intimacy between him and Nandini.

Old men who marry young girls are always suspicious. Was that the cause of his terrible anger? What will he do? I must be prepared.

Such thoughts troubled Kandamaran. However, an astonishing scene took place, contrary to his expectations.

When Senior Paluvettarayar entered, Nandini turned to him and smiled, blinking her large, dark eyes.

'My Lord! I was worried that you may be delayed much longer in your journey. Luckily, you have come back soon.'

On looking at her and hearing her voice, the old man's anger melted like wax in the flaming fire. He gave a stupid laugh.

'Yes, my job was done. I came back.'

He then looked at Kandamaran,

'What is this young fellow doing here? Is he composing love poems for you?'

After asking this, he laughed at his own joke.

Kandamaran's face turned red. Nandini laughed louder. 'He knows nothing about love or poetry. The only thing he knows is to fight and be wounded. Luckily, his wound is now healed. He was talking about returning home.'

'What can one say about the bravery of modern youth! I have participated in more than twenty-four campaigns and have borne more than sixty wounds. I was never bedridden. This youth was wounded on his back! That's why it has taken so many days.' He laughed mockingly.

'My dear, his wound in not merely physical. He is also mentally affected because of having been stabbed by his dear friend. That night he was wounded... Don't you remember what happened?'

Nandini looked into Senior Paluvettarayar's eyes with a meaningful stare. His mood changed.

'Yes, you are correct. I came here to give you some important news. He can also hear it. I believe a man has been arrested on suspicion as a spy at Mathottam in Lanka. Apparently, he had a sealed letter addressed to Arulmoli. Based on the descriptions, I think it could be this boy's dearest friend. That fellow must be really capable. See how he escaped our men and landed in Lanka.'

Both men did not see the expression that flashed across Nandini's face for a second.

'My Lord, I am not surprised about his escape. I have told you many times that your brother does not have the capability to command this Fort. His men are just like him!' Nandini ridiculed.

'When you said that about my brother, I did not believe you. Now, I agree. Listen to another odd story. Apparently, the signet ring with our Paluvoor symbol was with him. He refused to reveal how he came to be in possession of that signet ring.'

Nandini sighed lightly.

'How did he get our palm tree signet ring? What does your brother say about it?'

'If you hear what he said, you will laugh. He says that the signet ring must have gone to the spy from you.'

Upon saying this, Senior Paluvettarayar laughed a thundering laugh. Bushes trembled and the gazebo shook.

Nandini joined in his laughter.

'Do you know what else he said, your brother-in-law? It is even more funny! He says that while you were returning to Tanjore Fort in your palanquin, you met that handsome youngster. And he had even visited this palace. So, the ring must have gone to him through you or the sorcerer who comes to meet you often. My brother tells me all these imaginary tales to hide his mistakes!'

Senior Paluvettarayar laughed noisily once again.

'I should not have doubted your brother's intellect. I am surprised that you kept quiet, listening to all his accusations.'

Her facial expression changed once again; his lips trembled and his eyes turned fiery. Senior Paluvettarayar was one of the bravest men on earth, who had faced many lances and swords in several battlefields but he could not handle this petty anger of Nandini. His posture and words became vulnerable.

'My dear, did you think I was listening to him passively? I scolded him for his incompetence and almost reduced him to tears. Had you seen him, you would have felt sorry for him.'

Kandamaran, who was listening to all this, felt uncomfortable. He was filled with fear for Nandini and contempt for Senior Paluvettarayar. He wanted to leave. He cleared his throat.

'Sir!'

Nandini looked around.

'While talking about the talents of your brother, we completely forgot this young man. He wants to go home.'

'Yes, he can. His father must be worried that he stayed back at Tanjore for such a long time.'

'I wish to send a letter through him. May I do that?'

'What letter? For whom?'

'To the Prince in Kanchi.'

Senior Paluvettarayar looked at both Nandini and Kandamaran with distrust.

'A letter for the Prince! From you? Why?'

'Kundavai has written a letter to her younger brother and sent it through his friend. Why shouldn't the Young Queen of Paluvoor write a letter to the elder brother?' Nandini asked.

'Did Kundavai send the letter? How did you know this?' Senior Paluvettarayar asked.

'Why do you think I consult the sorcerer so often? I found out by his predictions. You are aware of the competence of your brother's men. It looks like they found out and reported the source of the signet ring which the spy had but they never reported about the letter sent by Kundavai.'

'Our men did not report about the signet ring. The Prime Minsiter who returned from Mathottam informed me.'

'At least, did the Prime Minister inform you about Kundavai's letter?'

'No!'

'My Lord! You must take heed of my warnings. Every official in this Empire is scheming against you. You must realize the truth now! I am not saying things just because of revelations by the sorcerer. I summoned the doctor's son arrested at Kodikkarai. He also confirmed the news that Kundavai had sent the letter to her brother in Lanka.'

She turned to Kandamaran. 'Sir! Please deliver this letter directly to the Prince at Kanchi. If he gives any reply, please forward it to me. Don't forget to invite the Prince to your palace at Kadamboor.'

'Can I inform my father that this is approved by Senior Paluvettarayar?' Kandamaran asked with some hesitation.

'You can. My wish is his will. Am I correct my Lord?' Nandini asked.

'Yes, yes.' Her confused husband could not say anything against Nandini's wishes. He simply nodded his head as if he understood.

After Kandamaran left, Nandini turned her mesmerizing look on Senior Paluvettarayar. She spoke in a honeyed voice.

'My Lord! I think you have lost your trust in me. My brother-in-law's jealousy has won.'

'Never! Nandini, never! I might lose my trust in my sword but not in you. I might lose faith in the heavens but, not in you.'

'Then, why did you question me like that in front of that boy? I felt so disgraced!'

Tears filled her eyes as she said this.

Senior Paluvettarayar was bewildered.

'My darling! Don't punish me like this!'

Wiping away her tears with his scarf, he picked up her hands to console her with mumbled words. 'But I do not understand some of your actions. Don't I have the right to ask?'

'You have all rights, it is my duty to reply. All I ask is that you should not question me in front of others. Now that we are alone, ask me whatever you want.'

'Why are you writing to Aditya Karikalan? Why do you want him to be at Kadamboor? Is he not the first enemy?'

'No. Aditya Karikalan is not our first enemy. That snake at Palayarai is our first enemy. I invited her to our house for a reason; I am writing to Karikalan inviting him to Kadamboor for that same reason. My Lord! Recall what I have said several times. I have told you that Kundavai has a secret plan. I have found out that secret. She is hell-bent on discarding the claims of everyone and place her darling brother Arulmoli on this throne at Tanjore. That is why she has sent a messenger to Lanka. That is why she has visited Tanjore. We must destroy her plans with counter-schemes. Now, do you understand why I am sending the letter to Kanchi?'

Nandini's questions totally confused the old man's intellect.

'Yes, I understand,' he mumbled incoherently, though he understood nothing.

'My Lord, this Empire has grown in greatness because of the service by you and your forefathers. I won't sleep even a wink, by night or day, till I place you on the golden throne of this Empire. Until that day, if you suspect me for any reason, please kill me with your sword.'

'My darling, do not torture me with such horrible words!' Senior Paluvettarayar said.

69

Blood-Thirsty Sword

Vandiyathevan reached the coastal city of Mathottam on the banks of river Palavi in Lanka. The city was very pleasing to the eyes with tall trees, lush green groves of mangoes, jacks, coconuts, palmyras, arecas, plantains and sugarcanes. There were numerous monkeys on the treetops and humming bees and baby-talk parrots everywhere.

The harbour was filled with large ships and goods were piled in mounds amidst the roaring murmur of sea waves. A city which used to be full of pilgrims now appeared crowded with soldiers bearing shields and swords.

The city had been transformed into a centre of war over the past hundred years. Armies coming from the Tamil land embarked and disembarked from this harbour. The city had changed hands several times under the Singhalese kings for a while and later under the Pandiya kings. Since Paranthaka's times, it was totally under the control of the Cholas.

Vandiyathevan tried to enter the fort but the soldiers took him into custody. As the commander of the Chola forces in Lanka, Bhoothi Vikrama Kesari, the elder chieftain of Kodumbalur was busy with the Prime Minister on that day, he ordered the guards to take away the letter and the Paluvoor signet ring from Vandiyathevan and place him in custody till he returned.

On the first day he had a good rest. On the second day, nuisance started. A cat came into his cell and disturbed his sleep. He threw it into the next cell and there followed a verbal fight between a man and the cat for quite some time. Finally, when the man in the next cell shouted as to who had thrown the cat into his cell, Vandhiyathevan maintained complete silence. When he heard a noise in his cell, he opened his sleepy eyes to see Alvarkkadiyan standing before him. He was somewhat confused to see him in here.

Why has this fellow come here? Has he come to help, or trouble me? Vandiyathevan called out to him.

'Nambi, I thought of you and here you are, right before me.'

'Young man! Were you thinking of me? You should be thinking of Lord Rama,' Alvarkkadiyan replied.

'I must really compliment you on your intuition; I was really thinking of Lord Rama and his disciple Hanuman, the monkey. When I thought of Hanuman, I remembered you!'

'Young man! Hanuman is the best among the devout. Don't compare me with the great Hanuman. Hanuman killed the demons in Lanka but I could not handle even a simple cat! See how the cat has scratched me,' Alvarkkadiyan pointed at his bleeding limbs.

'Oh Sir! Why did you pick a fight with a cat?'

'I didn't pick a fight with it. The cat picked a fight with me.'

'Nambi, I know a secret...'

'What secret?'

'That cat came to me too, it didn't scratch me. But it has attacked you. You know why? Because, it is a Saivite cat that does not like Vaishnava followers.'

'Really? Had I known this earlier I would have given it a severe blow with my staff. Anyway, how did you get caught here?'

'I showed them the Paluvoor signet ring, thinking that it would have magical powers in this city also but it turned out to be a mistake,' said Vandiyathevan.

'Yes, it is a blunder. Here, the commander is the elder chieftain of Kodumbalur. Don't you know of the rivalry between the clans of Kodumbalur and Paluvoor?'

'I did not know that!'

'I've come here to help you.'

Alvarkkadiyan now handed over the roll of palm leaf letter and the signet ring which the guards had taken away earlier from Vandiyathevan.

Vandiyathevan accepted them eagerly. Until that moment he had thought that Nambi was playing tricks on him to learn his secrets. But he changed his opinion now.

'Nambi, how did you get these?'

'The Commander gave them to me. We can leave whenever you are ready.'

'Sir, do you know the whereabouts of Prince Arulmoli?'

'Yes, I do. The Commander has asked me to go with you as your guide. I'll come if you agree.'

'Nambi, I would like to meet the Commander before I leave.'

'Sure.'

70

Rogue Elephant

Commander Bhoothi Vikrama Kesari, the elder chieftain of Kodumbalur (Vanathi's paternal uncle) was an elderly, experienced warhorse with personal experience of conducting numerous war campaigns thereby winning the confidence of the Chola Emperor. His younger brother faced defeat in an earlier Lankan war and lost his life. Therefore, as Commander of the Lankan war, he was eager to restore the name of his clan. Due to rivalry, Lord Paluvoor was raising several hurdles to the proper conduct of this war campaign in Lanka.

Vandiyathevan would have faced a tough situation had he been brought before the Commander with the Paluvoor signet ring. Fortunately, the Commander had reported to the Prime Minister about Vandiyathevan's arrival in Lanka as a messenger to Prince Arulmoli. The Prime Minister ordered the Commander to help Vandiyathevan and also sent Alvarkkadiyan to accompany him.

The Commander was impressed with Vandiyathevan and said so to Alvarkkadiyan.

'You are lucky to have this brave young man as your companion for the journey across the forest...'

'Sir, I don't need an escort; my wooden staff is enough.'

'Then, you can be his escort. Arrange for proper food for him before you leave. Food services are inadequate in Lanka. Mahinda's armies have destroyed all the irrigation tanks and canals affecting agriculture and farming.'

'This young man is very smart. Nambi, take him to our treasury and give him all the clothes and ornaments before you leave.'

Vandiyathevan bowed to the Commander in thanks.

'Princess Kundavai has ordered me to personally deliver some messages about Vanathi to the Prince.'

'I have never met a youth as intelligent as you!'

With these words the Commander embraced Vandiyathevan. He then spoke.

'You must leave as soon as possible.'

Vandiyathevan asked hesitantly, 'Sir, is this Vaishnavite gentleman accompanying me? Can I not leave without him?'

'It will not be easy for you to find Prince Arulmoli without Nambi. He is also carrying an important letter to the Prince. Better that you both journey together.'

After saying this, the Commander took Vandiyathevan aside and whispered in his ears.

'Nambi won't hinder your mission. But, be careful with him; find out what message he delivers to the Prince and report to me.'

Initially, Vandiyathevan suspected that Alvarkkadiyan had been sent to keep a watch over him. But now, *he* had been told to keep an eye on *him* instead. Vandiyathevan inwardly rejoiced at the reversal of roles.

Vandiyathevan and Alvarkkadiyan went eastward escorted by two soldiers. In the beginning, they passed through townships and villages but soon they had to go through the deep jungles. They found most of the tanks and lakes broken, with no water for farming, on account of the evils of war. They heard the frightening noises of wild animals— jackals, panthers, tigers, cheetahs, bears, elephants, etc.—in that forest.

Suddenly they heard a roaring sound, like the sound of sea waves, at a distance. Vandiyathevan was curious.

'There is no sea around here! Then what is that noise?'

'There must be a lake close by and elephant herds must be drinking water there.'

'Oh God! What if we are caught in the midst of that elephant herd?'

'There is nothing to worry about it. Elephants in groups won't harm us. They will simply pass us by without even glancing at us.'

All of them stopped under a tree. The soldier who was accompanying them quickly climbed the towering forest tree and looked out and cried out as he hastily climbed down.

'Sir, a single rogue elephant is pulling out trees, breaking branches and coming this way.'

'Oh! How to escape?' Nambi was terrified and began looking around.

Vandiyathevan turned to him.

'You just now said there was nothing to fear about a herd of elephants. But now you are afraid of a single elephant!'

'Dear man! A single rogue elephant is like a thousand wild elephants. None can face its fury.'

'We three men have spears and swords. You have your staff!'

'A thousand spears can do nothing to a rogue elephant. Look, there is a steep hillock. Let us climb up it and escape.'

After they had run a few yards, they realized that there was a deep valley before the hillock. The elephant was coming with a thundering roar reverberating from all sides.

It came closer and closer towards Alvarkkadiyan. If he took two steps backwards, he would fall into that deep valley. Bushes and shrubs prevented their escape on the sides.

Frightened, Vandiyathevan raised his spear but his hand refused to cooperate. Even thunderbolts from heaven could not stop that rogue elephant. At this moment, Alvarkkadiyan's actions provoked laughter.

Alvarkkadiyan was waving his wooden staff and shouting at the rogue elephant.

'Stop, stop! You will be ruined if you come any closer! I will kill you and bury you alive. Stop! Stop!'

71

Her Word Is Gospel

Alvarkkadiyan threw his wooden staff at the elephant and suddenly disappeared. They could see only his scarf on a tree branch.

The elephant came closer to the spot where Alvarkkadiyan had disappeared. Suddenly, the beast bent its forelegs as if it was kneeling down but toppled forward! A deafening noise echoing in all directions was heard and that mountain-like elephant disappeared, rolling down the valley raising a cloud of dust caused by the dislodged rocks and stones.

The elephant had fallen into the deep valley. The rogue elephant and the roguish Alvarkkadiyan had gone to their Creator in an instant!

A shiver ran through Vandiyathevan's body and he was upset beyond description. He stepped closer to the edge which had swallowed both the man and the beast and looked down. For a while nothing could be seen because of the cloud of dust.

Suddenly a voice was heard.

'What are you looking at? Why don't you give me a helping hand?'

Vandiyathevan jumped back on hearing this voice. To his astonishment, he found Alvarkkadiyan holding onto the roots of a large tree and swinging. Vandiyathevan's joy knew no bounds.

'Oh! Sir! You have sent that rogue elephant to heaven but you have stayed back in this heaven of *Trisanku*!' (Trisanku is a mythical heaven between the world of the Gods and the mortals.) Vandiyathevan clapped his hands and beckoned the two footmen. All of them lifted stocky Alvarkkadiyan with a rope.

'Come on! Get going! We must somehow reach the Royal Way

before nightfall. Where is my scarf? Where is my staff?'

'No hurry. Rest a little while longer, we can leave after you feel better,' said Vandiyathevan. They heard the howl of a jackal. Vultures and eagles began circling above.

'An elephant's death is not an ordinary incident. All beasts and birds will gather to feast on its dead body. We might become their side dishes, if we don't hurry up!' Alvarkkadiyan exclaimed.

The four men walked down that forest path as quickly as they could. A little after dusk, they reached the Royal Way, busy with people and vehicles.

The people living in those wayside villages and the shopkeepers were Singhalese. Tamil soldiers were patrolling the highway. They were living a fearless life under the Chola rule.

'Who has control over these areas?' Vandiyathevan asked.

'Chola armies have captured all areas up to Dampallae. Beyond that, Simhagiri mountains and the fortress is under the enemy, Mahinda.'

'What about the civilians in these areas?'

'The strategy adopted by Ponniyin Selvan in the warfare has not affected commoners. Buddhist Monks are happy about Ponniyin Selvan's war strategy. In fact, the Prince had ordered to repair and rebuild all the Buddhist temples damaged due to war. When I meet our Prince, I will tell him, "I don't like your actions one bit!"' Alvarkkadiyan said.

'Tell him that without fail! Who is this Prince to do things you dislike?!' Vandiyathevan spoke sarcastically.

'Young man, he has some sort of charming powers. Even his critics are hypnotized when they come before him; only one person has that power—the power to stand and talk in front of the Prince...'

'Whom did you mean when you talked about the person who can influence him?'

'The whole world knows that I am talking about his sister, Princess Kundavai. Her word is gospel to our Prince.'

'Oh! You are talking about Princess Kundavai of Palayarai. I thought you meant Young Queen Nandini of Paluvoor.'

'Nandini also has a unique power, but it is of a different type. Suppose a man is falling into hell, Kundavai will stop his fall and take him to heaven. Nandini's power is more exceptional, she will convince the falling person that hell is, in fact, heaven.'

How well he has estimated Nandini's character and her enchanting powers. Perhaps his claim that Nandini is his sister, could be true.

They walked for a while in silent thought till they heard the sound of galloping horses. The horses came closer being ridden at the speed of lightning, raising a cloud of dust like a mini tornado. Vandiyathevan immediately recognized one of the men seated on one of those horses.

Aha! That is Parthiban, trusted friend of Prince Karikalan in Kanchi. He does not care too much for me. How and why did he come here to Lanka? Where is he going?

The horses pulled up all of a sudden; Parthiban saw Vandiyathevan and spoke sarcastically.

'What is this, young man? How did you arrive here? They said that you had suddenly vanished from Tanjore. I was sure that the Paluvettarayars would have sealed your fate.'

'Can the chieftains of Paluvoor clan finish my story so easily?'

'Yes, of course. There is none to compare with you when it comes to saving your own life and somehow escaping...'

'Sir! I will save my life when it is necessary. I will readily give up my life when needed.'

'What happened to the assignment given to you by the Prince?' Parthiban asked.

'Accomplished, I have personally delivered the letters meant for the Emperor and the Princess.'

'Any news about Prince Arulmoli on your way? Has he come back to Anuradapura?'

'Sir, how will we know about such matters? We came by the

jungle path and a rogue elephant chased me. You know how I...'

'Enough of your story.' Parthiban cut him off and turned his horse around.

Alvarkkadiyan had been surreptitiously examining the other three horsemen as he was talking to Parthiban. When all had galloped away, he turned to speak to Vandiyathevan.

'Brother, did you notice those other three men with fiery eyes? Did you recognize any of them?'

'No. I have never seen any of them.'

'Of course. You could not have seen them. I have seen two of them, at midnight, near the war memorial of Thirupurambiyam. They were swearing a horrible oath.'

Alvarkkadiyan's whole body shivered.

'What was that horrible oath they took?'

'They swore an oath to destroy every rootstock of the Chola clan...'

'How did they manage to enter this island? Cunning fellows. How did they manage to join company with Parthiban?'

Alvarkkadiyan became quiet after posing these questions. Vandiyathevan remembered something that happened at Kodikkarai. Poonkulali's brother had taken two men across, to Lanka, in his boat. Were those two men part of these three? What was the connection between them and Parthiban?

They were now approaching Dampallae, the holy city of Buddhists.

72

The Elephant Driver

Vandiyathevan and Alvarkkadiyan entered the holy city of Dampallae. They saw astonishing sculptures of Buddha and Hindu gods. It was a festival day with a lot of pilgrims and Buddhist monks from far and wide including China. Street corners were filled with baskets full of lotus buds and champaka flowers.

Alvarkkadian approached a group of Buddhist monks to chat with them.

'There is a special festival in the Buddha Vihar (temple) in honour of two important Chinese pilgrims. They are returning after visiting Simhagiri.'

A beautifully decorated elephant was coming down the street with two Chinese pilgrims along with the elephant driver. The crowd gathered there, raised cheers.

'Did you see the elephant?' Alvarkkadiyan asked.

'Yes Sir, I saw. What a huge elephant! Shall we see if there is any ravine close by?'

'No need. Let us just stand by this roadside and watch.'

They waited by the roadside as the elephant procession came closer. The elephant went past. Vandiyathevan's eyes focussed on the pilgrims seated on the elephant wondering about the devotion of the Chinese pilgrims.

'Their pilgrimage is not disturbed even during war time. Prince Arulmoli has ensured their safety! Who else could have thought of it? But where is our Prince now? How to find him in this unfamiliar land?'

'Brother! Did you notice the elephant driver?' Alvarkkadiyan asked.

'The elephant driver! I didn't notice him.'
'Incredible! Did you notice the elephant driver's eyes light up?'
'What? Were any lamps lit in that elephant drivers's eyes?'
'What a peculiar fellow you are. Never mind, follow me.'

They followed the elephant and the procession behind it. The elephant stopped in front of the Buddha Vihara. The elephant driver whispered something in the elephant's ear and it knelt down with folded forelegs. The pilgrims descended. The Buddhist monks from the Vihara welcomed them with flowers.

The elephant driver took the elephant to some men standing there. After handing over the elephant to one of them, he pointed towards Alvarkkadiyan, said something to another and quickly walked away. The man with whom the elephant driver had spoken to approached Alvarkkadiyan.

'Sir, are you ready to come with me?'
'I've been waiting for you,' said Alvarkkadiyan.

The man took him to a wayside resthouse nearby. The man then climbed up a tree and kept watch.

'What is all this mystery about? I don't understand,' said Vandiyathevan.

'Be patient,' advised Alvarkkadiyan.

Two saddled horses were brought. Vandiyathevan became anxious about there being only two horses. What was the mystery about the elephant driver? Vandiyathevan tried to recall the face of the elephant driver but could not remember.

'Sir, who was the elephant driver?' asked Vandiyathevan.
'Can't you guess?'
'Was he Ponniyin Selvan?'
'You said that the pilgrims were returning from Simhagiri.'
'Yes.'
'Isn't Simhagiri still under enemy control?'
'Yes.'
'Is the Prince venturing amidst enemies?'

'Yes. Our Prince has visited not only Simhagiri but also the heartland of enemy territory with these pilgrims.'

'Why should he take such risks?'

'He is eager to see those towns and the wealth of sculpture and art in those places.'

'What enthusiasm! What a prince!'

Hoof-beats of galloping horses were heard. The footman who was watching, climbed down the tree quickly and unbound the two horses. He mounted on one asking Alvarkkadiyan to get on the other horse with instructions to follow the horses that would pass through that way.

'What about a horse for me?' asked Vandiyathevan.

'I have orders only to bring him.'

'Whose orders?'

'I cannot reveal that.'

'I must see the Prince immediately, I have important messages for him.'

'I know nothing about that, Sir.'

Alvarkkadiyan mounted the horse and said,

'Be patient, Brother! I will tell the Prince about you.'

'Nambi, are you not aware of the urgency of the message I am carrying?'

'Give that letter to me, I can deliver it.'

'That is impossible!'

'Then be patient. I cannot do anything else.'

Vandiyathevan boiled with anger. The Commander had asked him to keep an eye on Alvarkkadiyan when he delivered his message. It would not be possible now.

Some horses came closer and galloped past them at lightning speed; when both men on the horses took up the reins of their horses, an unexpected incident occurred. Vandiyathevan caught hold of the leg of the man on the horse and pulled him down to the ground; he quickly mounted that horse and galloped away as fast as it would go. Alvarkkadiyan followed. The fallen man made a hue and cry and threw his sword at Vandiyathevan but the sword flew past him and struck a tree.

Both the horses galloped at lightning speed following the horses ahead of them. Alvarkkadiyan felt happy and encouraged.

'Well done, Brother!'

73

Fistfight

The horses were galloping ahead in pitch darkness. Vandiyathevan wondered if Alvarkkadiyan had betrayed him as he was clueless about where they were heading.

Fortunately, moonlight showed them the way. Suddenly, he heard many human voices amidst cheerful sounds of dancing and singing. Light in the darkness showed soldiers camping merrily in the middle of the forest. Were they Cholas or enemies?

Vandiyathevan had very little time to think about this; one of the riders leading him suddenly turned around and came up close to him. The horseman slapped Vandiyathevan. He was completely disoriented. The man then plucked his knife and threw it away and landed him a heavy punch which unseated Vandiyathevan. Enraged, Vandiyathevan returned the blow on the man who had unseated him. The man did not accept the beating quietly. He showed his strength by striking back. By now both entered into a fistfight like demons and two huge fighting elephants.

Alvarkkadiyan and the other two men were curiously watching this amazing fistfight in the dancing moonlight. Very soon footsteps were heard; some soldiers came closer with lighted torches. Soon, a sizeable crowd gathered to witness the fantastic fistfight.

Vandiyathevan was thrown to the ground; the unknown assailant sat on his chest and snatched the roll of sealed letters. After taking the letter, the man jumped aside towards the torch light.

With measureless rage, Vandiyathevan shouted,

'Wretched Nambi! You have betrayed me. Get that letter from him!'

'Dear man! I cannot do that!' replied Alvarkkadiyan.

'I've never met a coward like you! How foolish of me to have trusted you.'

Alvarkkadiyan came closer to him whispering,

'You fool, the letter has reached the person it was addressed to. Why are you blabbering uselessly?'

Others noticed the face of the man who was reading the letter under the torch light. Loud cheers rose up.

'Long live Ponniyin Selvan!'

'Long live Ponniyin Selvan!'

Their cheers filled the forest. Birds nesting on the trees woke up, noisily echoing their ecstasy with wingbeats and shrill calls. More men came running to find out the cause for all the commotion.

When the victorious man noticed the bulging crowd, he looked around and said,

'All of you assemble for the feast.'

Upon this, the noisy crowd became silent and went to assemble at the large dining place.

Vandiyathevan was wonderstruck. All his pains were drowned in a sea of joy. This is our beloved Prince Arulmolivarman! What strength in his fists! How brisk he is! No wonder they say that even if you are beaten, be beaten by a champion. He has the charisma and dignity of Arjuna of the epics, strength of a Bhima of the legends. No wonder the whole world is full of praise for him!

Prince Arulmoli approached Vandiyathevan with a smile.

'Welcome friend! Welcome to beautiful Lanka! You have come so far crossing over seas, to join our brave Tamil soldiers in this far-off land. Are you happy about the chivalrous welcome given to you? Would you like some more fanfare?'

Vandiyathevan jumped with joy and bowingly said,

'My *beloved* Prince! I have delivered the letter sent by your gracious sister. My duty is over.'

'Well, your safety is my responsibility now. Did she give it to you personally?'

'Yes, My Prince. I had that good fortune. I journeyed day and night without stopping anywhere to bring it to you.'

'That is obvious or else you could not have come here so quickly. How can I thank you for your unique service?' Saying this, the Prince heartily embraced Vandiyathevan of the noble Vaanar clan. The gallant youth felt as if he was in paradise.

74

The Prince's Dinner Party

Thousands of Chola soldiers had assembled in that jungle. Gigantic stew pots filled with rice and beans were bubbling on huge stoves and meat was being cooked, the aroma spreading all around aroused the appetite of the soldiers. The soldiers were engaged in fun and frolic. When their darling prince joined them, their happiness knew no bounds.

Prince Arulmoli was seated on a tree-stump throne with his graceful garments and ornaments proclaiming his royalty. The Captain, Vandiyathevan and Alvarkkadiyan were seated near him. A play on a brave Tamil warrior who had fought against the Lankans was performed on this occasion to the enthralled audience.

The Prince and all others who watched the play cheered loudly with shouts of praise while the play was in progress. The Prince turned to Alvarkkadiyan.

'Did you both see the beautiful fresco paintings in the caves of Dampalle?'

'No, my Lord. We had no time. We can see those paintings and sculptures anytime. But, meeting you is not that easy. We met Parthiban at the royal highway but he informed us that you were not here.'

'Nambi, can you guess why he came here?'

'Yes, my Prince. Prince Karikalan has sent him here to escort you back to Kanchi City.'

'Absolutely right! You know the reason. Perhaps you also know the content of the letter brought here so safely by this friend of yours?'

'Your beloved sister has written that you should come back

immediately to Palayarai. Therefore, I brought this youth here safely to you through the forest trail; even there he tried to wrestle with a rogue elephant. I killed that wild beast with my wooden staff and brought him here safely.'

'Oh! Does that mean that you came to Lanka merely to guide him safely till he reached me?'

'No, my Prince. For my part, I have also brought you an urgent message.'

'What message?'

'Prime Minister feels that it is appropriate for you to remain here in Lanka for some more time.'

'All three elders send three different messages like this. What am I to do?' asked the Prince.

'My Prince, please forgive me for intervening. You must listen to the directive of your beloved sister,' said Vandiyathevan

'Why do you say that?'

'Because, your heart tells you to heed the orders of your sister.'

'I have been wishing for a brave young companion like you!' said the Prince with delight.

After the play, a sumptuous dinner was served. The Prince visited each table to enquire about their health and their families. The soldiers were in a sea of joy. Such acts of the Prince endeared him to one and all.

After socializing, the Prince went inside his tent along with Vandiyathevan and Alvarkkadiyan.

'See the enthusiasm of these soldiers! This whole island would have come under our control by now if only I was supported by the Paluvettarayars!'

On hearing this, Alvarkkadiyan said,

'My Prince! I am quite surprised about your concern for this place. But grave danger threatens the very foundations of the Chola Empire in the mainland!'

Vandiyathevan started pouring out what had been on his mind.

'Prince, the Paluvettarayar brothers keep the Emperor as if he was a prisoner. Some close relatives, high officials and chieftains have ganged up in a conspiracy. Your sister Princess Kundavai is mentally disturbed. Therefore, you should leave for Palayarai immediately!'

Then, Alvarkkadiyan confirmed what Vandiyathevan had mentioned. He also spoke about the midnight conspiracy that took place at the ruined war memorial of Thirupurambiyam.

'If treason or conspiracy is being contemplated, it is the Emperor who has to act. How can I venture into this matter without my father's consent?'

Vandiyathevan intervened,

'Prince, your father is sick and the Paluvettarayar brothers guard him like a prisoner. Your brother has also vowed not to visit Tanjore. Is it not your duty to safeguard the empire in such circumstances?'

'Why should the Prince go to Palayarai? I cannot understand this!' said Alvarkkadiyan.

The Prince was lost in thought for a while. 'Lust for land is a heinous crime. Because of this many sins are being committed on this beautiful earth!

'Do you know the history of Simhagiri Fort which I visited today?'

Alvarkkadiyan interrupted. 'No Prince, but isn't Simhagiri still under the control of enemy forces?'

'Yes, I have no intention of capturing that fort now. It would be a foolish waste of lives. There were two reasons for me going there. I had to fulfil my long-cherished desire to see the frescos of Simhagiri. My wish was fulfilled today...'

'The other reason...?'

'News reached me as soon as Parthiban landed at Triconamallee Hill. I avoided him today because...'

'Because...?'

'I also knew that the Prime Minister was at Mattotam. I expected some message from him. If two elders send word, I will have to obey the orders received first.'

'Prince! My suit has won. The first message you received is the one from your sister which I brought! You have to come with me to Palayarai,' said Vandiyathevan in a joyful tone.

'Prince, this fellow tricked you,' said Alvarkkadiyan.

'He did not trick me. I tricked myself. Both of you be patient for a while. Let's go to Anuradapura to meet Parthiban and decide after hearing what he has to say.'

75

City of Anuradapura

Prince Arulmoli, Vandiyathevan and Alvarkkadiyan left for Anuradapura early next morning. Vandiyathevan was brimming with joy and pride on accomplishing the task assigned by Princess Kundavai. His lifelong wish was also fulfilled by meeting the young Prince. He was astonished by the Prince's unconventional endearing approach and simplicity. He also understood the secret of his success. How simple he is with his men! He even won the love of the people he conquered in war.

They reached the outskirts of Anuradapura. A huge sculpture of Lord Buddha on the wayside drew their attention. Prince Arulmoli stopped near the statue and looked at it eagerly for some time.

'Well! What an exquisite piece of sculpture!'

Prince Arulmoli was focussing on the sculpture of Buddha and he touched the feet of the statue reverentially with his hands before mounting his horse.

'What is this? Is the Prince planning to convert to Buddhism?' remarked Vandiyathevan.

Ponniyin Selvan smiled,

'My devotion to Lord Buddha is not without reason. Those lotus feet of Lord Buddha gave me a message.'

'Oh! I did not hear anything!'

'It is a silent message.'

'What was the message?'

'The lotus feet of the Lord announces that I should visit the Lion Falls Lake at Anuradapura at midnight today,' said Prince Arulmoli.

They reached the city of Anuradapura at sunset. Vandiyathevan became speechless to see the beautiful ancient capital of Lanka.

As they came closer to the fortress, the crowd grew. Everyone—Tamils and Sinhalese, monks and householders, men and women, boys and girls—were in a jubilant mood, celebrating a carnival. Some of them were whispering among themselves after noticing the Prince. He made a sign to his companions and turned into a lane leading away from the *Royal Way*. He stopped beneath a grove of trees near a man-made hillock.

After dismounting from their horses, the three of them went to sit on some rocks overlooking the city.

'The biggest and most important festival is going on today,' said Prince Arulmoli.

'Everything is quiet with a big carnival amidst the war nearby,' said Vandiyathevan.

'Yes, people in the Chola Empire live and celebrate peacefully. Just as Krishna Jayanthi was celebrated in Palayarai these people are celebrating their carnival. These parts are also under the rule of Emperor Sundara Chola. Battles have to be fought on battlefields. Civilians should not suffer,' replied the Prince.

Being a festive occasion, no traveller was denied entry at the gates. All walked in freely. The guards were merely observing. The three men mingled with the crowds unnoticed.

Vandiyathevan noticed several mansions and buildings in various stages of construction and repair, thanks to the young Prince.

Why is he doing such things in a conquered land? Instead of looting and razing the enemy capital, why is this Prince rebuilding and holding carnivals?

Vandiyathevan brimmed with these thoughts.

They reached an old mansion with crumbling outer walls and dark windows. After dismounting, they walked towards the entrance. Prince Arulmoli clapped his hands thrice: a door opened like magic. The building seemed completely uninhabited. The Prince walked into that darkness. They reached the innermost courtyards of an ancient palace.

'We have to be a little careful here. Emperor Maha Sena might appear suddenly and chase us away!' spoke Prince Arulmoli.

'Who is Maha Sena?' asked Vandiyathevan.

'Maha Sena was the emperor who ruled this kingdom of Lanka six hundred years ago performing various good deeds for the people. People believe that his spirit still roams in this ancient palace. After him, no one has lived in this palace.'

Once inside, they were greeted by some soldiers to serve them. Refreshed after a bath and a simple meal, they went up to the terrace and viewed the city. Vandiyathevan turned to the prince and asked,

'Prince, you said that the statue of Buddha had asked you to go someplace at midnight?'

'Yes, we have to go there at midnight only. We still have time.'

Very soon a roaring sound, like the sea in a storm, was heard in the distance. Vandiyathevan turned to see a huge multitude of people moving continuously down the streets. In the midst of that sea of people, there were also hundreds of whale-like elephants.

'What is this? It seems like an enemy invasion!' said Vandiyathevan with some agitation.

'No, no! This is the biggest carnival of Lanka—the Parahara.'

Two eyes were insufficient to view this picturesque sight. Two million ears would not suffice to hear the music! The din raised by the drums, cymbals, horns, wind-pipes, tambourines deafened the ears. Such a beautiful carnival! The people in this crowd were in colourful costumes.

The tail end of the procession had turned the street corner; the noisy din of dancers and musical instruments as well as the roaring sounds of the crowd began to die down.

'We have just half an hour left for our appointment. Come, let us go!' said Prince Arulmoli.

They came down to the street and began walking in a direction away from the procession. The streets through which they walked were deserted. Very soon they reached the raised banks of a spreading lake. The lake was brimming with water, with gentle waves lapping at the shores under the bright moonlight. They climbed down the bank entering a beautiful garden; fragrance of various flowers assailed their noses. Man-made hillocks and reflecting pools could be seen here and there. One such elevated pool was carved like the face of a roaring lion: a cascade of water flowed out of its mouth to form another pool. The three men waited beside this pool.

Vandiyathevan was lost in thought,

All this is fine! But why and who has ordered the Prince to come here? Why did the Prince prevent me from bringing any weapons?

His mind flew across the sea towards Palayarai to Princess Kundavai and Vanathi. He tried to glean something by making the Prince talk.

'Prince, this place seems like the private garden of some old palace.'

Yes, this was a palace garden. King Dhutta Gamanu's palace was beside this garden a thousand years ago. Dhutta Gamanu's son, Saali, was walking in these gardens one afternoon. He saw a girl fetching water from these pools in a pot. He fell in love with her. He found that she was a girl from an ordinary background. He insisted upon marrying her in spite of her lowly social position. "Then you cannot ascend the throne!" roared his father. "I do not care for the throne," insisted the resolute son. Do you think any other prince in this world can say a thing like that?' asked Prince Arulmoli.

Vandiyathevan remembered the Ocean Princess who rowed her boat at Kodikkarai.

Is the Prince telling me this story with thoughts of that girl...? How can I raise a comment about Poonkulali?

Even as Vandiyathevan pondered about it, an astonishing thing happened. There appeared a cave behind the roaring lion's mouth. From that cave a hand holding a lamp appeared followed by the austere face of a Buddhist monk.

Vandiyathevan stood open mouthed as he watched this magical display. He held his breath wondering what could happen after that.

76

Throne of Lanka

The monk received the Prince and his companions.
'My heart is overjoyed to receive you here in this monastery. I welcome you on behalf of the Sangam of Buddhist monks. Who are these men standing here? Are they trustworthy? Will they be bound by the pledge?'

'Master, I trust these two as I trust my own hands,' replied the Prince.

'Then let them also come with us,' said the monk.

The monk was leading them. They entered the cave behind the cascade and walked into a narrow tunnel that twisted and turned for quite a distance.

Finally, they entered the main assembly with lights shining in all corners. The monks assembled there gave them a standing ovation raising slogans,

'May Buddha prevail! May the Order prevail!'

Their chief monk was seated on a dais. A jewelled, golden throne was before him. On a table beside the throne was a tray with a pearl-crown, a shining sword and a jewelled mace.

The Prince walked upto the abbot and bowed respectfully.

'Great Prince! This great congregation of Buddhists is happy to have your presence here today.'

All the monks in the congregation endorsed this with cheers of peace!

The abbot, Maha-thero, continued to speak.

'We are always obligated to your country which has given us

our Buddhist faith. But, since ancient times, the Cheras, Pandiyas and Kalingas who invaded our land committed many atrocities. They destroyed our Buddha temples, mansions, monasteries and dwellings. Till this day, no king has come forward to restore or rebuild those ruined places of worship. But Prince Arulmoli has taken up that divine task. This monastery appreciates this noble gesture of yours.'

The Prince bowingly accepted the good wishes from the Abbot who continued to speak.

'For many years the Perahara festival was not held in this city. In this worthy year you have ordered for the celebration of the great festival in a grand manner. We, at this monastery are extremely happy about this...'

Prince Arulmoli bowed his head once again.

'Great Sire, kindly command me for any other service to this Buddhist monastery!'

The Chief Monk smiled.

'Yes Prince! This monastery is confidently expecting more services from you.'

At this point the very aged senior-most monk of the monastery was carried in by the younger ones. He spoke with great difficulty,

'God bless you! Once, Asoka the great, the beloved of the gods ruled entire India under one canopy and spread the word of Buddha to the world. Now the gods decree that you shall rule a great empire like that and spread the word of Buddha. Prince, what is your reply?'

'Great Sire, the Divine Ones are all-powerful. But my humble mind is not able to comprehend their orders,' replied the Prince.

The great Abbot replied,

'Prince, this ancient throne that bore law-abiding kings over thousands of years now awaits you. Sit on this throne, wear this crown and hold the mace.'

Vandiyathevan was listening with rapt attention and was very eager to see the Prince accepting their divine order. But there was no change on Prince Arulmoli's face.

Like before, he spoke very calmly,

'Great Sire, how can that be possible? The king who sat on this throne and was crowned with these jewels is still alive, even though his whereabouts are not known...'

'Prince, the gods have ordained that the dynasty that rules Lanka now has to change... Men of this dynasty committed various heinous deeds and earned the curses of the Divine Ones: fathers killing their own sons; sons killing their fathers; brothers killing brothers; mothers killing their children. This dynasty which has committed such sinful deeds is not fit to rule and uphold Buddhist faith and law. Therefore, the dynasty has to change now. This congregation of Buddhist monasteries have the right to select the first monarch of the new dynasty. We, of this great congregation, select you. If you accept, we are ready to crown you this very night.'

The most profound silence prevailed in that assembly for some time. Prince Arulmoli rising from his seat greeted the assembly with folded palms.

'Great Sires, I bow before your magnanimity in presenting this ancient throne to me because of the love and trust you have for me. But your orders are beyond my capacity to fulfil. I came here to this island in obedience to the orders of my father, Emperor Sundara Chola. I cannot do anything without consulting him.'

The abbot interrupted.

'Prince, your father is unwell leading a life like a prisoner.'

'Yes, my father is unwell. Yet, I am bound by the orders of those who rule in his name.'

'We can also send an ambassador to Tanjore to get his consent.'

'What about the people of this land?'

'The people of this land will deem it to be a great fortune to have you as their king.'

'They will also agree. In this whole world more than any other opinion, I honour the opinion of my elder sister Kundavai. My mother gave me to this world, river Ponni saved my life, but my sister nurtured my mind and intellect. Even more important than her wishes are the command of a voice in my heart. My inner voice does not tell me to accept this exalted fortune. I beg you all to forgive me.'

Pin drop silence prevailed. After a while, the Abbot spoke once again.

'Prince, your words do not surprise us. We don't like to force you. You may respond even after a year. Never reveal about what happened here to anyone else. Don't share this secret even with your friends. Anyone disobeying or revealing these secrets will be subjected to terrible curses.'

After half an hour, Prince Arulmoli, Alvarkkadiyan and Vandiyathevan were once again walking down the moon-lit streets of Anuradapura. Vandiyathevan who had kept his mouth tightly shut during all the time inside the monastery, opened up all his pent-up thoughts.

'Prince, how could you refuse the throne of such a jewel of an island that was willingly presented to you?'

Prince Arulmoli simply smiled.

They were walking by the side of an old mansion. They heard someone clapping their hands across the street near the mansion. A figure stood over there.

'Come with me!' said the Prince as he crossed the street and went towards that figure followed by the other two. When they were halfway across the street, a loud rumbling was heard behind them. On looking back, they found the front porch of the old mansion was crumbling and falling down. If they had not turned to cross the street, the rubble would have fallen and buried them alive; fortunately, they escaped.

Vandiyathevan stood in the middle of the street looking at the rubble and wondering, while the other two had gone ahead. When he turned to join them, he could see the person who alerted them—a middle-aged lady standing in the moon-lit street. He couldn't believe his own eyes on seeing her. She looked very familiar.

How can this be possible? How could Nandini come to the streets of Anuradapura from Tanjore? Why should she come and stand here in the night like this?

In an instant, that figure disappeared like magic.

77

Is It Nandini?

Vandiyathevan walked quickly towards the spot where that woman was standing and staring. It looked like Nandini. Even before he reached, the woman vanished. When Vandiyathevan tried to follow her, the Prince stopped him.

'Prince, who was that woman?'

'That woman is the divine saviour of the Cholas.'

They looked at the spot across the street and saw a mound of debris formed by the crumbled porch of the old mansion. The debris could have easily buried a large elephant.

'My godmother appeared at the right time and saved our lives!' said Prince Arulmoli.

'Prince! Are you referring to that woman?'

'Yes, why did you try to follow her?'

'I thought she was the Young Queen of Paluvoor. Did you not see her?'

'It is your imagination. How could Nandini come here?' asked Alvarkkadiyan.

'I too noticed the facial resemblance. Come, let us go,' said the Prince.

They started walking in the bright moonlight. After some time, Alvarkkadiyan asked,

'Sir, what did that woman try to say to you using sign language?'

'She said that two enemies have come to kill me. But she said I have a long life.'

Vandiyathevan was shocked.

'Did she mean us?'

Arulmoli said laughingly,

'No, she did not specifically refer to you both. I won't be bothered even if it is you. She has saved my life several times before this.'

'Sir, I know who those enemies are. They are the men who came with Crown Prince Karikalan's friend Prince Parthiban, who came searching for you. Suddenly, two figures appeared on the terrace of that old mansion: it must be those men,' said Alvarkkadiyan.

'Nambi! Why didn't you say this before? You both go ahead, I'll come after searching that building,' said Vandiyathevan but Prince Arulmoli stopped him.

'You can't find them in that mansion. You both remain by my side till I order otherwise. Who knows what danger lurks where?'

'Sir, I won't leave you even for a moment!' replied Vandiyathevan

'I too won't leave you!' said Alvarkkadiyan Nambi.

Soon, they reached Maha Sena's palace to sleep. Moonbeams were dancing through the wide window.

Vandiyathevan vented out his anguish,

'Do you know how angry I was when you refused the crown? I felt like taking that crown and placing it on your head.'

Prince Arulmoli replied,

'My friend, wearing a crown is not that easy. We will talk about it later. It is very late; I can hear the people coming back from the Perahara celebrations. Let us go to sleep,' said the Prince.

'I cannot sleep. Only after I know the identity of that woman who saved us will I be able to sleep.'

'I don't know who she is. But I can tell you everything I know about her; come closer and sit by my side.'

78

Goddess Cauvery

Vandiyathevan and Alvarkkadiyan sat with eagerness near the Prince.

'When I was a young child, I went on a pleasure cruise on the Cauvery with my family. I was fascinated by the beautiful flowers floating on the water. But I was pained at the sight of those colourful flowers caught in the relentless swirls of water. I tried to save those flowers leaning over the side of the barge and I accidently fell into the river! Nobody noticed it. I was struggling for breath in the fast-flowing river.

Suddenly someone lifted me up. I was above the water in one instant. I saw the face of the person who saved me. Immediately the face was embossed in my mind. Later, I was given to someone else. Immediately I was surrounded by my parents, sister and brother pouring their love and affection on me. After awhile they raised a question as to who saved me. They looked around everywhere for that person. I too looked around but could not find that divine face. Then they decided that Goddess Cauvery herself had saved me. Since then, they have been offering prayers to Goddess Cauvery every year on that day.

I was always longing to see that Goddess. Whenever I visited the river, I would eagerly look around hoping to see her. As years passed, I lost all hopes of seeing her again. About a year ago, I came here to Lanka as the commander of the southern armies.

Commander Bhoothi Vikrama had already captured several regions of Lanka. Accompanied by a hundred men, I visited all the places under our control. In the course of those travels, we camped in a jungle very close to Elephant Crossing.

Suddenly one day a peculiar sorrowful cry was heard during the night, near that camp. We could not make out whether that cry was the call of a bird or a beast or a human. Initially our men in the camp ignored it. Later, the cry was heard even within the camp. Our men reported this to me. I brushed aside their fears. Any how, I was determined to find out the origin of the cries. One night, they crept upon the figure raising that cry. When they approached, that figure began to run away. It appeared to be a woman but they could not go near her. The cries continued every night. Our men were talking about it all the time. So, I decided to solve the mystery. The next night, I took a few men and started walking towards that cry. A woman emerged from behind the bushes. She looked at us for a second and started running. I ordered the men to stop and decided to follow her alone. She looked back and welcomed me. She was the divine mother who had saved me from the river when I was a child! I stood staring at her divine face!

"Mother! Who are you? When did you come here? I have been looking for you all these years! If you want to meet me, please come directly without wailing."

I asked her many more questions. That gracious lady never replied. Her tear-filled eyes touched my heart. She wanted to say something but could not. I realized that she was deaf-mute. Sadness gripped me. Suddenly, she hugged me and kissed me. The next moment, she let go of me and started running again. I did not follow her. My men in the camp posed a lot of questions. I convinced them saying, "She is mentally disturbed." And also advised them not to follow her or worry about her if she comes here again!

The next time I saw her, she took me to her hut in the middle of the jungle with all love and affection. An oil lamp was burning in that cottage with an old man lying down there. He had delirious fever and cold with locked up jaws and bloodshot eyes. He was babbling something...'

Vandiyathevan waited for a while and then asked impatiently, 'What happened in that cottage? Please tell us...'

'Nothing happened in that cottage. She dragged me out. She conveyed her message to me with various hand signals. "Don't stay in these areas. This delirious fever may attack you." I took her signs as a divine warning and moved camp the same night. My men also were very happy about that.'

(The fever referred to here is about the pandemic malaria which had no cure in those days.)

Eloquent Paintings

'That mute woman followed me everywhere I went. She saved me from several dangers. She would appear and disappear at lightning speed. I quickly learnt the art of talking to her in sign language. I could even read her thoughts and I could sense her presence even when she was not visible. Even now... both of you go back to your beds and pretend to sleep!'

She appeared through the moon-lit window with a soft hissing sound, making some signs. Prince Arulmoli followed her out of the wooden palace. Vandiyathevan and Alvarkkadiyan also followed them. They walked a long distance in the moonlight along a tree-lined path which led to a herd of elephants. Soon they realized that those were mere stone elephants upholding a stupa. The mute woman pulled a handle under one of the elephants and a door opened revealing a flight of steps. She lit an oil lamp and asked only the Prince to follow. The others waited a little way away. In the dim light of the oil lamp, the Prince saw the eloquent paintings on the walls depicting the life of a woman. That woman in the story resembled the mute lady with the lamp. Prince Arulmoli understood that the mute woman had depicted her life-story through those paintings.

The drawings showed a young girl standing on the shores of an island with her father riding the waves on a catamaran and fishing in the sea waters. Next, the girl was walking down a jungle, a young man resembling a prince was sitting on a tree; a bear was climbing a tree as the prince was looking elsewhere... The girl screamed to warn the prince. The bear was now chasing her. The prince jumped down and threw his knife at the bear. The Bear and the prince began wrestling as the girl was watching them. Finally, he won and came to the girl to thank her. She shed tears in reply. The fisherman father came to explain that she was mute. He befriended her and wandered through the jungle in the island hand in hand. He made a garland of flowers and put it around her neck.

One day a ship reached that island to pick him up. The prince consoled her saying he will quickly return after meeting his dear and near ones. She became very sad. Her father saw her pathetic state and took her to a place which had a lighthouse. From there they went in a bullock cart to a city which had a fort. They saw the prince standing on a palace balcony with a crown surrounded by richly dressed noblemen and women. The disappointed girl ran and ran to reach the seashore, climbed the lighthouse tower and jumped into the rough sea.

She was rescued by a man sailing in a boat. He took her to a priest thinking she was possessed. The priest smeared holy ash on her to ward off the evil spirits. At that time, a queen came to worship at that temple. The priest told the queen about that girl. The queen was pregnant and she recognized that the girl was also pregnant just like her. She took the girl to the palace in her palanquin. The poor girl soon delivered twin babies. The queen asked for one of the babies for herself. Though initially the poor girl refused, soon she left both the babies in the palace and went away at midnight without informing anyone.

For many years, she wandered in the forests. She would visit the city to see her children now and then, hiding herself behind the trees along the river.

Once, the King's child fell into the river. Nobody in the boat noticed it. She jumped into the river and saved the child. After handing over the child to the King she left.

All these incidents were painted very realistically on that wall. Prince Arulmoli was looking at those paintings with vivid interest and admiration. When he reached the last painting, he said,

'I am the one saved and you are my saviour!'

The woman embraced Arulmoli pouring kisses on his forehead.

She took him to another wall in the chamber. The paintings on this wall were not about incidents in her life. They depicted various dangers that might befall the Prince. She warned him with eloquent signs about those dangers.

Vandiyathevan and Alvarkkadiyan were watching all this from a corner. Vandiyathevan thought the woman's face looked a lot like Nandini's.

The woman took them out through some steep steps. They looked around to see a fire burning in the middle of the city.

'Oh! Look at Emperor Maha Sena's palace flaming up in fire!' remarked Prince Arulmoli. 'Perhaps we would have become fodder for the Lord of fire had we remained there!'

'How can you identify from this distance that it is the palace where we were sleeping?'

'The paintings in the chamber spoke to me.'

'I did not hear them.'

'Paintings speak in a unique and eloquent language. Only those who know that language can understand. They spoke of some family secrets of my clan. They warned me to go away from this Lanka island immediately.'

'Let us go to sleep and leave at daybreak,' said the Prince.

Next day, they reached the Mahameha Gardens in the middle of Anuradapura.

Towards one corner of the garden stood three horses in readiness. They started riding out of the town.

They were slowly riding along the *Royal Way* and saw a dust cloud at a distance and heard the hoof-beats of several horses galloping towards them.

Thinking them to be enemies Vandiyathevan asked the Prince to draw his sword to strike at them.

80

Amazing Sword Fight

Prince readily drew out his sword from its sheath. Huge great swords of immense length and weight were in the hands of Vandiyathevan and Arulmoli.

The Prince dismounted from his horse said, 'I cannot tolerate your high-handedness any more. Let me decide once for all!'

Awestruck, Vandiyathevan was not sure if it was jest or danger! 'Why hesitate?'

The Prince started swirling his sword with both his hands like the epic heroes Arjuna, Bhima and Abhimanyu.

A fierce dual ensued between the Prince and Vandiyathevan. Alvarkkadiyan was perplexed at this sudden act of Arulmoli. But he thought there must be some purpose behind it. Perhaps it was a trick to divert the attention of those coming down the road at lightning speed. He took their horses to block the road and waited by their side holding the reins.

The horsemen reached the site of the fight with tiger flags in their hands.

Commander Bhoothi Vikrama and Prince Parthiban were seated on two beautiful royal white horses. An elephant with a saddle on top, walked ponderously behind thirty horsemen.

The horsemen were annoyed by the road block made by Alvarkkadiyan.

'Who is that?'

'Move!'

'Make way!'

Soon, soft whispering and exclamations of surprise and amazement went back and forth among them as they came to a halt. The soldiers jumped down from their horses and stood keenly watching the fantastic sword fight on the road.

Commander Bhoothi Vikrama and Parthiban also started watching the fight. Parthiban was provoked to see Vandiyathevan fighting with the Prince Arulmoli and drew his own sword saying,

'Utter nonsense! How can we tolerate his foolhardiness?'

'Be patient, Parthiba. Let us also watch this fantastic sword display. It is a long time since I saw anything like this!' said the Commander.

A large crowd gathered to witness the amazing fight. Wonderstruck, Poonkulali stood amidst the crowd with shock and surprise. When the swords flashed here and there, her eyes also flashed in step with them.

Suddenly Vandiyathevan's eyes caught sight of Poonkulali and he lost his concentration for a moment. That one moment was enough for Prince Arulmoli to dislodge Vandiyathevan's sword from his hand.

The cheers raised by the men around was like a roaring ocean. Vandiyathevan tried to pick up his sword when the Prince ran up to tightly embrace him.

'You did not lose to my skilful sword. You fought equally. But you lost to the swordplay of a maiden's eyes! Nothing wrong about it! It can happen to anyone!'

Vandiyathevan tried to reply but Commander Bhoothi Vikrama and Parthiban came closer.

'My Prince! I had sent this youth to you. Hope he has not misbehaved. Anyhow I really enjoyed the fight!' said the Commander.

'Yes Sir! Just jest! I showed him what is war.'

On hearing these words of their beloved Prince, the soldiers raised cheers even louder. Patting Vandiyathevan the Commander said,

'Son, indeed it was a fantastic sword fight! Truly you are a good companion to the Prince. Our Prince often gets these sudden urges to fight. Those who cannot keep up with his duels can't be his longtime friends.'

The Prince addressed Parthiban.

'Parthiba, I knew that you had come here to meet me. How is my brother at Kanchi? How is grandfather? Please give me the message from my brother and grandfather.'

Commander Bhoothi Vikrama turned to the Prince, 'Let us go to the nearby resthouse and discuss.'

While walking towards the highway resthouse Vandiyathevan said

'Prince, I forgot one important message!'

'What is the message?'

'There was a smart girl standing in that crowd watching our fight. You even mentioned that I lost to the swordplay of her eyes. Do you know her? Please recollect, Sir! If you do not recall her name, her heart will break! You were about to get into your boat to board your ship at Kodikkarai. At that time, a lone girl rowed her boat and came ashore on the beach. You watched her with amazement and asked the Lighthouse Keeper, "Who is this girl?" He replied, "She is my daughter." And you said, "Is that so? I thought that she was the Ocean King's daughter—the Ocean Princess!" She has not forgotten your words. I would not have reached Lanka but for her help.'

'Now that you mention it, I vaguely recollect that incident. But what is this Ocean Princess of Kodikkarai doing here at Anuradapura?'

'Perhaps, she has come in search of you.'

As he said this Vandiyathevan turned back to look at Poonkulali. All her attention was focussed on the Prince.

By then they had reached the nearby resthouse.

Arulmoli looked at Parthiban and said,

'What is the message from my brother and my grandfather?'

'Prince, I have come here to escort you back to Kanchi as advised by your grandfather and brother. Your grandfather feels that you and your brother should be together at this time. Therefore, come to Kanchi before marching to Tanjore and destroying all those vile conspirators…'

Prince Arulmoli who was keenly listening to this message covered his ears and said,

'Never utter such alarming words.' He also expressed his disinterest in the throne.

'It is your brother's will and your wish. It is something between you two brothers. Visit Kanchi immediately. Both of you can discuss and decide,' said Parthiban.

'Parthiba, how can we decide without consulting my father the Emperor?'

'Commander, what is your suggestion? Our trusted prime minister has asked me to remain in Lanka for some more time. And you also endorse the idea. My sister has asked me to come immediately to Palayarai. What do you think?' asked the Prince.

'Prince, till this morning I was of the opinion that you should remain in Lanka. But, this morning, that girl who stands there brought some news and I changed my mind. I now think that you should go to Kanchi immediately.'

Prince Arulmoli now turned his eyes upon Poonkulali who was looking at him from behind a pillar.

'News from all directions is drowning me. What news has this girl brought now?' he asked.

'Let us listen to her,' said the Commander and beckoned Poonkulali to come near.

Poonkulali tried to say something, but she could not speak.

'Aha! The whole world has gone mute!' exclaimed Arulmoli.

That was enough: Poonkulali brimming with tears, ran away into the nearby grove of trees.

Vandiyathevan said,

'If permitted, I can go and bring her back.'

'Do that. Meanwhile, let the Commander break the news she had brought,' said Prince Arulmoli.

'My Prince, Senior Paluvettarayar has sent two large ships filled with soldiers to arrest you. Now they are anchored in a hidden spot in the mouth of river Thondai,' announced the Commander.

81

Conspirators

On hearing the news of his impending arrest by the Paluvettarayars, Prince Arulmoli smiled and remained calm.

'What can we do if they have come to arrest you upon the orders of the Emperor? Can we oppose?' said the Commander.

Parthiban yelled at the Commander on hearing these words, 'Fantastic! Is the Emperor in a position to give orders when the Paluvettarayar brothers keep him in confinement?'

'Nobody can meet the Emperor without their permission,' Vandiyathevan said.

'Commander, what is your advice?'

'Avoid the men sent by the Paluvettarayars. Board the ship brought by Parthiban and reach Kanchi immediately. I will go to Tanjore and meet the Emperor personally and assess the situation there...'

'Nambi, what is the right thing for the Prince? Should he remain in Lanka or go to Kanchi?'

'We should find the safest prison on this island and keep our Prince in it.'

'What nonsense is this?' asked the Commander.

'Is this time for jest?' asked Parthiban.

'Last night, when we were walking down the streets of Anuradapura, the porch of the mansion crumbled. Later, we were sleeping in one place and we left that place for some reason. Soon that place went up in flames. What was the cause for all these incidents?'

Parthiban spoke anxiously,

'Someone is trying to kill the Prince! That's why we have to take back our Prince to Kanchi.'

'Never! Rather than sending the Prince with you, we might as well hand him over him to the Paluvettarayars!' said Alvarkkadiyan.

'You fellow! What did you say?!' Parthiban asked angrily.

The Commander held him back,

'Nambi, why do you say this? Don't you know that Prince Parthiban is a true friend of the Chola clan?'

'I am well aware of it sir, but mere friendship won't suffice. I will post a question to Parthiban, let him answer. Day before yesterday, we saw two men in his company. Who were they? Where are they now?'

Parthiban was shocked and replied rather hesitantly,

'I met them at Triconamalle Hills. They promised to guide me to Prince Arulmoli. They disappeared suddenly at Anuradapura. Why do you ask Nambi?'

'They belong to a gang of conspirators. Look over there!' Alvarkkadiyan pointed towards a grove of trees.

He pointed to a spot away from the resthouse amidst the thick growth of trees where Poonkulali and Vandiyathevan were deep in conversation. Suddenly, Vandiyathevan swirled a dagger into the bushes—they heard a scream.

Vandiyathevan had gone in search of Poonkulali and found her in a grove, sobbing. He also found out the reason for her sobs.

'The Prince did not recognize me. He did not even look at me.'

'He remembers you very well. When I mentioned your name, he fondly called you Ocean Princess.'

'If he remembered me, why didn't he talk to me?'

'He spoke to you but you did not reply. You ran away.'

'I expected some pleasantries. He did not even look at me!'

'There is a reason for that, Poonkulali. These are difficult times for the Chola Empire, especially the Prince. I have vowed never to leave his side.'

'Do you like the Prince so much?'

'Yes. I like him a lot.'

'Me too!' said Poonkulali.

'I know that you like the Prince. That is why I came here to take you back to him. Come with me.'

'I won't come. I have told all the details to the Commander. I become speechless in his presence.'

'The Prince is very fond of mute women!'

'How dare you tease me!'

Poonkulali drew her dagger.

'Fine, I am going back,' said Vandiyathevan. As he took a step away, suddenly he turned back and plucked the dagger from her hands and threw it away near a bush.

A scream came from behind that bush.

'Somebody is planning to kill the Prince. Do you remember those two men who were taken by your brother from Kodikkarai to Lanka in his boat? You were also suspicious of them. How can we abandon our Prince at such a difficult time?' said Vandiyathevan.

Poonkulali thought for a moment,

'We have to find out who was hiding behind the bush?'

'Where to look for them in this vast jungle? Let us go join the Prince without delay.'

'Alright,' agreed Poonkulali.

Both walked towards the Prince.

Poonkulali stood there lost in deep thought.

'Ocean Princess! Do you remember me?' Poonkulali became oblivious to the surrounding when she heard the Prince's voice.

82

One and Only Duty

How could I forget our journey in my tiny boat across ceaseless white waves? How could I forget the mount like waves that took us sky-high one moment and hurled us down to the depths the next moment? How could I forget our victory over the sea lord's fury? How could I forget...?

Such thoughts were crowding Poonkulali's mind but she merely mumbled.

'Yes, I do.'

'I believe that you have told our Commander about two large ships filled with armed men that came up to river Thondai and anchored at a hidden spot. Is that true, Ocean Princess? Did you see those ships with your own eyes?' asked Prince Arulmoli.

'Yes, beloved Prince, I saw them. They also talked of arresting you and taking you back.'

'Did they speak anything about on whose orders they have come to do such a thing?'

'They said that it was on the orders of the Emperor.'

'Very good! Did they attribute any reason for that?'

'Yes. They said that you conspired with the Buddhist monks of Lanka to crown yourself as an independent king of Lanka.'

'Did they discuss anything else?'

'They said that the Commander should not be aware of their mission or else he will help you to escape. They wanted to find out your whereabouts to deliver the orders.'

'Good! You have really helped me a lot, Ocean Princess.'

Poonkulali moved away to a spot from where she could gaze

upon the Prince's face!

The Prince then turned to the Commander,

'Sir, you are a close friend of my father, I have the highest regard for you. Please help me discharge my duty.'

He made the same request to Parthiban.

The Commander looked at the Prince and said,

'You speak of fulfilling your duty: what does that mean?' he asked.

'At this time, I have to obey my father's orders. I want to surrender before them to discharge my duty.'

'Never! As long as I am alive, I won't permit that,' said Parthiban.

Calming down Parthiban, the Commander turned to the Prince and spoke,

'Beloved Prince! When the Emperor appointed you as the Commander-in-Chief of the Southern Armies last year, he said to me, "You are responsible to guard him from every danger. But if anything happens to him, the life from my body will part that very moment". Will the Emperor with such deep love for you send men to arrest you now?'

Prince Arulmoli interrupted at this point,

'I do not know if anyone can believe it or not but I believe it.'

'What are you saying, Prince?'

'It is true that I was plotting to covet Lanka's throne.'

Vandiyathevan felt perplexed.

'Last night, when Buddhist monks offered you Lanka's throne, you refused it. Nambi and I are witness to that.'

Arulmoli smiled at Vandiyathevan,

'Will those who conspire have witnesses to their deeds? I refused Lanka's throne mainly because you both were present!'

Vandiyathevan was stunned. The Prince continued,

'If you have any doubts, ask Nambi what our Prime Minister's message was for me. "Monks will offer you Lanka's throne; refuse it in the presence of reliable witnesses." Please confirm with him if what I say is true.'

On hearing these words, everyone in the resthouse was startled. Prince Arulmoli addressed the Commander,

'Sir, listen to me. It is true that I aspired for Lanka's throne. My sister fostered this desire in me. Therefore, I am a culprit. So, the Emperor has a valid reason for ordering my arrest.'

'Just a minute, Prince. If such a thought existed in your mind, it is the good fortune of this island. You are not accountable for that! Neither is your sister... It is Emperor Sundara Chola who is responsible. He has often said that he would like to see you seated on Lanka's throne. It was the Emperor who first sowed this idea in your sister's mind. So, you are no culprit...'

'Then why should I hesitate about going to my father? I will explain the true state of affairs to him. These two gentlemen can be my witnesses. It is my duty to follow whatever orders the Emperor gives me.'

Finally, Parthiban spoke to the Commander.

'No more wasting of time. Let us reveal the truth.'

Commander said,

'I will tell him the truth, be patient. You are aware that Senior Paluvettarayar married a very young girl named Nandini at his old age. He simply obeys every whim and fancy of hers. His ill-fate has reduced that great and brave warrior born of an ancient noble family to such an unfortunate situation.'

'Nothing new about it... Every town and village in Chola country knows about it.'

'The magic of that woman influences the Emperor also now. That is why he has given these orders of arrest.'

'Beware Commander! Don't malign the name of my father, the Emperor. As long as he is alive, any order from him is divine law.'

'Prince! We won't refute that. I came to know the whole truth about Nandini from Parthiban only last night; it is better that you know about it too.'

'Three years ago, in the final battle against Veerapandiya, we completely destroyed the Pandiya army at Madurai. Veerapandiya escaped into hiding. Nandini who had given sanctuary to Veerapandiya begged for his life. Kicking her away, Karikalan beheaded the enemy. Later, she appeared in Tanjore as the Young Queen of Paluvoor! We should be able to guess her intentions now. She has come to avenge Veerapandiya's death by totally destroying the Chola clan.

Vandiyathevan and Nambi will bear witness to the existence of a frightening gang that has sworn to totally destroy the Chola nobility. It is Nandini who finances that gang.'

'Commander, I am really surprised by all that you said. But it further confirms my decision to leave for Tanjore and be with my father who is surrounded with so many problems. Why do I need Lanka or its throne? No more discussions. None of you should stop me!' Prince Arulmolivarman spoke decisively. He then turned towards Poonkulali who was gazing at him with unblinking eyes.

'Ocean Princess, please come here,' he called.

Poonkulali came closer.

'You have been of great help to me. Will you please help me again?'

'Prince! What is this? I wait to fulfil your orders.'

'You have to be my guide and take me to those two ships waiting for me.'

Poonkulali who had been lost in her own thoughts decided to go as a guide.

'Prince, I will not stand in the way of your wishes. But I have some doubts about Poonkulali also. Let her ride ahead on our elephant. I insist on accompanying you till we see those ships on river Thondai. It is my duty too,' said the Commander.

Prince Arulmoli smiled. 'I won't be an obstruction to your duty.'

83

The Rogue Elephant

Prince Arulmoli was getting ready for departure. Parthiban came to take leave of the Prince.

'Prince, I leave for Kanchi without having achieved my mission.'

'Why leave in such a hurry?'

'I have to go to Kanchi and report to Prince Karikalan immediately,' said Parthiban.

'Parthiban and the Commander are cooking up some plot. We will come to know of it soon. This old man of Kodumbalur is primarily responsible for it,' said Alvarkkadiyan Nambi to Vandiyathevan.

'How could the Commander be responsible?'

'The Commander dreams of wedding his niece, Vanathi, to our young Prince and making him the king of Lanka. It was he who inspired the Buddhist monks to offer Lanka's throne to Prince Arulmoli. But he could not keep his efforts secret! The news reached Tanjore and that is why our Prime Minister came to Lanka and later sent messages through me!'

Finally, Prince Arulmoli, Commander Bhoothi Vikrama, Vandiyathevan, Alvarkkadiyan and four soldiers rode westward on high-bred horses. The elephant carrying Poonkulali followed them.

But, travelling along the Royal Way was not easy. Crowds gathered all along the way following them in a procession shouting, 'Long live Lanka's King Arulmoli!'

Prince Arulmoli summoned the chieftain of the country folk and asked. 'Why are you bestowing Lanka's kingship upon me?'

The headman bowed very reverently, 'My King, this territory

of Lanka has been suffering without a good king for several years. It is the wish of every citizen living on this island—Singhalese, Tamils, Buddhists, Saivas, monks and householders—that you should become our king. We have made arrangements to honour you with a banquet.'

The Prince could not say no to them; he was enormously delayed.

'Brother, it is obvious that the Commander had sent his men ahead to prepare for all these celebrations,' said Alvarkkadiyan.

The Prince was unhappy about this.

Poonkulali seated near the lotus pond was lost in thoughts. She was hoping that she could have been alone with the Prince during the journey and engage in conversation with him revealing the emotions in her heart. She was disappointed as there was no opportunity for that now. People surrounded him all the time! She was afraid of the blame of handing over the Prince to the enemies!

Soon Vandiyathevan came to call her, 'The Prince is already angry as the journey has been delayed. Come quickly without further delay.' Poonkulali rushed to climb on her elephant and follow them.

An unexpected incident occurred on the forest trail. An arrow was aimed at the Prince. But he was swifter than the wind and moved aside. The arrow pierced through Alvarkkadiyan's turban. All were shocked. The Prince now changed the strategy.

'I know the art of handling elephants. I wish to reach Tanjore with my life intact and prove my innocence to my father.'

'Your father will never suspect you of any crime!'

'Not just my father. I'd like to prove my innocence to all the people.'

'As long as I am riding a horse, all sorts of obstacles like that arrow might strike me. I will become an elephant-driver for a while again.'

The Prince jumped upon the elephant, asking Poonkulali,

'Ocean Princess, you don't mind me coming on this elephant with you, do you?'

'Lord, I must have done penance for this good fortune.'

'Will you be frightened if this elephant suddenly turns rogue and begins to run fast?'

'No at all beloved Prince...Not with you by my side...'

'There are ropes on both sides of the saddle on the elephant. Bind yourself tightly.'

'Why, my Prince?'

'This elephant is going to turn rogue. Don't panic, be careful.'

He gently rubbed the elephant on its forehead and softly spoke into its ears. Swiftly its walk turned into a run. The trees and shrubs of the jungle shook. The earth shook and shivered. Birds on tree-tops fluttered their wings noisily and flew away in panic. Beasts hidden in the forest emerged to run away in fright.

The Commander screamed, 'Oh God! The elephant has turned rogue!'

The elephant ran fast and very soon reached the Elephant Crossing.

After reaching the Elephant Crossing, the elephant plunged into the waves of the ocean like a mountain thrown by Hanuman of the epic Ramayana. It crossed the shallow waters and reached the forest on the northern shores.

84

Prison Ship

Poonkulali was not sure how far they had travelled. She wondered if they were still in Lanka!

Again, the Prince whispered into the elephant's ear. It immediately stopped on the shores of a tiny lake surrounded by trees. Poonkulali looked around to see if anybody was following them. But none followed. Prince Arulmoli and Poonkulali jumped down from the elephant. They sat on the banks of the beautiful lake.

Her lotus red face was reflected in the clear waters of the lake. Looking at her, the Prince said, 'Poonkulali, I like you very much! Do you know why I like you?' asked Prince Arulmoli.

'Everyone wanted me to act according to their wishes. You were the only one who readily agreed to act according to my wish. I will never forget this help, Ocean Princess!' finished the Prince.

Poonkulali went into a trance.

'The Commander and Parthiban were planning to delay my journey creating several obstructions on our way. He sent his men ahead of us and made the villagers arrange celebrations. Parthiban left for Triconanamallee Hill in a hurry to reach river Thondai before we could reach that spot. I know all their game plans. I defeated their purpose with your help...'

Poonkulali sobbed, 'My Prince, but I am a sinner—leading you to the enemies,' saying this she stood up with a jump.

The Prince gently held her hand to stop her from running away. Poonkulali was completely lost by the gentle touch of the Prince.

'Ocean Princess, I want to share something very important with you. I have no wish to wear a crown and rule a kingdom. I have a wish to board large ships and sail across several seas. There are many islands like this Lanka. I wish to go to all those places and look at the wondrous marvels of those countries.'

Poonkulali was listening with keen interest. 'Sir! When you go to all those places, could you take me with you?'

'I merely expressed my wishes. Who knows if they will be fulfilled?' asked the Prince.

She came back to earth from her dream-world. 'Sir, if that is your wish, why are you going back to Tanjore?'

'I was about to explain that but you diverted my attention, Ocean Princess. There is a mute woman wandering here and there on this island. Do you know her?'

'Yes, I know her, my Prince. I lost my mother when I was very young. She was the one who brought me up. She is my aunt-goddess. She lives in a rock cave on the Ghost Island between Lanka and Kodikkarai. I saw you for the first time on that island.'

'You saw me there?!'

'Yes. There are several beautiful paintings drawn by her in that rocky cave. I saw your face in those paintings. Later, one day when I saw you at Kodikkarai, I was astonished.'

'Oh! Now I understand. Ocean Princess, do you know about the relationship between me and that woman?'

'I do not know.'

'Poonkulali, she is my elder mother. Lawfully, she should have become the queen of Tanjore.'

'Prince! Is it so?'

'Some secret sadness was always distressing my father. Now, I have found the truth. My father thinks that my elder mother is dead and that too because of him. If I tell him that she is alive, his mental agony will ease off. In this situation, I must reach Tanjore as soon as possible. I immensely value your help.'

'Prince it is my good fortune. But, why do you need my help

in all this? If you had spoken to the Commander, he would have arranged for you to go to Tanjore.'

'No. I do not wish to share my father's personal secrets with them. I need another favour of you. Several dangers will cross my path. If some such misfortune happens to me on this journey, or I am unable to meet my father, you must meet the Emperor and reveal all these matters. If he wishes, take her to him.'

'No misfortune will cross your path.'

'If something were to happen to me, you must do as I have told you.'

'I promise, my Prince.'

'How can I entrust this important mission to anyone else? Tell me.'

'You have entrusted this job to me. The job is done. Can I take leave of you?' asked Poonkulali in a tear-laden voice.

'Be patient, we have not yet reached river Thondai. Climb up on this elephant and be with me till we see the tiger flags of the Chola ships,' said the Prince.

Their journey started again.

They had reached the mouth of the river. Poonkulali jerked in surprise, 'What is this?'

'What is the matter?' asked Prince Arulmoli.

'The ships which I had seen earlier with tiger flags are not here, anymore. It appears as though I tricked you to bring you here. This will confirm the Commander's suspicion.'